PRA ... ELS

"A wild ride."   —Lora Leigh, #1 *New York Times* bestselling author

"Passionate, inventive, sexually explicit."   —*USA Today*

"One of the strongest sports romance series available."
                                        —Dear Author

"Endearing characters, a strong romance and an engaging plot all wrapped up in one sexy package."   —Romance Novel News

"Both sensual and raw . . . Plenty of romance, sexy men, hot steamy loving and humor."   —Smexy Books

"Holy smokes! I am pretty sure I saw steam rising from every page."
                                        —Fresh Fiction

"Hot, hot, hot! . . . Romance at its best! Highly recommended! Very steamy."   —Coffee Table Reviews

"Burton knocks it out of the park . . . With snappy back-and-forth dialogue as well as hot, sweaty and utterly engaging bedroom play, readers will not be able to race through this book fast enough!"
                                        —*RT Book Reviews*

Titles by Jaci Burton

WILD, WICKED, & WANTON
BOUND, BRANDED, & BRAZEN

Wild Rider Series

RIDING WILD
RIDING TEMPTATION

RIDING ON INSTINCT
RIDING THE NIGHT

Play-by-Play Series

THE PERFECT PLAY
CHANGING THE GAME
TAKING A SHOT
PLAYING TO WIN
THROWN BY A CURVE
ONE SWEET RIDE
HOLIDAY GAMES
(an eNovella)

MELTING THE ICE

STRADDLING THE LINE
HOLIDAY ON ICE
(an eNovella)
QUARTERBACK DRAW
ALL WOUND UP
HOT HOLIDAY NIGHTS
(an eNovella)

UNEXPECTED RUSH

Hope Series

HOPE SMOLDERS
(an eNovella)

HOPE FLAMES
HOPE IGNITES

HOPE BURNS
LOVE AFTER ALL
MAKE ME STAY

Anthologies

UNLACED
(with Jasmine Haynes, Joey W. Hill and Denise Rossetti)

EXCLUSIVE
(with Eden Bradley and Lisa Renee Jones)

LACED WITH DESIRE
(with Jasmine Haynes, Joey W. Hill and Denise Rossetti)

NAUTI AND WILD
(with Lora Leigh)

NAUTIER AND WILDER
(with Lora Leigh)

HOT SUMMER NIGHTS
(with Carly Phillips, Erin McCarthy and Jessica Clare)

eNovellas

THE TIES THAT BIND
NO STRINGS ATTACHED

WILD NIGHTS

UNEXPECTED RUSH

JACI BURTON

BERKLEY BOOKS, NEW YORK

BERKLEY

An imprint of Penguin Random House LLC
375 Hudson Street, New York, New York 10014

This book is an original publication of Penguin Random House LLC.

Library of Congress Cataloging-in-Publication Data

Names: Burton, Jaci.
Title: Unexpected rush / Jaci Burton.
Description: Berkley trade paperback edition. I New York : Berkley Books, 2016.
I Series: A play-by-play novel ; 11
Identifiers: LCCN 2015043380 I ISBN 9780425276815 (paperback)
Subjects: I BISAC: FICTION / Romance / Contemporary. I FICTION / Romance / General.
I GSAFD: Love stories I Erotic fiction.
Classification: LCC PS3602.U776 U54 2016 I DDC 813/.6—dc23 LC record available
at http://lccn.loc.gov/2015043380

PUBLISHING HISTORY
Berkley trade paperback edition / February 2016

PRINTED IN THE UNITED STATES OF AMERICA

10 9 8 7 6 5 4 3 2 1

Cover photo by Claudio Marinesco.
Cover design by Rita Frangie.
Interior text design by Kristin del Rosario.

Penguin
Random
House

To my husband, Charlie,
for his never-ending patience, his understanding of my weird moods
and his acceptance of pizza as a staple when I'm on deadline.
Love always and forever, babe.

ONE

"MEN SUCK."

Harmony Evans tossed her purse on the kitchen table of her mother's house and pulled up a chair next to her best friend, Alyssa. It was Thursday night—family dinner night at Mama's house. Everyone was coming over, as it always was at Mama's. Right now she'd prefer to be sitting in the corner of a dark bar, nursing a dirty martini. She was going to have to settle for sweet tea because, short of death, you did not miss Thursday-night dinner at Mama's.

She'd already come in and kissed her mother, who was holding court in the living room with Harmony's brother, Drake, and several of his friends, giving her time to catch up with Alyssa.

Alyssa laid her hand over Harmony's and cast a look of concern. "Oh, no. Is it Levon?"

Harmony wrinkled her nose, preferring never to hear the name of her now *ex* boyfriend again. "Yes."

"Did you dump him?"

"I did not break up with him. He gave me the classic 'It's not you, it's me' speech. He's doing so much international travel with the law firm, and he just can't devote enough time to the relationship, so it wouldn't be fair to lead me on when he knows he can't commit. He went on with more excuses but it was all blah blah blah after that." She waved her hand back and forth.

Alyssa's gaze narrowed. "What a prick. Why is it so damn hard to find a man of value, one who will respect a woman and give her honesty?"

"I have no idea." Harmony pulled one of the empty glasses forward and poured from the pitcher that sat in the middle of the table, already filled with tea and ice and loaded with so much sugar she'd likely be awake all night. At this point, she didn't care. She'd work it off in a gym session tomorrow. "All I know is I'm glad to be rid of him. It was bad enough his bathroom counter had more product on it than mine did."

Alyssa laughed. "It's for the best, Harmony. What does a man need on his counter besides a toothbrush, soap, deodorant and a razor?"

"According to Levon, there was stuff for his beard, trimming devices, facial scrub, moisturizer—separate ones for his face and his body. An entire manicure set for his nails, to use when he wasn't off getting mani-pedis of course."

"Of course," Alyssa said, then giggled.

"Oh, and the scents. Let's not forget his entire rack of colognes."

Alyssa nodded. "The man did reek, honey."

"I think he owned more perfume than I do."

"Never a good sign. See? You dodged a bullet."

"I did."

Alyssa lifted her glass. "Let's toast to that."

They clinked glasses. "To men we're lucky to have not ended up with," Harmony said.

"What are we toasting to?"

Harmony looked up to find Barrett Cassidy standing at the kitchen table. He was her brother Drake's best friend and teammate, and since the guys both played for the Tampa Hawks football team, and Barrett also lived in Tampa, it meant she'd often see Barrett at Mama's house for dinner. Along with several other members of the Hawks football team.

One of the nicest things about living in Tampa, as a matter of fact. She'd often thought it fortuitous that her brother had been drafted by the hometown team. It had kept him close to home all these years, and of course, one couldn't complain about the awesome eye candy her brother brought home now and then.

Especially Barrett. Most especially Barrett.

"We're toasting the end of Harmony's relationship with a man who was absolutely not right for her," Alyssa said.

Barrett arched a brow, then gave Harmony a sympathetic look. "Really. Sorry about that."

Harmony shrugged. "Nothing to be sorry about. Alyssa's right. He wasn't the man for me."

"Then I guess I'm . . . happy for you?"

She could tell this was uncomfortable for him. "Come on. Sit down and have a glass of iced tea with us."

"I'm not sure I want to wade into these waters. Breakups are not my territory."

"Oh, come on, Barrett. Surely you've dumped a woman before," Harmony said, pouring him a glass. When he didn't answer, she added, "Or you've been dumped."

He pulled out a chair and sat. She'd never realized before how utterly . . . big he was. He'd always kept his distance from her, preferring to hang with Drake, so this was the closest she'd ever been to him. Both he and Drake played defense for the Hawks. Like her brother, Barrett was absolutely pure muscle. But she never paid attention to Drake. Barrett, though? Oh, yes. Just watching the way his muscles flexed as he moved was like watching liquid art. She could stare at his arms for hours, but she tried not to ogle. Too much, anyway.

"I've been dumped before, sure," Barrett said. "And maybe I've broken up with a woman or two."

Alyssa leaned close to Harmony. "He's downplaying being the one who dumped the woman."

"I heard that, Alyssa."

"I meant for you to hear me, Barrett. You're just trying to be the good guy right now because we're roasting the not so good guys."

Barrett narrowed his gaze. "I told you I shouldn't be sitting here. If you both want to bad-mouth my species—which you have a right to, since some asshole broke up with you, Harmony—then I should leave. Also, I'd suggest something stronger than iced tea. It helps."

So maybe he had been dumped before. It sounded like he knew how to get through it.

"It's okay, Barrett," Harmony said. "Me getting dumped is definitely not your fault. I'm not as broken up about it as I should be, all things considered. So you're safe here."

Besides, looking at Barrett could definitely make her forget all about Levon and his prissy bathroom counter. She wondered how many items Barrett kept on *his* bathroom counter? She'd just bet not many.

She turned her chair toward him, determined to find out. "Actually, I have a ridiculous question for you, Barrett."

He turned his gorgeous blue eyes on her and smiled. "Shoot."

"How many items currently reside on your bathroom counter?"

Barrett cocked a brow. "Huh?"

Alyssa laughed. "Very good question."

"I don't get it," Barrett said.

"We're conducting a poll about men and their bathrooms," Alyssa said. "Indulge us."

Barrett finally shrugged. "Okay, fine. Uh . . . soap, of course. Toothpaste and toothbrush. Deodorant. Maybe a comb?"

Harmony smiled when Barrett struggled to come up with anything else. She knew he was an absolute male of the not-so-fussy-about-his-grooming variety.

He finally cast her a helpless look. "I don't know. I've got nothin' else. Did I fail?"

"Oh, no," Harmony said. "You most definitely passed."

"You should go out with Barrett," Alyssa suggested, nudging Harmony. "He's a nice guy, and he obviously doesn't keep thirty-seven things on his bathroom counter."

Barrett laughed. "Yeah, and Drake would kill us both. Well, he'd definitely kill me."

The idea of it appealed, though. She'd had such a crush on Barrett when Drake had first introduced them all those years ago. And now? Hmm. Yeah, definitely appealing.

"What my brother doesn't know won't hurt him—or you. What do you say, Barrett? Care to take me out?"

BARRETT WAS AT A LOSS FOR WORDS. HARMONY WAS his best friend's little sister.

Only she wasn't so little anymore.

He and Drake had been friends since sophomore year of college and had bonded then. They'd celebrated when they'd both been drafted by Tampa. Both of them played defense, they'd been roommates in college, and they'd become friends. It had been that way ever since.

He'd been coming to Drake's mom's house ever since college.

Harmony had been just getting out of high school back then. She'd only been a kid. Now she was a woman, with a career of her own, and she'd just been dumped by some guy obviously too stupid to know what a treasure he'd had.

She was beautiful, with dark brown skin, straight dark hair that teased her perfect shoulders and those amazing amber eyes. She had the kind of body any man would want to get his hands on, curves in all the right places, and that sweet, kissable mouth . . .

And he had no business thinking about Harmony at all because there was a code—no messing with your best friend's sister.

Absolutely not. No. Wasn't going to happen.

He pushed back his chair and stood, looking down at Harmony as if she was Eve in the garden and she'd just offered him the forbidden apple. "I know the rule, Harmony, and so do you. I think I'll go check out what your mom made for dinner tonight."

He might be tempted, but there was too much at stake. He was going to step away from the sweet fruit laid out in front of him before he decided to do something really stupid and take a taste.

Because going down that road would spell nothing but doom.

TWO

AFTER BARRETT WALKED AWAY, HARMONY STARED AT
his retreating form, confused as hell by what he'd just said.

"What was that all about?" Alyssa asked, pulling Harmony's
gaze away from Barrett's fine ass.

"I have no idea." She pushed back from the table. "But I'm going
to find out."

Mama's house was much bigger than the one they'd grown up
in. First thing Drake had done when he'd gotten his initial pro
paycheck was buy their mother a new house. She'd objected, saying she liked her old one just fine, but Drake had insisted her old
house was crumbling down around her. He hadn't felt right about
her staying in it, and she had finally relented.

Mama was a proud woman. She didn't need anyone to take care
of her. And for years, she'd been the one taking care of both Drake
and Harmony. But their old house had been a wreck, so Harmony
had been so glad Mama agreed to the new one.

There was a crowd around her brother and Barrett right now, and the last thing she wanted was to nudge herself in the middle of Barrett and Drake. Drake was overprotective and had been since their dad died when Harmony and Drake were young. Mama had raised them alone, but Drake, being two years older, had put himself in some sort of parental role, which had been ridiculous at the time, but after Dad passed, Harmony had felt lost and leaned on Drake for support. He'd been her closest ally and her best friend.

Until she'd turned fifteen and had fallen madly in love with Kellan Smith. Drake had done everything in his power to squash that romance.

In hindsight, a good move, but at the time she'd hated her brother for getting in the way of the love of her life.

Fifteen-year-olds often didn't make the best decisions. Kellan had been fine looking, and had moves a young Harmony had never before been subjected to.

Nor should she have been, since Kellan had been nineteen at the time.

Drake had cornered Kellan and threatened to not only kick his ass, but have him arrested. When Kellan had dumped her, she'd been devastated.

She hadn't found out about Drake's threats until later. And she'd been pissed.

Her brother had always been up in her business. Which she supposed had been fine when she was a teenager, but she was twenty-five years old now. Way too old to have him monitoring who she saw and who she didn't.

And she still needed to know what Barrett had been talking about, so she waited until Barrett wandered into the backyard by himself with a beer in his hand.

She followed him, one eye on her brother, who was preoccupied with the television, laughing with some of the other guys from the team.

Satisfied Drake didn't have his eyes trained on her, she slipped out the back door.

Barrett stared out over the garden.

She stepped up next to him. "A little too noisy in there for you?"

He frowned at her. "What are you doing out here, Harmony?"

"Trying to get you alone so I can ask you what you meant by the rule."

He took a long swallow of his beer. "The rule. The guy rule."

Somehow she knew she wasn't going to like this rule. "What guy rule?"

He turned to face her, his body so imposing. She imagined he was quite threatening on the football field. But to her, he was just Barrett. Sexy, incredibly hot Barrett.

"The unspoken rule about not messing with your best friend's little sister."

She gave him an incredulous stare. "You can't be serious."

"I am."

"That's the most ridiculous thing I've ever heard. I'm not a child, Barrett. I'm a grown woman who can make her own decisions. And you're a grown man capable of making your own decisions as well."

He looked unmoved by her statement. "You're Drake's sister. That makes you off-limits."

"Unbelievable. What is this, medieval times? Who comes up with this shit? Do you guys get out a notebook in the locker room and make lists?"

He didn't smile. "This is serious business, Harmony. And no, we don't make lists. It's an unwritten, unspoken rule. Every guy knows it."

If her eyes rolled any harder, they'd roll clear out the back of her head.

"It's a stupid rule."

"Nevertheless, it's there. And I'll honor it."

Before she gave herself a headache, she walked off, back inside. Alyssa joined her. "What did he say?"

She poured herself another glass of iced tea, still wishing it was that dirty martini, because this day was getting more bizarre by the minute. She took several sips of tea and leaned against the kitchen island. "It's some moronic man code about not getting involved with your best friend's sister."

Alyssa gaped at her. "What? That's dumb as hell."

"Which is what I told him."

"Did you also tell him you've had a crush on him since the first time Drake dragged him into the house, back when they were in college?"

"I most certainly did not." She'd never told anyone—other than her best friend—about her years-long crush on Barrett.

"You should tell him. Maybe that would change his mind."

"I don't think so. And don't you tell him, either."

Alyssa made crisscross motions over her heart. "Your secret goes to the grave with me, sister. You know that."

Said crush had ebbed and flowed over the years. She'd been nineteen the first time she'd laid eyes on Barrett. She'd taken one look at tall, dark-haired, blue-eyed Barrett and had fallen instantly in lust.

Even though he'd been a few years older than she was, she hadn't cared. No other guy had existed for her after that. Barrett had been nice to her, though he had largely ignored her, as older guys did to nearly invisible teens.

Still, her crush had endured.

During her college years she'd found other guys who actually noticed her. Then she'd replaced her fantasy of Barrett with real men.

Like Levon.

She snorted.

"What?" Alyssa asked.

"Just thinking about my journey in the man department over the years."

"Oh. Yeah. You've chosen some true keepers, Harmony."

Harmony pursed her lips. "It's not my fault. I'm smart, I'm kind, I'm generous, I'm funny, I'd like to think I'm a proud, damn fine-looking woman, and I'm hot as hell."

"Hell yes," Alyssa said.

"And yet for some reason I keep attracting these losers."

Alyssa gave her a look of commiseration. "It's not like I'm dating winners of the year, either. It's hard to find a good man."

They looked at each other and grinned.

"And good to find a hard one," they said simultaneously, then laughed.

"Too bad Barrett is off-limits," Alyssa said. "That man is the definition of hardbody."

Harmony didn't believe in off-limits. She wasn't giving up just yet.

THREE

BARRETT STOOD OUTSIDE, THINKING.

Thinking and watching Harmony and Alyssa inside in the kitchen, both of them talking and laughing.

Not that he was paying attention to Alyssa. Alyssa was pretty and had a banging body. But it didn't seem to matter, since his gaze was focused on Harmony, on the way she put her entire body into it when she laughed, the way she tilted her head back, exposing the soft column of her neck, the way she reached for Alyssa's hand when she had something important to say.

The woman had expressive body language. It wasn't the first time he'd caught himself watching her, noticing her hair, the way she walked, the subtle curve in her hips or even her slender fingertips. And then his mind would wander to those fingertips and her hands, imagining her wrapping her hand around his neck while he explored her mouth, or raking her pretty fingernails down his bare chest or using her sweet soft hands to stroke his—

Jesus. Had he really paid attention to all those things? He had been, for a while now. And then she had to go and ask him to ask her out on a date. It was like she'd read his mind, as if she'd known all the fantasies he'd been having about her lately.

Which he had no goddamned business having.

Because of the rule.

Drake was his best friend. They'd been like brothers both on the field and off. He'd never step on that friendship by touching his kid sister.

But that was the problem, wasn't it? Harmony wasn't a kid anymore, and hadn't been for a long time.

He just hadn't noticed she'd grown up—until recently. He wasn't sure when it had happened. Maybe earlier this year, at the New Year's Eve party Drake had thrown at his mom's house.

They always liked to congregate here. Mainly to keep Mama Diane company, and hell, Diane liked a good party as much as anyone.

That New Year's Eve Harmony had worn some slinky silver dress that clung to her curves, revealing cleavage and skin, and she hadn't brought a date that night.

Neither had he, which meant he'd been scoping out the single women at the party.

He hadn't meant to scope her out, but when he'd walked in the kitchen and she'd been bent over the dishwasher, revealing silken legs and sexy thighs, all he could think of was spreading her legs and . . .

He jerked his attention away from the window, realizing he was standing out in the backyard with a fucking hard-on.

What the hell was wrong with him? He could still remember the day she'd gotten her braces off. She'd started late and she'd told him high school with braces had been a nightmare. She'd been so excited, and had told him she couldn't wait to show whatever boyfriend she'd had at the time.

She'd been barely what? Nineteen? Barely legal. He hadn't paid attention to her. He just remembered smiling at her and telling her she looked pretty.

She was more than pretty now. She was a knockout.

And he was never, ever going to touch her.

Downing the last swallow of his beer, he went back into the house and grabbed another from the fridge. Fortunately, Harmony and Alyssa had exited the kitchen, so maybe he could avoid her the rest of the night.

He made his way into the living room, where Drake and some of the other guys were playing video games. First he stopped at the dining room table to kiss Mama Diane's cheek. She was chatting with one of the neighbors.

She patted his cheek. "Where'd you disappear to?"

"Out back. Your vegetable garden is looking healthy."

"And don't think of running off with my tomatoes."

He laughed. "You know me so well, Mama Diane."

"Yes, I do. You hungry?"

"Always."

"You boys are always hungry. Dinner will be ready soon."

"Thank you."

He winded his way over to the sofas, where there was a fierce game of war going on. At least on the television. Drake was in the middle of the action, killing aliens along with Bubba Sinclair and Lionel "Mean Man" Taylor, both part of the Tampa defense. It was almost always defensive players over for dinner on Thursday nights when they were in town.

Defense was king. It's why he'd always loved being part of a defense. Keeping the other team from scoring was what he did best.

And all these guys were beasts.

He loved them as much as he loved his job.

He couldn't wait for the season to start. Tampa was going to kick some ass this year.

Barrett watched the battle until a skirmish was completed. During a break, Drake leaned back on the sofa, tilting his head back. "You want in on this?"

"No, I'm good."

"Afraid I'll kick your ass?"

Barrett laughed. "I think you know better than that."

"Oh, I do, do I? Get said ass over here and let's see who's better."

"You all turn that off now," Mama Diane hollered. "Dinner's ready."

In an instant, the game was turned off, and so was the TV. They all gathered in the oversized dining room at the huge table— one of Mama Diane's few requests once she'd acquiesced on the new house.

It was stuffed pork chops tonight, one of Barrett's favorites, along with green beans, amazing mashed potatoes and baked apples.

Barrett made it a point to sit next to Drake, and as far away from Harmony as possible.

She shot a smirk in his direction when she took her seat at the opposite end of the table, as if she knew exactly why he'd chosen that spot.

She could think what she wanted to. The farther away Harmony stayed, the better.

He concentrated on his food, and the conversation about this season.

"Where's that fine boyfriend of yours, Harmony?" Mama asked.

Harmony lifted her chin. "We broke up."

"What? Why?"

Harmony focused on her dinner. "From what he told me, it was more about his business, and he didn't have much time to spend with me."

Barrett watched Drake lay down his fork. "Wait a minute. Levon broke up with you?"

"Yes, Drake. He broke up with me."

"What the—" Drake, ever mindful of the no-cursing rule in Mama's house, restrained himself. He picked up his fork and waved it at Harmony. "I need to have a talk with that man. Tell him how to appreciate what a fine treasure he had in you."

Harmony leveled a glare at Drake. "No. You do not need to interfere. It's over between Levon and me."

"Did he hurt you?"

"He hurt my feelings. That's about it."

"Then I'll have a talk with him."

"No, you need to leave it alone, Drake."

Drake looked over at Barrett. "I'll be having a discussion with Levon."

The one thing Barrett knew about Drake was that he was extremely overprotective of Harmony. Yet another reason he would never get involved with Harmony.

Not to mention the guy code.

Fortunately, the conversation soon turned to football.

"Look, we started out strong last season, and finished weak," Drake said. "We'll have to do better even before this season starts. Drafts and free agency helped, and we've all worked hard getting our bodies ready during the off-season."

"Everyone's healthy this year," Mean Man said. "That's gonna work to our advantage."

Barrett nodded. "I'm ready. We're all ready. We're solid going into summer workouts."

"I don't know about the rest of you, but I'm itching for the upcoming season," Mama Diane said. "I can hardly wait for the games to start. How about you, Harmony?"

Harmony nodded. "Absolutely. Wouldn't miss it. I expect you guys to be good this year."

"We're always good."

She shot a look over at Barrett. "Prove it."

The guys all laughed.

"She's looking at you, Barrett," Drake said. "There'd better be some takeaways."

Barrett met Harmony's gaze. "There will be."

"I'm counting on a strong defense this year," Mama Diane said.

The conversation continued over dinner—and after—when the guys piled into the kitchen with the plates and bowls to clean up.

The one thing everyone understood was, if you came for dinner, you were responsible for cleanup.

Mama Diane and the crew were used to cooking for large crowds. When he'd first started coming over here, he asked if it was an imposition to add him in. She'd told him she'd come from a large family and always wanted one of her own, but after her husband passed away, she'd never remarried, and she'd had Drake and Harmony to look after. And then Drake had gotten into sports and all his friends came over as kids, and continued to during high school, then college and pros, and it had been a dream come true for her.

But she'd taught them right way that it was their responsibility to do the dishes.

It was the same thing at his house, so it was a rule he understood well.

And since Mama Diane and her sisters were great cooks, no one complained.

After dinner, everyone piled back into the dining room for pie. Multiple pies, actually. Strawberry rhubarb pie, apple pie, pecan pie and cherry pie.

Barrett chose the apple pie. With ice cream, because pie without ice cream was practically a sin.

After he'd had his fill, he rinsed his dish and put it in the dishwasher, then hung out in the living room with everyone.

"How's the house coming along?" Steve asked him.

"I close on it next Tuesday."

Drake turned to him. "Have you decided yet what you're going to do with it?"

He shook his head. "I haven't hired a contractor. It's a great house in a perfect location. It just needs a complete gut job and a total remodel."

Harmony shifted away from the conversation she'd been having with Alyssa. "I didn't know you bought a house."

"Yeah. I'd been looking for a while. Found this place on the water, but it's older, so it needs a lot of TLC."

"What it needs is a bulldozer," Drake said with a laugh.

Barrett laughed, too. "You're right about that, but the location was perfect. It's right on the water and has a boat dock. The property is in great shape and the dock is solid. It's just the house that needs some work."

"A lot of work," Drake said.

"Okay fine. A lot of work. I need to find a contractor."

"Harmony could help you with that," Mama Diane said. "Have you forgotten what she does for a living?"

He'd honestly never paid much attention, other than it had something to do with mini blinds or shutters or paint or something. "Um . . ."

Harmony rolled her eyes at him. "I'm an interior designer, Barrett. I own my own company. And because of that, I have contact with a variety of contractors."

He'd had no idea. "No shit."

"Language, young man."

"Sorry, Mama Diane." He turned his attention back to Harmony. "No kidding."

"No kidding. Why don't you take me by your house, and I can assess your needs? We can go from there."

Well, shit. The last thing he wanted was to spend any time in close proximity to Harmony. Especially alone. Not after what had happened earlier. "I don't know."

Mama Diane leveled a frown at him. "Are you insinuating my baby girl here can't handle the job?"

Double shit. "No, ma'am. I wasn't insinuating that at all. It's just that the place is such a mess, I don't want to burden her. I'm sure Harmony is very busy."

Harmony gave him that all-knowing smirk again. The one that said she knew damn well he was trying to weasel his way out of being alone with her, he'd gotten caught in a lie and now he was going to have to backpedal his ass off.

She gave him her sweetest smile. "It's hardly a burden, Barrett. It would be my pleasure to look over your place and offer my expertise."

"You should definitely use her," Drake said. "She's good at what she does."

It was all Barrett could do not to cringe at Drake's choice of words. His gaze lifted to Harmony's and her lips curved.

"Yes, Barrett. You should use me."

Goddammit.

Figuring he was truly fucked, he finally nodded. "Thanks. That would be great. I'll text you and we'll set something up."

"Perfect."

Somehow he felt like he'd just been ensnared in Harmony's web. And he was about to get eaten alive.

FOUR

ONE OF THE THINGS BARRETT ENJOYED ABOUT THE off-season was more time to spend on the charities he'd organized. Together he and Drake had funded a community center for kids, and they were going to spend some time there this afternoon.

It was summer, so it would be busy with all of the kids out of school. One of the main objectives in setting up the community center was to have a place for both boys and girls in the middle school age group to hang out over the summer.

He remembered being that age, being bored and having nothing to do, and it really hit him hard when Drake had told him about being subjected to gang influence at that age. He wanted these kids to have an alternative.

He parked in the lot and noticed Drake's car was already there. He quickly made his way inside to join his friend. At the security desk he flashed his ID.

The guard smiled. "I know who you are, Mr. Cassidy," the guy said. "Go on inside."

"Thanks."

He heard a lot of noise coming from the gym, which made him grin. He peeked through the door and saw a bunch of kids playing basketball.

"Hello, Barrett."

He turned and smiled at Greg Green, the administrator of the community center. They shook hands.

"How's it going, Greg?"

"Good. I'm glad you and Drake stopped by today. We have a full house this summer. Drake's in the computer room with Bianca."

Barrett followed Greg down the hall toward the activity room. Drake was in there, sitting with a group of boys and girls.

God, every year as he got older these kids seemed so much younger. They all looked up when he entered.

"Hey, how's it going?" he asked.

He was always happy to see the smiles on the kids' faces. He was even happier that they were more focused on their computers than they were on him.

He knew Bianca, because as one of the trustees of the center, he'd been involved in the initial hiring of all the employees. These were all great people. The community center ran year-round, hosting before and after school programs when school was in session.

Bianca waved to him. Drake got up and came over.

"I'm sorry to tell you that you missed lunch today," Greg said with a curve of his lips. "It was really good, too."

"Please don't tell me that you had mac and cheese on the menu today," Barrett said.

"Okay, I won't mention it."

"Now I feel even worse. What are the kids working on today?"

"They're learning Excel. I'm always amazed at how fast these kids can pick up programs. In so many ways, every generation is smarter than the one before."

"That's great. I'm glad we can teach them useful skills."

"And keep them off the streets at the same time," Drake said.

"Yes."

They left the room and moved down the hall. "We have a swimming coach from one of the high schools working with them on lifeguard lessons next week at the pool. We already have a waiting list for that. The counseling sessions are going very well with many of our students. I think you'll be pleased with the progress."

Barrett nodded. "I've read the monthly reports, Greg. I couldn't be happier with how the center is operating."

"I agree," Drake said. "The kids are happy, the community is happy, and we sure are."

"Good. I hope you plan to stay awhile and interact with the kids. I know they'll be thrilled to spend some time with you."

"That's what we plan to do," Barrett said.

They spent the next several hours joining in different activities, from arts and crafts to computers to old-fashioned board games. The kids put Drake and him through their paces.

Near the end of the day Drake and Barrett joined a number of the kids outside for a game of flag football. They divided into teams, with Drake and him on opposite sides. Barrett really loved that the girls were playing, too. And from what he'd seen when he'd peeked into the basketball game in the gym earlier, these girls were athletic.

He and Drake had a great time going against each other, not surprisingly, since they were both so competitive. So were the kids, but there was a lot of laughing as he and Drake knocked into each other during their game. Barrett blocked him hard and pushed him back, and Drake shoved Barrett to the ground.

Drake held out his hand for Barrett, who glared at him. "Flag football, remember?"

Drake grinned. "Oh, yeah. Must have forgotten that."

By the time their makeshift game was near the end, they were tied. Now Barrett's sense of competition had really set in. He huddled with his kids.

"We've got this. Their defense is weak. I've got the blocking. Ray, you toss it to either Layton or Rachelle, whoever is open."

They all nodded and broke the huddle, then set into game formation. At the snap, Barrett went hard after Drake, shoving him to the ground.

"Goddammit, Barrett," Drake said through clenched teeth.

Barrett just laughed, helped haul Drake to his feet, then they watched the play unfold.

Ray had tossed the ball to Rachelle, who was running like a sprinter on fire down the field toward their makeshift end zone.

She scored and everyone cheered. Hell, even the other side cheered for her.

"Girl's got some speed," Drake said.

"She sure has."

At the end of the game they all came together. "You played tough," Drake said. "You're all athletes, and you should be proud of yourselves."

Barrett took in the grins on their sweaty faces. "Come on. Let's go get something cold to drink."

He slung his arm around Drake as they followed behind the kids. "I'm exhausted."

"Me, too. And what the hell was up with that hit, man. My hip hurts."

"Baby."

"Kiss my ass."

Barrett laughed as they made their way back into the center.

They cleaned up a little, got something to drink, and found Greg.

"Those kids will wear you out," Greg said.

Drake nodded. "They sure will. But we had fun today."

"They appreciate you stopping in. And so do we. You're welcome anytime."

They shook hands with Greg, then headed out to the parking lot.

Barrett felt exhilarated. "Now I'm ready to take on the world."

Drake laughed. "Good. Come back to my place."

"I need a shower first."

"Okay. Go shower, then meet me at my place."

"All right. See you in a few."

He drove to his condo, took a quick shower and put on clean clothes, then went to Drake's. He rang the bell and Drake answered. He'd already showered and was dressed.

"I can't believe you're ready."

"Whatever, man. Doesn't take me long to look this good."

Barrett rolled his eyes.

Drake grabbed his keys. "Come on. Got an errand to run, then we'll go grab something to eat."

"Sounds good. All that kid play made me hungry."

Drake headed downtown, which was strange, because they never went downtown to eat. But he was game for whatever Drake had in mind. Maybe he had a meeting with someone and he had to do it downtown.

Drake pulled into a parking garage in some upscale building. He parked and shut off the engine, then turned to Barrett. "You should come upstairs with me."

Barrett shrugged. "Sure."

He wondered who would meet with Drake after five p.m., but it wasn't his gig. He was just along for the ride—and the food that was going to come after.

They rode the elevator to the fifteenth floor to the law firm of somebody somebody and somebody whose names Barrett immediately forgot.

"Got a meeting with your lawyer?" Barrett asked.

"Not exactly."

The receptionist was gone for the day, and Drake seemed to know where he was going, since he turned left down the hall and went right to the door of—

Uh-oh. That name on the door looked familiar.

Levon Powell.

A very good-looking man dressed in a very expensive suit sat at a very expensive desk. He was on the phone, and when he saw Drake, he said, "Let me call you back."

Levon stood, then smiled. "Drake. What brings you here?"

"You know why I'm here. It's about Harmony."

"What about her?"

This was so not a good idea. Barrett wanted to be anywhere but here right now.

"You broke up with her."

"Yes, I did."

"Why?"

Levon tilted his head to the side. "I think that's between Harmony and me."

Barrett could feel the tension emanating off Drake. "You messed with my sister's feelings. You hurt her."

Drake advanced, and Levon held up his hands. "It wasn't like that. It was a mutual breakup."

Barrett needed to put a stop to this. He grasped Drake's arm. "Drake. Let's go."

"You stay away from her," Drake said.

"Hey, I intend to. We're finished."

"Hell yes, you are. And if you ever speak to her or come near her again, we're going to have a problem."

"Man, we don't have a problem. It's over. Mutual, remember?"

Barrett could tell Drake was pissed at Levon and wanted to get physical with him. He felt the need to step in, so he laid a gentle hand on Drake's chest.

"Like Levon said, it's over, right?"

Drake nodded. "Yeah."

Barrett sent an apologetic look Levon's way, then waited for Drake to walk out the door before expelling the breath he was holding. When they got into the elevator, he turned to Drake. "What the hell was that all about?"

"That was about my sister. I needed to make it clear to Levon that I had my eye on him, that no one messes with Harmony."

"From what I gathered, they were over and it was a clean break. No harm no foul, ya know?"

"Whatever. It pisses me off when men think they can fuck over a woman and there are no consequences."

He had no idea what to make of this. "I think Harmony is fine about the breakup."

Drake turned to him as the elevator doors opened. "He dumped her, man. What kind of asshole does that?"

Barrett resisted the urge to laugh, knowing the level of anger his best friend had. "Honestly? Lots of guys."

They walked out to Drake's car. "Well, that's not cool. And now he knows to stay away from her."

Barrett got the idea that Levon wouldn't be going anywhere near Harmony ever again. Not that he ever planned to anyway.

He loved Drake like a brother, and had for a lot of years. But sometimes he didn't understand his best friend. He was so over-protective of his sister. As far as he understood, Levon might be a jerk, but he hadn't hurt Harmony physically.

He'd never go after some guy who had broken up with his sister, Mia. Not unless the guy got physical with her or hurt her in some way.

At least he didn't think he would. Then again, Mia had never talked about anyone she dated.

Maybe this was why. He had no idea what kind of reaction he would have if he knew anything about his little sister's dating life. But he didn't believe he'd be over the top like Drake. Sometimes relationships broke up. That's just the way it went. And you got over it.

Harmony seemed okay about it.

Drake's phone rang and he picked it up on his car speaker.

"Yo."

"Are you out of your fucking mind?"

Harmony's voice. And she didn't sound very happy with her brother.

"Dunno what you're talking about," Drake said.

"I just got a call from Levon, and he said you came to his office and threatened him."

"Not true," Drake said. "I had a chat with him."

"Drake. Seriously. What the hell did you say to him?"

"Hey, I'm near your place. We'll stop by."

"Drake."

He hung up on her, then turned to Barrett and grinned. "She loves me."

"I don't think she loves you very much right now, man."

"She will when I explain it to her."

Barrett understood siblings, since he had plenty of them.

This should be interesting.

Within ten minutes they rolled into Harmony's town house complex. Drake parked and they got out and went to the door.

Harmony answered, still in her work clothes.

She looked good. He didn't want to notice how sharp she looked in that dress that outlined her curves.

"You are insane. Hi, Barrett," she said, as she held the door for them to come in.

"Hey, I was just protecting you."

She shut the door behind her as they walked in.

"I do not need you to protect me. Not now, not when I was a teenager, not ever."

Barrett followed the two of them past the living area and into her kitchen. He noticed she had paint supplies in her bathroom, and the white bathroom was now being painted a shade of green.

"Redecorating the bathroom, Harmony?" he asked.

"What? Oh, the paint. Yes. I'm changing the color."

Drake's lips lifted. "She paints or redecorates whenever she's upset."

"I do not. And don't change the subject. What the hell were you thinking storming into Levon's office like that?"

"I was thinking of punching him in his smug, asshole face. But I didn't. I just told him to stay away from you."

She let out a long sigh. "He has every intention of staying away from me, considering we just broke up, idiot. And you scared the shit out of him."

"Did I? Good. Then he'll leave you alone."

"He threatened to call the police, Drake. I had to talk him out of that and I told him you would never come near him again."

"He's a pussy."

She rolled her eyes. "You need to stay out of my life, out of my business, and most especially my love life. I don't know how many times I need to tell you that I'm an adult now and I can take care of myself. Can I make that any clearer to you?"

"Okay, fine. You know if Levon had any balls, he'd have told me to go fuck myself and we'd have thrown a few punches and everything would have been okay."

Barrett tried not to snort at Drake's twisted sense of logic.

Harmony raised her hands in the air. "Really? Really, Drake? I don't even know what to do with you. That's the most uncivilized, barbaric, ridiculous thing I've ever heard. You have to stop interfering in my life."

Harmony's voice had gotten progressively louder.

"Okay, okay." Drake went over and put his hands on her shoulders. "I'm sorry. It won't happen again."

She stared at Drake. "I'd like to believe that, but I know it's not true. Please call Levon and apologize."

Drake laughed. "Not gonna happen. But I promise to not bother him again. Is that good enough?"

"I guess so." She sighed. "I'll call him again to reassure him. Which by the way, I do not want to do."

Drake shrugged. "You don't have to talk to him at all. I took care of it."

"No, you made it worse."

"I love you, baby sis."

She shook her head. "I love you, too. But dammit, Drake, you make me crazy."

Drake pulled her into a hug. "That's why you love me."

Siblings. Barrett shook his head.

Harmony stepped away from her brother and glared at Barrett. "And don't you stand there and shake your head. You were there with him and you let this happen."

"I take no responsibility for trying to control Drake."

"Whatever. You two get out of my house. I have painting to do."

Drake turned to leave and Barrett followed, then stopped to take a peek in the bathroom. "So you really redecorate whenever you're upset?"

"Out, Barrett," Harmony said.

He grinned, then followed Drake to his car.

FIVE

HARMONY WENT OVER HER SCHEDULE IN HER OFFICE. The space wasn't much, since she'd only been in business for a year, but so far, things had really taken off. Her calendar was full, she'd hired an assistant, and word had gotten out to local contractors that she was damn good at what she did, which meant even more referrals were coming her way.

Just the way she'd envisioned when she'd gone into business for herself. She'd interned with some of the best designers she knew, and she'd learned a lot. But in the end, she'd wanted her own firm. A risky move, for sure, but if there was one thing Harmony had in droves, it was confidence.

Which could end in her downfall, but failure wasn't a word she acknowledged.

"You've got a final walk-through with the Greens tomorrow afternoon."

She nodded at Rosalie, her assistant. "I've got that on my calendar. Did they install the crown molding in the living room?"

"I was over there this morning. Molding is in place and the trim painters are there. Kitchen is finished, master bedroom and bath have been completed. Everything on the checklist has been checked off. Oh, and Jeff called and said he'd meet you there this afternoon at three for you to do a walk-through with him."

"Perfect." Jeff Golan was one of her favorite contractors. He was no-nonsense, like her, and he got things done on time, which was why he was one of her favorites.

She'd also gotten a text from Barrett, which had actually surprised her. They were meeting at his house tonight, since he had practice today.

She knew he was reluctant about it, but nothing put the fear in a man like her mother.

She smiled at that. Even her formidable brother could be brought to his knees by one death stare from Mama.

Technically, she should bring a contractor with her tonight, but she wanted to make Barrett uncomfortable. What better way to do that than to come alone?

It would serve him right for not thinking of her in the first place. Did the man not know *anything* about her?

He was going to find out.

She handled her appointments, which lasted until after five. She still had time to head back to her town house and freshen up before she had to meet Barrett.

She looked in the bathroom mirror. *Yes, and maybe change clothes, too*, she thought with a wicked smile.

She went into her bedroom and opened the closet, choosing . . .

Oh yeah. Definitely the red dress. Professional, but still one that would make Barrett take notice.

She'd make sure he wouldn't ignore her anymore.

She programmed the address of his house into the GPS in her car and headed out. The house was located near the west side of the bay, on the water. It was a gated community, so she gave her name to the attendant at the gate, who let her in.

The streets were well maintained with beautiful mature shade trees and well-manicured lawns. She drove down a few streets, made a left and found Barrett's house. She parked, got out and looked at the exterior of his home.

Incredible on the outside. It had a white stucco exterior and gray tile roof. The front landscaping was perfect—not overbearing yet not sparse, either, with a sizable front yard.

So far, so good.

She walked up the well-tiled path leading to the front door and rang the bell. Since there was a black Escalade in the driveway, she knew Barrett was already there.

He answered the door looking utterly delicious in brown cargo pants and a tight white T-shirt. She'd barely noticed him the other night when he'd come over with Drake, mainly because she'd been in panic mode and her focus had been entirely on her brother and his idiot move with her ex-boyfriend. Now, though, her attention was fully on Barrett.

It had to be a sin to look that damn fine.

"Hey," he said. "Thanks for coming." He held the door wide and she stepped in.

"It's my pleasure." She took a look around, tilting her head back to note the tall ceilings in the entry and formal living room.

"How are you doing after the other night?"

She rolled her eyes. "I don't even want to talk about my brother right now. Or possibly ever."

"Okay, then. I'd offer you something to drink, but I don't

actually live here yet, so I've got . . . nothing—including a refrigerator."

She laughed. "It's okay. I'm fine."

She looked around the living room. "This is nice. Dated, but nice."

"Why don't you just walk through and do . . . whatever it is you do?" he asked.

Her lips quirked. "I'll do that. Thanks."

She made her way into the kitchen, which was spacious, but also had white laminate countertops and faded oak cabinets. And white appliances.

She grimaced. "The only thing this room has going for it is space. It needs to be gutted."

"Yeah, I'm not really happy with it, but the one thing I liked about it was the size."

She took photos and made notes on her tablet. "Do you cook?"

"I can cook. I'm not a great cook, but I know my way around a kitchen."

"Enough to know the difference between a gas stove, electric and an induction cooktop?"

"I'd rather have a gas stove. With six burners. And double ovens. If my mom comes to visit, she's going to want to do some serious cooking. I want to make sure she has the kitchen to do it in."

"Or that you might get lucky some day and have a woman come cook for you in your fancy new kitchen?"

"I would never insist a woman cook for me. My mom just loves to cook. And if a woman I was dating came to my place, I'd share in the cooking duties."

She gave him a dubious look. "Sure you would."

He looked exasperated with her. "I told you I can cook."

"Many a man has uttered those words and failed me, Barrett."

"I'm not that guy."

Again that look. "Now you're challenging me."

She waved her hand at him in dismissal and walked away.

He followed. "Fine. I'll cook for you. But if you're going to gut my kitchen, it won't be here."

She enjoyed the fact he was pissed off about the whole cooking thing when it had been nothing more than a throwaway comment.

"I'll invite you to my place, Barrett. You can cook for me there."

"Wait. What? How did this conversation turn into a me cooking for you at your place event?"

She turned around. "I don't know. How did it?" Deciding to let him think on that one for a while, she asked, "Tell me what you like in terms of countertop surfaces. Granite? Quartz? Marble? Concrete, or something else?"

"Granite. Dark. Solid wood cabinets. Also dark."

She made notes, then motioned to the wall separating the kitchen from the other rooms. "We'll also take down this wall to open the space into the living room."

"You know best," he said.

With a smirk, she nodded and made a note as they made their way into the family room.

Mirrored walls in the family room. And carpet. Yuck. With two sliders—and drapes.

Who decorated this thing? It was awful.

"It's so dark in here," she said, grimacing. "We need to bring some of that fantastic outside light in here."

"Any thoughts on how to do that?"

"Yes." She made a note on her tablet. "You have tall ceilings in here. We'll knock out some of the walls and add more windows, top to bottom. We'll do a bi-fold door near the pool to bring in even more light. And all of this carpet has got to go. I'd suggest marble or tile in here because of the pool. The last thing you want is people traipsing inside with their wet feet onto carpet."

"Agree with you there."

She opened the sliding glass door and walked outside. It was super spacious, with a pool, a hot tub and a fantastic view of the water, but she had an idea.

She turned to him. "Another option to think about is a sunroom off the formal living area to the side. You have the space, and you could entertain, even when it rains." She walked over to the slider leading into the other side of the house. Barrett followed.

"Right here," she said. "I could see a bar over there, lots of tables and chairs and we could mount a TV. You're on the water and you want to extend your outdoor area as much as possible."

He could envision what she said, could already see the bar, could see his friends there watching sports or playing poker. "I like the idea."

"Of course you do. I have great ideas, Barrett." She headed back outside, past the pool, making notes along the way.

"Landscaping needs a little cleanup and refreshing. Some taller bushes here, a few extra trees there. You don't want to obliterate your awesome views of the water, but you also need your privacy. You're well-known in the area. You don't want every gawker on a speedboat snapping pictures of you partying with your friends."

"I hadn't thought about that."

She lifted her gaze to his, confidence evident in her smile. "That's why you have me. Trust me. I'll think of everything for you. All you have to do is play ball."

He cocked a brow. "Really."

She tipped her finger under his chin. "Absolutely. I'll take care of everything and when I'm done, this place will be the house of your dreams, Barrett. All you have to do is tell me what you want, and I'll make it happen for you. I'll even give you things you never dreamed of."

Barrett sucked in a deep breath of humid summer air. Harmony was going to have to stop putting those ideas in his head. Thoughts of her giving him everything he ever dreamed of went well beyond just this house.

She'd shown up in that little red sundress that clung to her curves and showed off her spectacular legs and made him think of her as a woman, not a girl.

He didn't want to think of her as a woman.

He didn't want to think about her at all.

He didn't know why the hell he'd agreed to this. It was painful.

She pulled her gaze away from his and looked down at her tablet as if she hadn't just wrapped his balls in a tight sling and cut off his circulation.

"Let's go look at the bedrooms."

He wasn't sure his dick could handle being in the bedroom with her. Any bedroom.

Especially following her up the stairs, watching the way her hips swayed back and forth as he followed behind her. And that ass. She had the most perfect ass and getting his hands on it suddenly seemed like the best idea ever.

No.

Worst idea ever, and he had better self-control than this.

To avoid any more mental temptation, he moved up beside her.

"There are three bedrooms to the right, master is to the left."

She nodded. "Okay. Let's check out the extra bedrooms first."

The three bedrooms were spacious, which was another of the things he liked.

"Do you want the bedrooms carpeted?" she asked as they walked into one.

"No. I hate carpet."

She smiled. "Me, too. We can discuss tile or wood floors up

here. With the humidity, I'd suggest tile. There are lovely porcelain tiles that look like wood flooring."

"Sure. Whatever. As long as it isn't carpet."

"Done." She made a note and stepped into the upstairs bathroom, her nose wrinkling.

"Ew. This will need a redo."

"Most everything in the house does." He already knew going in
that the entire house was going to need renovations. He just wasn't
a decorating kind of guy, so he had no idea where to start. He had
to admit that, so far, he liked everything Harmony suggested.

"We'll retile the bath, put in a new tub and shower, double van-
ity and repaint. Who thought purple in the bathroom was a good
idea for paint?"

"No idea. Maybe kids did it."

She made a note while shaking her head. "At least it's a spacious
bathroom."

She walked out and made her way down the hall. His lips
quirked. He had to admit, he agreed with all her ideas. More than
that, he liked them. And he had no idea why that surprised him.

Maybe because he hadn't known this was her job. Or that she
was so knowledgeable about what she did.

When she opened the door to the master, she nodded. "Great-
sized room. Horrible carpet. And floral wallpaper—yikes. That
definitely has to go. You need more light in here, so I say we widen
the windows to bring in more of that killer water view." She walked
out onto the deck.

"This is fantastic, Barrett."

He stepped out onto the oversized deck with her. "What? You
actually like something?"

She laughed, and the sound of her throaty laugh shot straight
to his balls, making them quiver.

"I'm only rough on the house as it is now because the more

critical I am on the front end, the more kick-ass it'll be when it's finished."

"I'll have to trust you on that."

She laid her hand on his biceps. "I told you to trust me, didn't I?"

He liked the feel of her hand on him. He didn't want to like it. "Yeah, you did."

She squeezed his arm. "I'll make this place amazing. But this deck? Other than needing to be refinished, I wouldn't touch a thing about it. It's incredible."

"Yeah, it's what finally sold me about the place. Being able to come out here at night and look out over the water is my perfect idea of 'end of the day.'"

"Maybe you need a mini fridge in your bedroom so you can grab a cold one to take with you to sit out on the deck."

He grinned. "Can you do that?"

She laughed. "I could, but I'm not putting a mini fridge in your bedroom."

"Damn."

"Come on, let's look at the master bath."

He followed her into the bathroom, another place that was a total wreck, but he liked the size of it.

She stared at it without saying a word for the longest time, then wrinkled her nose.

"What?" he finally asked.

She looked up at him. "Do you take baths?"

"No."

She leaned against the counter. "I thought all athletes did that. You know, to soak their sore muscles."

"I can do an ice bath at the locker room after a game. And there's a hot tub outside if I need a hot soak. So no, I don't need a bathtub."

"Someday you're going to get married and some woman's going to want to take a hot bath."

"Future Mrs. Cassidy can get naked in the hot tub if she wants a hot soak. That's why you'll make it all nice and private in that area, right?"

She pondered the thought. "I suppose."

"Look at it this way. Let's say it was you moving in here and you were creating this bathroom for yourself. What would you do?"

She looked over the bathroom again.

"What I really want to give you is an oversized shower against the wall there. You're a big guy and you need that. But if I do that, it means eliminating the tub. I could push the wall out to the north and put in a soaker tub, but that would eat into your closet space, and I don't want to do that, because a master bedroom needs a big closet. You'll still have a tub in the other upstairs bathroom, so for purposes of resale I think you're fine. You just won't have a bathtub in here, which I think is okay, because you'll have a monster shower. And I'll put in a steam shower for you."

"That'd be cool."

"I thought so."

"And if it were you buying this house and the master didn't have a tub?"

She pondered again, staring at the existing tub/shower combination.

"I think I'd look at the obscenely large shower that was also a steam shower and fall madly in love. Because if I wanted a bath, I could either use the tub down the hall, or soak in the hot tub. And I'd rather have a super large closet, which I'm going to give you."

He pondered the options she'd given him, realizing the decision was his to make. "Let's do the steam shower."

"Okay."

They went back downstairs and she pulled up a seat at the

existing peninsula in the kitchen. Barrett sat next to her, sitting quietly while she made notes.

Finally, she pivoted on the barstool and looked up at him. He was struck by the gut punch connection he felt when his gaze met hers, the liquid warmth in her eyes when she gave him a direct look.

It was damned uncomfortable, super hot and made him want to pull her out of that chair and onto his lap so he could touch her and put his mouth on her. But he couldn't look away from her.

"I regularly work with several very good contractors. However, if there's someone else you'd rather use, that's fine."

Her knees bumped against his leg. He swore she was doing it on purpose.

"I don't have anybody in mind. I'm fine with whoever you recommend."

"Great. I'd like to have Jeff Golan come over and do a walk-through, going through everything you and I discussed to make sure he can do everything I want done. I can do that without you being here, unless you want to be."

He shook his head. "Not necessary. You know what I want."

Her lips ticked up. "Yes, I do."

That knowing smile again. She was killing him.

"Jeff will come up with an estimate of the costs. Since I'm the designer, Jeff and I will work closely together during the renovation and I'll make sure the design elements stay on track. If anything comes up, I'll stay in touch with you."

He nodded. "That works."

"Obviously you won't be able to live here during the renovation, since we're essentially changing every room."

"That's fine. I hadn't planned on moving in until after renovating."

"Good. I'll talk to Jeff tomorrow and we'll get things started."

He stood. "Thanks for doing this, Harmony. You made it all easy."

"Oh, it won't be easy, trust me. You'll have to make a lot of design choices and I'm going to be honest here. I think you'll find a lot of them a frustrating and boring pain in the ass. Renovating is often exasperating as hell. But I'll try to make the process go as smoothly as possible."

"Thanks for that. Training camp and preseason will be coming up soon, so the last thing I want to focus on is paint color."

She laughed. "I can imagine. I'll be here every step of the way to shoulder much of that burden for you. But remember, Barrett. This is your house. Not mine. So you will have to make most of those decisions."

"Yeah, I know."

"Okay, then. I'll have a contract drawn up and get that over to you tomorrow. Now, there's only one decision you have to make right now."

"What's that?"

She gave him a wickedly sexy smile. "When are you coming over to my place to cook dinner for me?"

"You were serious about that?" He was hoping she'd forgotten.

"Of course I was. You didn't think I'd lay down a challenge and not expect you to back it up, did you?"

She waved one of her sexy legs back and forth, forcing him to look at them, and at her feet.

Hell, she even had pretty toes.

He should say no. He definitely should say no. To hell with her challenge. He knew better.

The code.

But it wasn't like he'd be dating her or anything. He just had to prove he could cook. Then he could get the hell out of there and away from her. And they'd be working together on this project, so, like it or not, he was going to have to get used to the idea of being close to her. It might as well start over dinner.

"I have practices and then some meetings. How about Saturday?"

She offered up a benign, innocent smile that didn't fool him for a minute. "Saturday sounds fine."

He walked her out to her car and opened the driver's door for her. She turned to him. "Text me a list of items and I'll shop, since you won't have time."

"I'll have time."

She sighed. "Text me a list of items, Barrett. I'll take care of it."

He liked that fire in her eyes when he irritated her, hated to admit that he wouldn't mind stoking it with passion.

And when his thoughts went down that road, he knew it was time to get far, far away from Harmony.

He leaned in, for some reason needing to poke her a little. "Hey. I've got it covered."

She inhaled, then let it out in a heavy sigh. "Fine."

She slid into her car, her dress riding up her thighs and giving him a glimpse of her smooth silky legs as she climbed in.

Dammit. He was sure she'd done that on purpose.

He shut the door and she drove off.

He walked back inside the house, deciding he needed a minute or two to cool down before he left. He walked outside and stood staring out over the Intracoastal Waterway.

This was going to be rough. He was attracted to Harmony in ways he hadn't expected. Normally he could fight an attraction, but she was smart and beautiful and hot and sexy and every time he was around her the chemistry between them grew more explosive.

She was also Drake's little sister, and like it or not, that fact was going to have to stay front and center in his mind.

SIX

BARRETT WAS HAPPY TO BE WORKING OUT WITH HIS teammates. They weren't officially at camp, but working out together to get in shape for training camp next month. He breathed in the energy of his teammates while he stretched and got down to business.

Barrett and Drake and most of the guys on the defense often got together at the gym during the off-season to work out together. Now it was summer and OTAs were over, so they brought in some of the rookies and free agents to join their daily workout routines. The team facility was always the best place to get a hard workout in and run drills on their own.

They generated a tough sweat as they pushed one another hard for the better part of three hours. Barrett and Drake worked with a few of the defensive rookies, putting them through their paces to see what they had.

It was going to be a good team this year.

"You up for going out tonight?" Drake asked as they made their way back to the lockers.

"What did you have in mind?"

"I know a couple of ladies."

Barrett laughed and shook his head. His best friend always knew a couple of ladies. He knew more than a couple of ladies. Drake was popular with women. At six foot four and with his dark good looks and the way he smiled, for some reason women were attracted to him.

That man always had a woman on his arm.

A flash of a dark-skinned, dark-haired beauty entered Barrett's head.

No. Absolutely not. He wouldn't even entertain the idea of Harmony.

"Sure. Let's do it."

"All right," Drake said, flashing his signature grin. "Let's meet at Skye at nine."

"You got it."

Barrett went home and did some work on his computer, then took a short nap. It had been a long workout day, and he knew going out with Drake meant it would be a long night of partying. If he got lucky, maybe he'd be up all night with a smoking-hot woman.

After he grabbed something to eat, he got dressed and headed over to Club Skye, one of the hottest clubs in Ybor City. The parking lot was jam full of cars, but he and Drake often frequented the club and had VIP status, so he left his keys with the valet and since he knew the folks at the door, he didn't have to wait in the lines. Drake had texted him that he was already inside at a VIP table, so he found his best friend, unsurprisingly having already accumulated about five women at the table, along with Steve Mittman and Mean Man Taylor.

"What took you so long?" Taylor asked. "You have to stop and get a pedicure?"

Barrett laughed. "Yeah. Make sure I'm all pretty for the ladies."

One of the women, a cool redhead, slid up and put her hands on his shoulders. "You look pretty enough to me."

The women here were always forward, anxious to be seen with a football player. Most of the time it suited him just fine. These women knew what they were after, and there were no games involved.

"What's your name?" Barrett asked.

"Raquel. And you're Barrett Cassidy. I'm a big fan of the Hawks."

"Nice to meet you, Raquel."

Barrett took a seat next to Drake and the guys. Raquel had decided to sit on his lap. He didn't have much of a problem with that. She wore a short, barely there dress that slid up her perfect thighs, so he rested his hand on her butt while he and the guys talked football.

Tunes were rockin', the hard liquor was flowing, and it was a good night. They all went out on the dance floor for a while, and Barrett was treated to Raquel's moves.

She had plenty of them, which included her cupping his crotch and squeezing his dick.

Then she draped her arm around his neck, ground her pussy against his cock and talked dirty in his ear.

And he didn't have a hard-on. What the hell was up with that? He'd only had one whiskey, so it wasn't as if alcohol was affecting him.

He could have Raquel either in the private area of the VIP lounge or out in his SUV if he wanted her. He could take her home and he knew they could have a good time together. She'd made herself more than available. But for some reason, she left him cold. Maybe it was because his thoughts kept straying to someone warmer, with liquid amber eyes and curves that kept him up at night.

Try as he might, despite Raquel's roaming hands and killer body, his mind was firmly on Harmony tonight.

Which was all kinds of wrong, but there it was.

He stayed about two hours, then leaned over and told Drake he was heading out.

Drake frowned. "What's wrong?"

"Nothing. Got an early meeting with my attorney in the morning, so I can't be hungover."

Drake nodded. "I'll see ya."

Much to Raquel's disappointment, he had to tell her he was heading out—alone.

He breathed a sigh of relief when he walked out of the club and to his SUV.

He normally got into the club scene, and while he'd enjoyed hanging out with the guys, the women just weren't doing it for him tonight.

Maybe because only one woman was doing it for him.

And he had to find a way to get her out of his thoughts so he could go back to life as normal.

SEVEN

BARRETT SPENT MOST OF SATURDAY TRYING TO TALK himself out of going over to Harmony's place.

In the end, he couldn't figure out a legitimate reason why he shouldn't go that wouldn't make him look like a total wuss. So he decided he'd suck it up and do it. They could be friends. She was going to be working with him, so this was as good a time as any to get used to being around her.

He got into his SUV, turned up his radio and hit the highway.

He did the grocery shopping first, then drove out to her place. When he'd last come here with Drake, he'd paid no attention to where they were. Now he took the time to notice the community. Pretty nice complex with a good view of the water. He could see why she chose this location.

He parked and grabbed the grocery bags, walking the short distance to her door. He rang the bell and waited.

She didn't answer.

He frowned and rang the bell again.

She finally opened the door, wearing a yellow and white sundress that was tight on top and full at the bottom and made him notice her body in ways he had no business noticing.

"Hey," she said with a smile. "I was on the phone. Sorry it took me so long."

"Not a problem."

"Come on inside. It's hot out there."

He walked in, thankful she had the AC cranked up. "Feels good in here."

"It'll feel even better once you have something to drink. You can unload those bags on the counter." She led him past the small living area.

He stopped and peered into the bathroom.

"Got it painted, I see. The green looks good."

"Thanks."

"So, whatever had you upset is out of your system now?"

Her lips quirked. "Yes."

"Good to know."

He stepped into the kitchen and laid his bags on the counter.

"What would you like to drink?"

"A beer would be good."

"Coming up." She opened her refrigerator and pulled out a beer, handing it to him.

"Thanks." He took out the chicken and slid it into her refrigerator, then pulled up a seat at her kitchen island and popped open the beer, taking a couple long swallows.

"Nice place."

"Thank you." She smiled. "I fell in love with it as soon as I saw it, and I knew it had to be mine. The view from the bedroom balcony is fantastic. I'll give you a tour later."

He wasn't sure he wanted to be anywhere near her bedroom. She was already too tempting as it was. "That sounds great."

She took a peek inside the grocery bags. "Interesting."

His lips curved as he took another swallow of beer. "I'm going to rock your world tonight."

She swiped her fingertip along the condensation sliding down her glass of iced tea. "I look forward to that."

Her warm brown eyes melted him when she said those words, and his dick got hard.

Dammit.

"I meant the food, Harmony."

She blinked an innocent smile. "Of course you did."

"We discussed the rule."

She shrugged. "That's your rule, Barrett. Not mine."

Damn she was frustrating. "It's a rule I intend to adhere to."

She reached across the island and patted his hand. "Whatever you say. So, would you like to see my town house? It'll give you an idea of my decorating style."

He got the idea she'd just patronized the hell out of him, and he wasn't sure how to feel about that. But he wasn't about to continue that line of conversation, so the best thing to do was let it drop. "Sure."

"This is obviously the kitchen. I bought into the town house before it was built, so I chose the countertops, backsplash, cabinets and all the hardware."

The kitchen was spacious. It had dark maple cabinets with dusky gray quartz counters and stainless steel appliances. The white and gray glass herringbone backsplash seemed to work well with everything else and wasn't wild or crazy.

She moved around the island. "The flooring is actually a porcelain tile that looks like hardwood. I had it put in throughout the house."

It was a dark terra cotta color, and really looked like wood flooring. "I like it. I definitely might want to consider it for my house."

"I thought you might. Easy to clean, holds up much better to our high humidity than wood floors. We'll talk about it when it comes time to order flooring."

She led him into a spacious second living area.

"This is the family room, where I spend most of my time because of the view. It has a balcony as well." She went to the doors and opened them, walking him out onto what was a decent-sized deck.

"I sacrificed backyard for two decks and a view," she said, as she stepped out next to him.

The view of the water was pretty awesome. "This is nice. But I guess no dog for you, huh?"

She laughed. "Sadly, no. My hours are so erratic I don't think it would be fair to get a dog anyway."

He turned to her, leaning an elbow against the wood rail. "I remember when I first met you. You told me that after you graduated college you were going to get your own place because you wanted a puppy and your mom was allergic, so you couldn't have one at her house."

She frowned. "I said that? I don't remember."

"You told me that the first day we met. You told me a lot of things, because you talked all the time and never shut up, but that's the one thing that stuck with me the most."

She laughed. "I did have a tendency to talk a lot, especially when I was nervous."

He cocked a brow. "I made you nervous?"

"Exceedingly."

He knew he shouldn't, but he couldn't help stepping closer, breathing in that sweet, citrusy scent that always seemed to surround her. "You don't seem nervous now."

She stepped in as well, her fingertip tracing circles around his forearm. "I am most definitely not nervous around you now, Barrett. Back then I was young and inexperienced and not accustomed to being around extremely attractive men like you."

This was dangerous territory and he knew better than to court that kind of danger. He should put his defenses up and maintain his distance.

But damn if he wanted to right now. Not when Harmony's mouth was painted a sweet, kissable shade of plum, and her tongue swept out to lick across her bottom lip, tempting him to lean in and take a taste. Or maybe even a bite.

She leaned in, expecting it. So easy to grab hold of her and take what she offered, what they both wanted.

But then he thought about Drake, and how betrayed his best friend would feel if this happened between Harmony and him.

Nope. Not gonna happen. He took a step back. "So how about I cook us some dinner?"

He read the disappointment on Harmony's face, but she immediately masked it with a smile. "Sure. I'm anxious to see if you can really cook."

He moved in beside her as they headed downstairs. "Honey, I never say what I don't mean."

She lifted her gaze to his. "I'll file that comment away for some future date."

He had no idea what she meant by that, but when they got back into the kitchen, she started unpacking the grocery bags.

"I have no clue what you intend to do with all that stuff, but I'm happy to help."

He shook his head. "Oh, no. You laid down the challenge and told me men fail you in the kitchen. You just sit there and watch. I've got this."

HARMONY HAD NO IDEA WHAT BARRETT WAS GOING TO cook for her today. He'd asked her if she had an outdoor grill, which she did, so she knew he'd be grilling whatever he cooked, which suited her just fine, since it was hot and she wasn't keen on the idea of using the oven.

She watched as he used the meat mallet she'd provided for him to pound the hell out of the boneless chicken breasts until they were small rectangles. Then he melted butter in a bowl and added lemon juice and zest and set it aside.

"What are you going to do with that?" she asked.

He looked up at her. "You'll see."

He took another bowl and mixed parmesan cheese, fresh basil, garlic and more butter.

Whatever it was he was doing with that concoction, it made her hungry.

He laid the flattened chicken breasts out and filled them with the parmesan mixture, then folded the chicken over and secured each one with a toothpick.

"Oh I see," she said. "Stuffed chicken breasts."

"You got it."

He got out wooden skewers and soaked them in water while he sliced a red, yellow and green bell pepper, a red onion, zucchini and a yellow squash. He mixed up a marinade of olive oil, salt, pepper and garlic, then tossed the vegetables in the marinade.

"We'll let those sit for a few minutes while I start cooking the chicken."

He stepped out onto the downstairs balcony where she had her grill.

Huh. Maybe he did know what he was doing after all. If so, he'd be the first man she'd ever known who had.

Typically, when she dated a guy, she did all the cooking while he sat back with a drink in his hand, metaphorically scratching his balls, waiting to be served.

She had no problem with traditional gender roles. She knew how to cook and she did it well. She actually enjoyed it. But she was also a professional career woman and she worked as damn hard as men did. Just once she'd like to date someone who appreciated that, who understood how hard she worked and would surprise her by having dinner on the table when she came home.

Hell, she'd be happy dating a man who would offer to do the dishes.

Her friend Alyssa was right. Harmony knew there were awesome men out there, the kind who could appreciate her. She just hadn't found one yet.

Though, focusing her attention back on Barrett, she found a glimmer of hope as she sat back, sipped her tea and watched him prepare the meal.

So unusual. But yet another reason to like this man.

He came back inside, and as he walked by she breathed in the grill scent on him.

Actually kind of an aphrodisiac.

"So where did you learn to cook?" she asked, as he pulled the vegetables from the marinade and laid them on a plate.

"My mom. And surprisingly, from my older brother Flynn. He's taught me a few new cooking tricks over the past year."

Her lips ticked up. "Not the typical types of things one hears uttered from the mouth of a big, well-muscled man."

He laid his hands on her kitchen island. "Now that's a sexist statement."

"Probably. But still, you just don't look like the cooking type."

"There's a cooking type? Do you ever watch cooking shows?"

"Frankly, no."

"Trust me, there's no cooking type. There are people from all walks of life who enjoy cooking, from kids to women—" He leveled a devastating smile on her. "Even men with muscles."

She could tell she'd hit a raw nerve. "I'm sticking my foot in my mouth with this conversation, aren't I?"

"Maybe a little. Which is the only reason I'm here today cooking you dinner."

She didn't buy it. "The only reason?"

He picked up the plate of skewered vegetables and made his way to her back door. "Trust me, Harmony. It's the one and only reason."

She smiled as she checked out his retreating form.

Only reason her ass. He could have said no, and he didn't. He was here because he wanted to be here.

"Guy rule" be damned. She intended to take full advantage of their evening alone together.

EIGHT

CHICKEN WAS DONE, AND JUST IN TIME BECAUSE THE vegetables had a nice grilled edge to them. They looked tender and just about cooked to perfection.

Barrett might not be a master cook, but he'd learned enough from his mom and from Flynn to work his way around a kitchen, and definitely a grill.

He liked food. All his brothers did. His mother made sure they could take care of themselves in the cooking department, at least as far as the basics. And now that Flynn was opening a restaurant, Barrett had learned a thing or two about upping his game beyond just eggs, burgers and tossing a steak on the grill.

Like tonight's dinner. When he'd been out in San Francisco visiting Flynn several months back, his brother had showed him how to fix the stuffed chicken breasts with grilled vegetables. Not hard, really. It had become one of his staple meals.

As he loaded the finished chicken and vegetables onto plates to carry inside, he wondered why no guys had bothered to fix a meal for Harmony. Even bacon and eggs could be impressive if done the right way—and at the right time.

Men were such douchebags sometimes. And the old ways of thinking that women were supposed to do all the cooking were long gone. His mother, a former career attorney, had made sure to teach all her sons that rule. She might have given up her career to stay at home with her kids, but that didn't mean she did all the work around the family ranch.

Everyone pitched in. Which didn't mean the boys did the outside work while Mom and his little sister, Mia, did the cooking and cleaning inside the house, either. According to Mom, guys were more than capable of cooking a meal, doing the dishes, and scrubbing toilets. Just as women could operate the tractors outside.

Barrett had grown up doing it all. He'd like to think he was pretty well-rounded.

He carried the plates inside and laid them on the dining room table. Harmony had already set the table.

"Perfect timing," she said, coming into the dining room from the kitchen. "I just opened a bottle of wine."

"I'll go wash my hands, then we can eat."

He dashed into the bathroom to wash up, then met her back in the dining room.

"I have to admit, this all smells really good," she said, as he pulled a chair out for her at the table.

He took a seat next to her, anxious for her to take a bite of the chicken.

Instead, she lifted her glass of wine and tipped it toward him. "Thank you for coming over to cook dinner for me."

He tipped his glass to hers. "You can thank me after you've tasted it."

Her lips curved. "Are you nervous?"

"No. Confident."

"Good. I like my men confident."

Her men. Barrett was not one of her men. Never would be. But he was confident—he just needed her to eat the damn food so he could get the hell away from her sweet scent and the temptation to run his hands over her soft skin.

She finally set her wineglass on the table and cut into the chicken. He waited while she took a bite and swallowed.

Her eyes closed and she made a sound—a moaning sound. He resisted groaning in response.

"This is excellent."

He slanted a smile at her and started eating.

"Okay," she said after she'd had several bites of the chicken and the grilled vegetables. "You can cook."

He took a couple swallows of wine. "Did you think I was lying?"

"No. I don't know. Maybe I did. I'm frankly surprised. My last . . . well, let's not go there."

"Let's do. Tell me about bathroom counter guy."

"Levon? He was . . . high maintenance."

"In what way?"

"His clothes had to be impeccably pressed. I'm pretty sure the only things that ever went into the washing machine were his underwear, and even that is suspect. Everything else went to the dry cleaner's. His house was spotless. He had cleaning people come in three times a week."

Barrett raised a brow. "A bit of a neat freak, huh?"

She cut into another piece of chicken, then waved her fork at Barrett. "That's an understatement. He yelled at me once because I forgot to take my shoes off at the front door. He didn't want his precious mahogany floors scratched. And I was wearing tennis shoes at the time."

"What an asshole."

She laughed. "Yeah, kind of. At least not the kind of man I wanted in my life long-term. I like a neat and orderly house, but if I want to toss my purse on the dining room table, I'd like to know the man in my life isn't going to have a nuclear meltdown over it."

"Definitely the wrong guy for you."

"I agree."

They finished dinner, carted their plates into the kitchen and loaded them into the dishwasher. Barrett picked up the bottle of wine from the dining room table and they settled into the living room.

What he should be doing is making a fast exit. But he didn't want to be rude by eating and running, so he'd stay a few minutes longer. Then he'd make a clean getaway, having fulfilled his obligation.

She kicked off her sandals and pulled her legs up on the sofa, then picked up her glass. "You got the contracts?"

"I did. Already signed them. They're in my car. I meant to bring those inside with me."

"No hurry. But the sooner we get those executed, the sooner we can get started and finished. I know you'd like to move into your house."

He nodded. "The condo's a little tight for me. I'm on the road a lot during the season, but off-season it gets claustrophobic."

"I'm sure it does, big guy like you in a condo."

"Yeah, it wasn't exactly my best move. I should have leased a town house, kind of like what you have here. You have more space than I do."

"I wanted more room than a traditional condo. The town house affords me that. I would have preferred a house, but then there's all that lawn maintenance."

His lips curved. "Not a fan of mowing?"

"I don't mind it, but my business has taken off, and I often have evening and weekend meetings. I'd like a bigger place with space for an office. Maybe sometime down the road I'll opt for the house. Right now, letting the homeowner's association deal with it works for me."

He studied her in her cute little dress and her perfectly manicured turquoise toenails and matching fingernails. She had tiny feet, too, her heels smooth as polished stone.

"I can't imagine you pushing a lawnmower."

She cocked a brow. "Is that right? Who do you think mows the lawn at Mama's house in late summer when you and Drake are out of town at some road game?"

"Don't you have a lawn service?"

She laughed. "Mama would never allow a lawn service. She thinks it's a frivolous expense."

"That sounds like her."

"And with her bad back, she can't handle the mower anymore. So I do it. Which is another reason I didn't buy a house. I have to make the time to do the yard work at Mama's. No way I could find the time to do that at her house and mine."

He made a mental note to mention that to Drake. If Drake could convince Mama Diane to move into a new house, he could wear her down on a lawn service, too.

"You're just a tough girl, aren't you?"

"It's not that hard to mow the lawn, Barrett. Or run a weed whacker. Mama did it for years until her back issues. We Evans girls are made of strong stuff."

"And yet you look tiny and fragile."

She snorted out a laugh. "I also take kickboxing classes, so don't mess with me."

"That sounds like another challenge."

"You might be all big and muscular, but we could go a few rounds. Who knows? I might be able to take you down."

An instant visual of Harmony—naked and sitting on top of him—hammered his brain.

That would be one hell of a takedown. A tangle of limbs, her writhing on top of him, her sweet body undulating as she rode his dick . . .

Goddammit. What was it about this woman—this particular woman—that stirred him up like no other woman had before? He'd never had a problem walking away from a woman. Some were the right woman, and some weren't. And when they weren't, he never looked back.

So what was he still doing here, and why hadn't he left yet? He stared at the now empty bottle of wine on the table.

This was the time. He'd done what he'd been asked to do. They'd shared a meal. Dishes were done. They'd had after-dinner wine and conversation. He could make a polite exit.

"Oh, but speaking of things that maybe I can't do, I was wondering if you'd help me with something while you're here."

So much for his exit. "Sure."

"It's upstairs in my bedroom. Follow me."

She slid off the sofa and he followed her upstairs, careful to stay right next to her so he wouldn't be tempted by visuals of her legs or her butt.

She walked into her bedroom, and he prepared himself for some kind of assault, like her pushing him against the wall and rubbing her body all over him.

He was strong. He could withstand temptation. He'd just tell her no—politely but firmly, while reminding her about his friendship with Drake.

"Okay, so here's the deal," she said, pulling him from his righteous fantasy. "I bought these shutters for the bedroom windows, and I thought I could save on installation costs by doing it myself. The problem is, it's kind of a two-person job because these things are heavy. I was wondering if you'd be willing to give me a hand."

Okay, so no assault. Instead, a home improvement project. He hadn't even been in the vicinity of guessing her motivations.

"Oh. Sure, I can do that."

She grinned. "Awesome. Thanks."

She hadn't stripped down or pushed him against the wall or rubbed her body on his. Instead, she led him into her spare bedroom, where two boxes sat on the bed.

So maybe that seduction fantasy had been all in *his* head, not hers.

"These are the shutters?" he asked, focusing instead on the task at hand.

"Yes."

He picked up the boxes—she was right, they were heavy. He carted them one by one into her bedroom and laid them on the floor.

In the meantime, she'd grabbed a cordless drill while he unpacked the boxes. Then she disappeared again, and he had no idea where she wanted these. He assumed the two windows on either side of the bed, since that's where they'd seem to fit, but he didn't want to make assumptions, so he started reading the instructions.

When she came back upstairs with a ladder in her hands, he got up and took it from her.

"Jesus, Harmony. I could have gotten that for you."

She lifted her gaze to his. "I don't have the expectation that you're the man and I can't do anything for myself. I planned to install these shutters myself. It's just the windows are higher than I expected, the shutters are heavy and I was a couple hands short."

"You know, I get that you're all female empowered and all that shit, and I have no doubt you can move mountains on your own. But it's still okay to ask for help if you need it."

She arched a brow. "I just did, jackass."

He wasn't insulted. He liked when she got feisty and stood up for herself. It made him like her even more. He didn't enjoy women who were doormats, who let a man walk all over them. Harmony obviously wasn't that woman and he respected her for it.

So he laughed and took the ladder from her. "Okay, let's take down these curtains."

"They let too much light in," she explained.

He set up the ladder against the first window, climbed up and pulled the curtains off the rod, then used the drill to remove the screws. He shoved the screws in his pants pockets and dropped the drapes onto the floor.

"And when I sleep, I want to sleep. Plus, the shutters are prettier."

When he just stared down at her, she quirked a smile. "Okay, I can see you don't care at all about the reasons for the change in window treatments."

"Not so much." He climbed down, kneeled on the floor and broke open the plastic package in the box. He took her hand, flipped it over so her palm was up, and dropped the screws in her hand. "Hold these and follow me."

He picked up the first shutter frame and positioned it against the window.

"Screw."

She handed him a screw and he drilled it in. It went that way for a while, until he had the frame mounted, and then the shutter.

"You make it look easy," she said after he finished the first window.

He smiled at her as he picked up the ladder and moved over to the second window. "I'm a lot bigger than you, so for me it is easy. I can see how this would have been unwieldy for you."

"I can handle most any project around the house. I'm handy with power tools. I hung the drapes myself."

"You did a good job." He took the curtain down and mounted

the shutter on the second window. When he was done, he folded the ladder and took a step back so she could inspect his work.

"These shutters are beautiful, just as I envisioned. I don't know what I was thinking putting drapes in here. It was a wrong decision. This is so much better."

"Glad it worked for you."

She closed the shutter louvers and darkened the room. "Perfect. I won't have any trouble falling asleep now."

"And I won't have to worry about you tossing and turning at night."

She laughed. "Yeah, I can imagine that's going to occupy a large amount of mental space in your head."

He carried the ladder and the tools back downstairs and put them in their places in her neat and orderly garage. She actually had a toolbox out here with more than enough tools to handle any task.

Good for her. He came back into the house.

"So was that another decorating project to deal with you being upset?"

She cocked her head to the side. "A . . . Oh. No. It was actually something I've wanted to do for a while now. I just needed two people to get it done. The painting, however, was definitely a redecorating project. I like to paint or redecorate and it helps me think and work through problems."

He kind of had an idea where this was going. "Problems like ex-boyfriends?"

"Maybe something like that."

"Gotcha. So any other 'honey dos' you want done before I take off?"

She leaned against the kitchen counter. "No. All the light bulbs are currently in working order. Though I can replace those myself."

He moved in closer to her. "I'm sure you can do most anything yourself."

She pushed off the counter and stepped toward him. "Yes, I can. Though some things are more fun done with someone else."

He knew exactly what she was talking about, and the look she gave him not only gave him dirty thoughts, but made his cock come to life.

He took a step back. "Harmony."

She took a step forward, pressing her hands against his chest. "Barrett."

The last damn thing he wanted was her hands on him. It was also everything he'd thought about lately. Her hands on his chest. On his cock. Along with her mouth.

Fuck.

He grasped her wrists. "Not a good idea."

She lifted her gaze to his. "Why not?"

"You know why not."

She raised a brow. "If you tell me right now that you're thinking about my brother, I'm going to seriously question which side of the field you're playing for."

He took her hand, slid it down his chest and laid it on his now-hard cock. "That has nothing to do with your brother, and everything to do with you. Which is a problem."

She let out a soft laugh, then rubbed his erection with the palm of her hand. "Yes, a pretty sizable problem from what I can tell."

He wanted her hands on him. He wanted to take this further. He wanted to kiss her pretty mouth and slide his tongue inside to taste her.

He wanted a lot of things, but he'd learned a long time ago that he couldn't have everything he wanted, and some temptations were better left alone.

Harmony was one of those temptations. And he owed it to Drake to keep his hands off his sister. So he took a step back, regretting every inch he moved backward.

Harmony cocked a brow. "You sure about that?"

"Not really, but it's a choice I'm going to have to make."

"Because of Drake."

He nodded.

"Okay. I'm not going to throw myself at you, Barrett." She walked him to her front door, then turned to face him. "But I think it's the wrong decision. And when you're lying in bed tonight with your cock aching and hard, think about that decision and what you could have had tonight. Because we're two grown-ass adults and you should be able to make your own choices about who you see—and who you take to bed."

His cock was already hard. But this was complicated. "Good night, Harmony."

She opened the door for him. "Good night, Barrett."

He walked outside, blasted by the hot, humid air, which didn't improve his frustrated, irritated mood at all.

As he slid into his SUV and started the engine, he turned the AC to arctic, hoping it would cool down his desires on the drive back to his place.

Unfortunately, the cold AC made him think of Harmony being in the car with him—naked—the air vents blowing on her nipples, arcing into tight points. She'd rub them, teasing him as he drove.

Shit.

By the time he pulled into the garage of his condo, his dick was rock hard, throbbing, and he needed some relief.

Too bad he'd walked away from a very willing and receptive Harmony.

He'd made the right choice, even if his dick didn't think so at the moment.

He threw his keys on the kitchen counter, grabbed a beer from the refrigerator and, leaving the lights off, walked into the living room. The drapes were drawn, so he stared through the French doors into the darkness.

He wished Harmony was standing next to him. Her scent still lingered around him, so he took a deep breath and closed his eyes, imagining her moving in front of him to put her arms around him, pressing her breasts against him. Her hair would tickle his chin and he'd grab a handful of it, tilt her head back so he could take her mouth in a deep kiss.

His cock strained against the zipper of his jeans. He set his beer down on the coffee table and returned to the back door. In the dark he had plenty of privacy, so he unzipped his pants, drew them and his briefs down over his hips and pulled out his cock.

His gaze was fixed outside, but that's not what he was looking at. He was firmly implanted in his imagination, where Harmony had dropped to her knees, her hands taking hold of his cock just as he had hold of it now. As he began to stroke, so would she, only her hands were smaller and softer than his.

She'd sift his shaft through both hands, looking up at him as she tilted his cock toward her lips. And when her sweet pink tongue darted out to lick at the crest, he groaned.

"Yes, suck it," he whispered to himself, caught up in the fantasy of her mouth covering his cockhead.

He stroked the shaft, fisting it in his hand and drawing it through, imagining it disappearing in the warm recesses of Harmony's mouth. He shuddered at the visuals of her lips compressing over his flesh, of her tongue darting over his cockhead.

He could go all night doing this, fantasizing about her sucking him. But dammit, he could already feel his balls tighten, could already feel them quiver in anticipation of his climax.

He reached over on the table for a tissue and held it in one hand while he pumped his shaft harder and faster in his fist, wishing

Harmony were here. He'd want her to watch him get off. Hell, he'd want to watch her get off. Now that'd be something he'd enjoy. Her, naked and spread-eagled on his sofa, her sex open to his view while she pumped her fingers inside and teased her clit. God, he wanted to see her naked so damn badly.

"Fuck." The visuals were all too much. He let loose a stream of come into the tissue, his hips pumping hard as he groaned and shuddered through an orgasm that was filled with images of Harmony crying out while she came, too.

Spent, he crumpled up the tissue, pulled up his pants and went into the bathroom. He flipped on the light, flushed the tissue and stared at himself in the mirror while he washed his hands.

"You could have had her, dumbass. Instead of jacking off into a goddamn tissue, you could have been inside of Harmony."

Except for that number-one rule—she was Drake's sister.

He stared down at the sink and shook his head. Yeah, he'd gotten off, but he felt no more satisfied now than he'd been before.

With a disgusted sigh, he turned off the bathroom light and left the room.

HARMONY GOT READY FOR BED, ALREADY ANTICIPAT-ing the awesome night's sleep she was going to have now that Barrett had installed the shutters for her.

She washed her face, brushed her teeth and turned off the lights, smiling as the room was bathed in utter darkness. As she stared up at the ceiling, she thought about tonight.

She had put on a brave, aggressive front for Barrett tonight, making sure to show off her confident side. But inside, when she'd touched him, she'd been a quivering pile of gooey marshmallow just waiting for him to touch her back.

And when he hadn't, her confidence had taken a hit.

But she wasn't the type of woman to take one setback and give up. Because Barrett had definitely been interested. Hard as granite interested. Just the thought of him getting hard over her made her wet.

God, the man was so damn stubborn, though. He could have been in her bed tonight. Instead, now she lay here, frustrated, every nerve ending taut with tension.

She slid a hand inside her top to fondle her breasts, imagining what it might have been like tonight if Barrett had pushed her against the wall and kissed her.

She could feel his lips on hers, soft and firm, taking command, rubbing his hard cock against her pussy as his tongue warred with hers.

With a whimper, she tucked her other hand inside her panties to cup her sex. She gasped and rubbed her clit, visualizing how it would have gone down tonight had Barrett stayed.

He was a demanding, powerful man, the kind who would take what he wanted from a woman. She could well imagine him drawing her underwear down and putting his mouth on her pussy, licking and sucking her until she came.

The visuals slammed into her as she quickly rubbed her clit. She was so wet, so hot, and when she came, she moaned his name, begging him to fuck her over and over. Her climax was a crazy release, and one she welcomed. One she'd desperately needed.

She rested her hips on the bed and let herself float down from that amazing high.

"Dammit, Barrett," she said to the ceiling. "We could have had such a hot time tonight."

With a little pressure, she could wear him down.

She respected him wanting to honor his friendship with Drake, even though his loyalty was a bit misplaced. If she'd been seventeen or something, then definitely.

But she was no child, and Drake was already overprotective enough about every aspect of her life. She would not let her brother call the shots over her romantic life.

She wanted Barrett.

She intended to have him.

With renewed confidence, she turned on her side and closed her eyes.

NINE

HARMONY AND JEFF BOTH TOLD BARRETT THE CREW would show up today to start demo on his house, and he wanted to be there to watch. Plus, Harmony had called and made an appointment with him for this morning to meet about some design stuff.

What he hadn't expected was for Harmony to be at his house. When he parked his SUV on the street, she was outside in the driveway talking to Jeff. She was holding a stainless steel cup in her hand and waving it around as she talked. Obviously an animated conversation was going on, and she wasn't happy about something.

He grabbed his cup of coffee out of the car and headed their way.

"These delays are costing the homeowners money, Jeff."

"I agree, Harmony, but there's nothing I can do if they keep changing their mind about finishes every third day. First they wanted black granite for the countertops. Now they've decided on marble. So we have to cool our heels and wait for the marble to come in, which, by the way, is back-ordered. I had no choice. I had to send the crew on to another job. Everything else in the house is on hold until we can install the counters."

Harmony took a deep breath, then nodded. "You're right. You're right. I'll talk to them."

"Great. And when you do that? Tell them if they change one more thing in the house, it's going to set back the final date for move in."

"I'll do that. Thanks for being so patient about this."

Jeff shrugged. "I'm used to it."

She finally noticed Barrett standing there and turned to him with a smile. "Good morning. You ready to see your house demolished?"

He returned her smile while he shook Jeff's hand. "Hopefully just the inside parts."

Jeff laughed. "Promise you we'll only take the pieces out that are supposed to come out. You're welcome to wield a sledgehammer if you'd like."

"No thanks. I'll stay out of the way and leave it to the experts."

"What?" Harmony said. "This is typically where all the homeowners want to dig in and destroy something."

"I've done plenty of renovating at my parents' house. I've slung my share of sledgehammers in my lifetime. I'll pass."

"Then come enjoy the destruction," Jeff said. "But if you change your mind, the sledgehammer is yours."

Barrett grinned. "Thanks. Or maybe Harmony will want to take a swing."

"Ha." She held up her cup. "I'll just sip and observe."

"My crew's already in the house and I'm heading that way," Jeff said. "Come on in when you're ready."

Jeff disappeared inside, while Barrett cocked his head to the side, taking in Harmony's black dress with white polka dots, along with her high heels. He tried not to notice her sleek, long legs or the way the dress cut across her breasts.

Too late. He already noticed.

"You're wearing that to a demo?"

She laughed. "It's not like I'm going to actually be *doing* the demo."

"Yeah, but it'll be dusty and dirty in there."

"Trust me. I know my way around a renovation. I'll stay out of the dust zones."

"Maybe you should wait outside. Or better yet, not be here."

Her lips quirked. "Trying to get rid of me, Barrett?"

"Nope. Just trying to look out for that pretty dress you're wearing."

"You noticed my dress."

Her smile nearly knocked him out. It was pure sex and promise. Damn her for being so desirable without even trying.

"I noticed your dress could get dirty. That's all."

"Uh-huh. Sure you did." She linked her arm through his. "Come on, hot stuff. Let's go inside and take a look at the magic happening."

They walked through the front door and into the main living area, which so far, was unscathed. All the action seemed to be happening in the back of the house, mainly in the kitchen.

"Come on this way," Harmony said, leading him into the dining area. "We'll be out of the way in here, but we can still watch."

Jeff had a crew of four in the kitchen, and as Barrett sipped his cup of coffee, he watched them do a total teardown in a matter of a half hour, from removing appliances to ripping out the cabinets and the countertops. Next to come up was the hideous floor.

"Impressive."

Harmony grinned. "I told you Jeff and his team were good."

Jeff came over. "We're about to take this wall down, so you two might want to either back away or make yourselves scarce. It's going to get dusty in here."

"That's our cue to leave," she said. "Thanks for the show, Jeff."

"Yeah, it was fun to watch," Barrett said. "Kitchen already looks larger."

"This whole place will look bigger in a few days once we take out some walls and flooring and start cutting out for windows."

Barrett nodded. "I'll check back in, but I don't want to get in your way."

"You won't be in the way," Jeff said. "It's your house. Come by anytime."

"Thanks."

He and Harmony walked outside.

"Do you want to come to my office so we can go over some design plans?" she asked.

"Sure."

He followed her over to her office and pulled in front of a nice storefront that had the name of her company—Evans Interior Design—etched on the front.

He met her at the door and opened it for her.

"Thanks."

Inside was an explosion of fabrics and tiles and books spread out on a large tabletop.

"Oh, you're here."

A young woman, probably around the same age as Harmony, approached her. She was petite, with dark hair pulled into a high ponytail and a gorgeous smile that she leveled in his direction.

"Rosalie, this is Barrett Cassidy. Barrett, this is my assistant, Rosalie Juarez."

Rosalie grinned and held out her hand. "I know who you are, Mr. Cassidy. I'm a big fan."

"Call me Barrett. Nice to meet you."

Rosalie nodded and turned her attention to Harmony. "The countertops are in on the Robinson project. I called the contractor to let them know. Delia Spring also called and is interested in doing a living room redesign. I told her you'd get back to her."

Harmony nodded. "Thanks, Rosalie. Can you get back to Delia and make an appointment with her? I think I have time tomorrow morning but double-check my calendar."

"Will do."

Harmony motioned to Barrett. "Come on back to my office and we'll go over some design features."

Her office was located in the back of the shop. Her desk was neat and tidy, with a laptop and pens and a pad of paper.

"Have a seat," she said, closing the door behind them.

The office had windows on all sides, and was spacious enough even for him. He pulled up a chair and instead of sitting behind the desk, she grabbed her laptop and pulled up the chair next to his.

"We'll start by going over a few items you'll need to select. Once I get an idea of your likes and dislikes, we'll take a look at some of the samples we have out in the showroom."

"Sure." He wasn't thrilled about being here and having to do this, but Harmony had told him on the phone that she wasn't going to pick his countertops or his flooring or paint color, so he was going to have to do it.

Fortunately, she had everything organized, so it went pretty fast. They were out in the showroom within an hour, where he chose the type of granite countertop he wanted, along with the flooring and backsplash—with Harmony's guidance, of course.

"I think you'll be happy with the porcelain tiles," she said, as she finished making notes in her tablet. "They have the look of hardwoods, but with your pool and all the rain we get, they'll hold up better."

"Agree."

"I think we'll wait on paint color in the kitchen and living area until the floors go down and the appliances and counters are in. It'll give us a better feel for how the space looks."

"You would know best."

She smiled up at him. "Why yes, I would."

He picked up his phone to check the time. "So are we done here?"

"Why? Anxious to get away from me?"

"No, actually, I have a thing to do today."

She arched a brow. "A thing?"

"It's a team thing. Not really a team thing, since I'm the only one doing it today."

"Okay, Barrett, you're being vague."

"Sorry. It's a community outreach program for at-risk teens. There's a facility near the stadium that the team supports."

"Oh, okay. I know that one well. Drake's involved with it, too. He's spoken there a few times. Great program. Are you giving a talk over there today?"

He nodded. "Yeah. Some of the kids are in a summer program, so I'm going to talk with them about sports—and grades. I figure if you talk about sports to them, they might actually listen to how important school and grades are."

"That's fantastic. I'd love to go with you. I know the coordinator there."

"You do?"

"Yes. We went to college together. And we can grab some food while we're out."

He liked how she'd inserted the "we'll eat together, too" part of the day. "Are you sure your schedule will allow that?"

Her lips curved. "Still trying to get away from me?"

"No. I just don't want to make you late for any appointments."

"Trust me, Barrett. I know exactly where I'm supposed to be at any given time. I've got time for this. Plus, I want to see what you do with these kids."

He shrugged, knowing he wasn't going to get out of bringing her along. "Sure. Let's go. It'll be fun."

More time with the seductress in her sweet dress, while he tried not to ogle her sexy legs in front of middle school kids.

Yeah, it'd be about as fun as a hard-on with no relief in sight.

TEN

HARMONY KNEW SHE'D BACKED BARRETT INTO A COR-
ner by inviting herself along to the community center. But she'd
actually wanted to go. She hadn't seen her friend Lachelle in a long
time. Both of them had hefty schedules, plus Lachelle had eighteen-
month-old twin boys, so trying to get a night out with her friend
was nearly impossible these days.

So when she walked through the doors of the community center, she couldn't help the smile on her face or the way she leaned
into Barrett. She was so excited to see her friend.

"Lachelle and I were roommates freshman year at Florida State,"
she said to Barrett as they waited at the front desk. "We became
friends right away, and were inseparable through all our years of
college together."

Barrett grinned. "Like Drake and me."

"Yes. Exactly like that. Though she majored in social work and

I did interior design. We didn't exactly have sports in common like you and Drake did."

"Your brother and I didn't share the same major. Drake did media studies and I did political science. The difference in our majors had no effect on our friendship. I think Drake and I would have been friends even if we hadn't had football in common."

Harmony adored how much Barrett loved her brother. It was one of the things she admired the most about him. He was loyal to Drake, and Drake hadn't experienced much in the way of loyalty and friendship growing up. There were the guys in gangs who had claimed to be his friends, who wanted him—no, more like coaxed him—to be a part of what they considered their brotherhood. To someone like Drake, who had been displaced and had grown up fatherless, that kind of male leadership had appealed.

Mama had told him absolutely not and had told him she'd kick his ass. Fortunately, he'd had football to focus on, to keep him honest and straight. Along with Mama, who had been fierce with her love as well as her discipline.

Once out of high school and into college, he'd had football, his studies and loyal friends like Barrett to keep him focused.

She was grateful.

"He's lucky to have someone like you in his life."

"I don't know. I've always felt like the lucky one."

Harmony got an inkling right then of why Barrett was so hesitant to do anything with her. Barrett had to know how protective Drake was over the family, and especially her. Barrett was also protective of his friendship with Drake and wouldn't want to do anything to jeopardize it. And she'd never want to do that, either.

But he was also going to have to understand she was her own woman, with a life separate from her brother's.

It was going to be a dilemma.

"Harmony."

She turned to see Lachelle walking toward her. She didn't know how her friend did it with everything going on in her life, but she was gorgeous, with her long black hair in dreads and her painted red lips and her long legs encased in a sunny copper dress. She looked as bright and beautiful as she had back in college.

"Girl, it has been too long," Harmony said.

Harmony embraced her friend in a tight hug.

"I know," Lachelle said. "Totally my fault. Between Davis and the twins and work, I'm buried. I'm so sorry I had to cancel our girls night out a few weeks ago."

"Don't even worry about it. Next time we'll do a playdate on a Saturday with you and the kids. I want to see them anyway."

"Sounds like a plan. And then we'll leave the kids with Davis and we'll go have margaritas."

Harmony grinned. "An even better plan."

Lachelle turned to Barrett. "I'm sorry, Barrett. It was rude of me to ignore you."

Barrett gave Lachelle a wide smile. "Not a problem. I know better than to get in the way of two friends getting reacquainted."

"This much is true. Anyway, I'm so glad you came today. The kids are so excited to see you."

"I'm looking forward to seeing them."

"Then let's get started. Why don't you head to the gym, and I'll gather up the kids."

Harmony went with Barrett into the gym. Bleachers were set up and Barrett had a podium with a built-in microphone.

"Nervous?" she asked.

He let out a short laugh. "No. I've done this before. And I like kids. They're always honest and will tell you exactly what's on their minds."

She turned to face him. "So you prefer someone being forth-right. Telling you what they want. What they're thinking."

"Yeah. Makes it easier, don't you think?"

"Absolutely."

She was about to tell him exactly what she wanted, but the doors opened and an influx of middle schoolers poured in.

Definitely not the right time. She stepped away so Barrett and Lachelle could take the podium.

Once all the kids had taken seats on the bleachers, Lachelle stepped up to the podium and the microphone.

"Good afternoon. As you know, we often have industry leaders and people who we feel can relate to what you're all going through. Today, I'm so pleased to introduce Barrett Cassidy, a player with our own Tampa Bay Hawks."

There was loud applause, and, Harmony noted, squeals from the girls.

She couldn't blame them.

Barrett came out from behind the podium.

"I speak loud enough; I don't think I'll need the microphone."

He got close to the kids and pulled out one of the metal chairs, sitting down in front of them.

"I'm not going to blow smoke up your asses and tell you all that I know what any of you have been through."

Harmony looked over at Lachelle, who shrugged at Barrett's use of profanity.

Whatever it took to reach them, she supposed.

"I didn't grow up in poverty, or in foster care, or homeless, or in any of the situations I know many of you have faced. I know a lot of you are sports fans, so you know my family name. You know who my father is, who my brothers are, and where I come from. I had it easy growing up. I got to go to great schools and an amazing college here in Florida. But I've known a lot of my brothers on the team who did grow up like you. And I learned a lot of my work ethic from them, as well as from my father, who did come from poverty. And he taught all of his sons to never take anything for granted. That it's not just all about sports and money and how to make a quick buck. It's about what's in your head as much as it is what's on the playing field.

"He taught all of us to pay attention, to learn, that using your head to get ahead is what's most important. Does that make sense to any of you?"

He got a lot of nods.

"Look, I know it may seem easy to steal, or to want to use your bodies or your hands and feet in whatever way you can to make money. But it's a temporary thing. If you want to be successful in life, the best way to do that is to use your brain. It'll last a lot longer than your body will."

"But that's not what you did, is it?"

Harmony tracked the voice, someone on the far top tier of the bleachers.

Instead of calling out whoever said it, Barrett said, "You mean because I chose football as a career?"

There were a lot of nods and *yeah*s from the crowd.

"I can see why you'd think that. But if you look at my background, you'd also know that I graduated college with a 4.0 GPA. I graduated, unlike a lot of athletes, whose only desire in college is to see how fast they can get drafted into their professional sport. My degree is in political science. I know that my body will only last so long on the football field. I've known a lot of rookies who got injured their first or second years. Career-ending injuries, and all their dreams died on the football field. I'm smarter than that. I'm investing my earnings and I have a plan for my post-football career.

"It's important to think beyond who you are today to what you can do with your life. You maybe started out your lives with disadvantages, but that doesn't mean you have to stay down. You aren't a product of your past any more than I am. I had a great upbringing and many advantages. So did a lot of athletes. I've seen a lot of those athletes piss away those advantages on drugs, bad investments and bad decisions. Bad decisions can cost you your future. You're at the crossroads of your future right now. You're in charge of your lives right here. Today. Good choices and smart thinking can turn your lives around. All you have to do is make smart decisions. No one can live your life for you or make those decisions for you."

Harmony was so impressed. Barrett was doing an amazing job, letting these kids know that their futures were in their own hands, that they could do anything if they wanted to.

"He's very good at this," Lachelle whispered to her.

"Yes, he is."

"You'd be surprised how many athletes come in here and talk smack to these kids about sports, and how they need to be physically fit and get out there and play ball and it's all bs," Lachelle said. "That's not what they need to hear. They need to hear exactly what Barrett is telling them. To use their minds, to think about their futures."

Lachelle was right. Harmony had been surrounded by plenty of troubled kids growing up. She wished some of them had heard Barrett's speech. It might have saved a few from walking the wrong path.

Then again, she also believed in choice. And some of them were going to make the wrong choice no matter what.

Barrett took questions and there were a lot of them. He handled them all perfectly, and Lachelle stepped in and helped when

Barrett didn't know the answers. Then he surprised all of them with tickets to one of the Hawks preseason games for them and their families. Everyone excitedly cheered.

It took Lachelle a while to get them settled down, especially since Barrett insisted on spending time chatting one-on-one with any of the kids who wanted to, which was quite a few of them.

But eventually Lachelle insisted it was time for the kids to go back to class, and Barrett reminded them to engage their brains. They all waved good-bye to him on their way out of the gym.

"I can't tell you how much what you said will stick with some of these kids," Lachelle said.

"I wish it would stick with all of them."

Lachelle laid her hand on Barrett's forearm. "You can't save them all, Barrett. If you reach only a handful of them, it'll be enough. Trust me."

"Have you got a few minutes?" Lachelle asked Harmony. "I have a meeting in about a half hour, but I've got new pictures of the boys."

"I wouldn't miss seeing those. Providing Barrett has time."

His lips curved. "I have time."

"Awesome," Lachelle said. "Follow me to my office."

Harmony started moving, then realized she felt a little dizzy. It was awfully warm in the community center. She'd noticed it while she was listening to Barrett's speech. She should probably mention it to Lachelle, but then again her friend was likely already aware of the glitchy AC system.

They made their way into Lachelle's office. "Sorry," Lachelle said. "It's kind of tight in here. We don't really get spacious offices."

"This is fine," Barrett said. "I can lean against the doorway."

Harmony made her way inside and sank into the chair. Now she was feeling nauseous. It was brutally hot outside today, and now that they were sitting in this tiny box of an office, it was even warmer.

She swallowed, fighting back the rising tide of nausea as Lachelle brought her laptop over and faced it toward Harmony. "The one on the left is Marcus, and on the right is Mateo."

She blinked to clear her vision, which was currently a bit wonky. She smiled at the two adorable toddlers in the photo as Lachelle flipped through a slide show. "I cannot believe how big they've gotten since I saw them last."

"Future linebackers if you ask me," Barrett said.

Lachelle laughed. "My husband is hoping for point guards or power forwards."

"Oh, a basketball guy, is he?"

"Indeed."

"They have long legs," Barrett said. "I'd say your husband has a pretty good shot at those positions."

"And he's six foot six, so I'm hoping they get their height from their daddy, and not from me."

Harmony was trying hard not to fall out of her chair. Or sweat all over it.

"What do you think, Harmony?" Lachelle asked.

She blinked and lifted her gaze to her friend. "What?"

Lachelle laughed. "Head already somewhere else?"

"I'm sorry. Just staring at these cute babies. I can't wait to cuddle them."

She was going to have to make an exit.

"We'll definitely do that soon."

Lachelle's phone rang. "Oh, I have to get that."

Harmony waved her hand. "I'll talk to you later."

She pushed out of the chair, using the edge of the table for support. She turned to Barrett, who suddenly seemed out of focus.

"Ready?"

"Yeah."

She looped her purse over her arm and followed him out the door, hoping like hell she didn't pass out in the hallway.

But she only made it to the end of the hall before she felt the walls closing in on her.

She couldn't breathe, and she was so dizzy she couldn't move another step. She leaned against the cool wall.

Barrett was right there.

"Harmony. What's wrong?"

"Dizzy."

He slipped his arm around her, his strong body giving her the support she needed. "Let's sit you down somewhere."

She shook her head and laid her hand on his chest. "No. Not here. Lachelle will see me and fuss. Need to get out of here."

"Okay."

He pulled her against him, using his body to support her while he walked her outside.

God, it was so hot out here. She was glad she hadn't eaten today, so she wouldn't throw up.

Hadn't eaten.

Dammit.

Thank God he'd used remote start to cool the car down. She was so hot. Barrett got her into the SUV and hurried over to the other side. Her hands were shaking as she fumbled in her purse.

When Barrett climbed inside and started the engine, she was ever so grateful for his phenomenal air-conditioning system in the vehicle.

"Do I need to take you to the hospital?" he asked.

She shook her head. "Low blood sugar." She found the energy bar that had been buried in the bottom of her purse. "Need to eat."

She was afraid she was going to pass out before she could get a bite of the bar into her mouth. Her hands were trembling so badly she couldn't even unwrap it.

"Here," he said, his voice calm and gentle. "Let me do that for you."

He unwrapped the bar and broke it in half. "Eat. We're heading to a restaurant right now to get some fluids into you."

"O . . . okay."

She took a bite, then another, still feeling nauseous. The last thing she wanted right now was food, but she knew it was what she needed most.

By the time Barrett pulled into the parking lot of the restaurant, she felt marginally better—at least better enough that she wasn't in danger of passing out. But she was still shaking.

He put the SUV in park and turned the vehicle off, then leaned over to her. "You okay?"

"I'll be fine now."

"You wait right there while I come around to your side to help you out."

She nodded, undoing her seat belt while he came around. He opened the door, then reached both hands around her waist and hoisted her out of the SUV.

"I'm going to set you down on your feet."

"I'm really okay, Barrett."

"Yeah, sure you are. I'm still going to hold on to you."

Her lips curved. "I'm really not going to mind if you do."

She was still feeling a bit off balance, and she knew if he hadn't been with her back at the community center, she'd have slid down the wall into a heap.

That wouldn't have been her finest moment.

He kept his arm firmly around her waist as they entered the restaurant. To anyone else, they looked like a couple in love who couldn't keep their hands off each other. To her, right now Barrett was her lifeline.

Fortunately, the restaurant wasn't crowded, so they were seated right away. Their waitress came over.

"What can I get you two to drink?"

Barrett looked over at her.

"I'll have a large orange juice."

"Iced tea for me," Barrett said, fingering the edges of the menu in kind of a nervous fashion.

He continued to do that until the waitress came back with their drinks.

"Are you two ready to order?"

"We'll need a few minutes," Barrett said.

The waitress nodded and wandered off. Harmony took a couple of long swallows of the juice, already feeling a lot better now that she'd eaten half the energy bar.

But Barrett continued to stare at her as if he expected her to fall on the floor and die on him any second.

"I'm really okay."

"Are you sure? I could still take you to the hospital."

She shook her head, then took another sip of juice. "I've had low blood sugar my entire life, Barrett. I know how to manage it. It was just a stupid thing on my part today. I was running behind because I had to deal with some e-mails before I left the house this morning, and I totally forgot to eat or drink some juice. I know better. And then I went along with you to your event, and I completely forgot I hadn't eaten. This is entirely my fault. Thank you for being there for me."

He raked his fingers through his hair and blew out a breath. "Christ, Harmony. You scared the shit out of me. The way you were shaking, and sinking down that wall. And I had no idea you had hypoglycemia."

She appreciated his understanding of the terminology. "It's not something that tends to come up in idle conversation."

"Yeah, well, maybe it should. So people who care about you can . . . you know, care about you. And *for* you, in case you forget to eat."

She couldn't repress her smile. "Thanks. For caring. And for the suggestion."

Their waitress came by and she ordered food. Now that the crisis had passed, she was hungry, so she ordered a chicken salad and bread.

"You should have something more than that."

"Trust me, it's more than enough to sustain me." She studied the look of concern on his face, the way he watched every sip of orange juice she took.

So she was very grateful that their food arrived fast. She wasted no time digging into her chicken salad while Barrett had a double cheeseburger and double order of fries.

"Good thing you can work all that off, huh?" she asked as she took a sip of the water she'd asked the waitress for.

"Good thing. How's your chicken salad?"

"Fantastic. Would you like a bite?"

He shook his head. "I think I've got enough to handle over here. And you need to eat all of that."

Once she'd plowed through her salad and eaten it all, she set her plate to the side and took another few sips of water. She felt good now—great, actually. There was nothing like the relief she felt once she got past a particularly rough episode.

She knew better than to skip breakfast, but every now and then stupidity reared its ugly head. She wouldn't let it happen again.

She made a mental note to replace the energy bar in her purse.

"Better?" Barrett asked after he'd polished off the last of the fries.

"Much. Thank you for taking the time to feed me."

"It was either that or the ER, and you didn't seem too happy about that idea."

"They would have just hooked me up to an IV. The chicken salad was much tastier."

Their waitress brought the check. Barrett pulled out his wallet and paid.

"You ready?"

"Yes." She stood and followed him out the front door. When she slid into his SUV, he turned to her.

"What's on your agenda the rest of the day?" Barrett asked. "Any meetings?"

"One. And a wild amount of paperwork, e-mails and phone calls."

He turned his key in the ignition, then slid on his sunglasses. "Cancel them."

She shot him a look. "Excuse me?"

"Cancel them all. I'm kidnapping you."

She laughed. "I don't think so."

"You've had a rough morning. I'm going to give you a relaxing afternoon."

Now that was a tempting idea. The meeting was with a supplier, and could easily be shuffled. She could answer e-mails in the car on the way to . . . wherever it was he was taking her. And the phone calls she could shift off to her assistant.

"Done."

His lips curved. "I like a cooperative captive. We'll stop by your place so you can pick up a few things."

She shifted in her seat to face him. "Are you sure I won't call for help?"

At a stoplight, he drew his sunglasses partway down, those

gorgeous eyes of his offering up such sexy promise it was all she could do not to self-combust with an orgasm right in the passenger seat.

"Now why would you want to do that?"

Oh, it was on.

ELEVEN

BARRETT WAITED IN HARMONY'S KITCHEN WHILE SHE went upstairs to pack a bag.

This hadn't been his intended plan for the day, but sonofabitch, she'd scared him today when she'd almost fainted in the hallway of the community center. Sure, she'd had a meal and she seemed fine now, but he still wasn't convinced. He intended to hang out with her for the rest of the day and make sure she was going to be all right.

Despite wanting to keep his distance from her, he wouldn't abandon her when she needed him. And today, whether she said she was okay or not, she needed him. So he was going to spend the remainder of the day assuring himself that she was indeed over her hypoglycemic episode.

And while he was at it, he'd also see to it that she had another few meals.

She walked into the kitchen, bag in hand. She'd changed out of her dress and into flowery capri pants and a white tank top that showed off her pretty damn buffed arms. At least her muscle tone meant she typically ate well and worked out. That meant something to him.

"Okay I packed a swimsuit and another change of clothes." She cocked her head to the side. "You aren't like . . . flying me to Jamaica or anything, are you? Because I have three appointments tomorrow."

He laughed. "As fun as that sounds, no. We're going to the Sandpearl Resort over at Clearwater. Spend the day at the beach, in the water, and we'll eat. They have a great pool and an even better restaurant."

"As delightful as *that* sounds, I have a pool here. And just how many times do you think you need to feed me today?"

"As many as it takes to quell this panicked feeling in the pit of my stomach."

She stepped up to him, laying her hand on his arm. "I can't tell you how sweet your concern is, Barrett, but honestly, I'm okay now."

"I know. But you can take the rest of the day off. Sun's out, and the beach is calling. We'll get a cabana and you can chill."

"Okay. We'll chill. Sounds fun."

"Good." He took the bag from her hands. "Let's go."

HARMONY HAD NO COMPLAINTS ABOUT TAKING THE rest of the day off. There was nothing like relaxing in front of the Gulf. When they got to the resort, she was surprised to discover Barrett had booked them a room.

"Easier to change clothes that way," he said, as he led them up to their room.

Now that she was feeling one hundred percent herself again, she was intrigued. "Of course."

He'd gotten them an oceanfront room, which couldn't have been easy considering this was the height of summer vacation time. But she wasn't about to complain about the amazing view once she stepped fully into the room. She headed straight for the balcony and walked outside. The heat was oppressive, but the balcony was shaded and there was a lovely breeze. Plus the view of the Gulf was spectacular.

Barrett stepped beside her, and the spacious balcony suddenly seemed closed in.

Not that she minded having his big, gorgeous body next to hers.

"Ready to hit the beach?" he asked.

"Absolutely. I'll go change."

She picked up her bag and went into the bathroom to change into her bikini. She pulled on her cover-up and slid into her beach flip-flops, then came out of the bathroom to discover Barrett had already changed into his board shorts and a tank top.

She wondered what he would have thought if she'd come out of the bathroom while he was naked. She certainly wouldn't have minded seeing all that muscle in the buff. And maybe their afternoon would have turned out completely different.

She grabbed her sunglasses and sunscreen, then turned her phone to silent mode. She'd already told Rosalie she was out for the day and given her instructions to shift her appointment and answer some calls for her, so she was cleared until tomorrow.

After this morning's debacle, she was actually looking forward to a little downtime.

She followed Barrett to the elevator. They rode down to the lobby and walked out to the pool area.

"I thought we'd get a private cabana on the beach, unless you hate sand."

She laughed. "I don't hate sand. Sand is fine with me."

They walked out onto the beach and Barrett stopped at the rental shack. He filled out the paperwork and they were shown to a private spot that was more like a small room. She'd expected an umbrella and a couple of lounge chairs, not this open-air room with a roof, a sofa, chairs and a sliding door that closed for privacy. Sweet.

"This is nice," she said, sliding onto the lounge.

"Yeah. I like privacy."

A cocktail waitress appeared. "What can I get you two to drink?"

Barrett ordered a beer.

"I'll have an iced tea for now."

"Anything to eat?" their waitress asked.

"Nothing for me," Harmony said.

Barrett shook his head. "We're good, thanks."

After their waitress left, Barrett said, "How am I supposed to get you drunk and appropriately sugared up if all you're going to drink is iced tea?"

She laughed. "I'm fine for the moment. And I promise to tell you the second I get hit with a hunger pang."

"Promise?"

She crossed two fingers over her heart. "Promise."

Content to sit under the shaded roof of their private room for now, she pulled off her cover-up, kicked off her sandals and slid fully onto the lounge, enjoying the view of not only the ocean, but Barrett as he drew his shirt over his head, revealing his amazing torso.

The man had one hell of a body. He was well muscled, with incredibly wide shoulders, impossibly chiseled biceps and triceps and a lean, tapered waist. She itched to run her fingers over his amazingly sculpted abs.

His legs were just as well defined as the rest of him.

As she scanned her way up his body, her gaze landing on his gorgeous face, she found him ogling her in the same way.

Only he was frowning.

"What?" she asked.

"You keep checking me out like that and I'm going to pick you up, carry you to the water and toss you in."

She laughed. "I don't need a cooldown, Barrett."

"You sure as hell look like you might."

He was still eyeing her, his gaze hot and direct and seemingly unable to focus only on her face. She had to admit she liked that he looked at her body. She wanted him looking at her in that way that told her he was interested. If he was interested, then maybe she could offer up some . . . temptation.

She stood, stretching. "Okay. Maybe we should get our toes wet. How about a walk along the water?"

"You want to put on some sunscreen first?"

"Absolutely." She dug into her bag and the first thing she did was wind her hair into a bun on top of her head. Then she pulled out her sunscreen and lathered it on her legs and arms. She made sure to take her time, stretching each leg out on one of the chairs to smooth the lotion on her legs.

She might have heard Barrett groan when she rubbed the sunscreen over her chest, her fingertips lingering at her cleavage. She resisted the urge to smile.

Finally she handed the tube to him. "Would you do my back?"

He heaved in a giant breath of air. "Sure."

When she felt his warm fingers along the top of her shoulders, it was her turn to take in a breath. He'd touched her today when he kept her from falling, but that was him caring for her in a medical crisis. Now it was different. Now it was his fingertips gliding over her skin, a soft caress that made her close her eyes and wish they were up in their room, both of them naked and exploring each other's bodies.

She'd really love to get her hands on his body. All of his body. But for now, she'd enjoy this moment and the gingerly way he seemed to touch her, as if he thought she was fragile. Or maybe he was trying to avoid too much contact.

"Everything okay back there?" she asked as he moved down to her lower back.

"Fine."

His voice was tight, his tone clipped, as if he wasn't having the best time putting lotion on her body. Since most men who weren't at all physically attracted to a woman would have no problem putting sunscreen on them, she knew the reason Barrett was uptight about this was because he was attracted to her.

Her lips curved upward in a satisfied smile. This day was turning out better and better.

He finally handed the lotion back to her. "Done."

She turned around, gracing him with her brightest smile. "Thanks. Ready?"

"Unless you need me to rub some of that on your butt."

She cocked a brow. "Would you?"

"Hell no."

She laughed. "Come on. It's blistering hot out here. Let's go cool our feet off in the water."

She wasn't intentionally torturing him, but if he suffered a little and it moved him in the right direction, then she wouldn't mind that.

She wanted him interested in her. And he was definitely showing signs of interest.

So far, so good.

Now she just had to turn up the heat a little.

TWELVE

GO TO THE BEACH. WHO THOUGHT THAT WAS A GOOD idea?

Oh, right. He had. Barrett made a mental note to do extra squats in the gym tomorrow to torture himself in punishment for this lame-ass idea.

Harmony was a few steps ahead of him as they walked the water's edge, her bright red bikini showcasing every one of her perfect assets.

Mostly, her perfect ass, which was round and curvy, and all he could think about was getting his hands on it.

He should have suggested they spend the afternoon in a frigid movie theater, where she'd have all her clothes on. And maybe a sweater, too.

The problem was, he liked the water, and figured maybe she could relax and unwind, they could have a few drinks and she could eat. He hadn't thought this through to the part where she'd be in a bikini and he'd have to endure seeing all her gorgeous skin exposed.

She bent over to pick something up, giving him an even better view of her ass and causing his imagination to spring into overdrive.

He could already envision gripping her hips and driving his cock into her while she was bent over the sofa in their private tent area, sweat pouring off of him as he made her come, over and over. He could hear her soft cries, feel her pussy clench around his cock as she came.

His cock hardened and he had to banish the images.

Down, boy. Nothing was going to happen, especially out here.

Or, ever. Not with Harmony.

She turned and waited for him to catch up.

Yeah, it was just as bad from the front because beads of perspiration caressed her breast, drawing his focus there and making him wish they really were alone, so he could lick the droplets, pull aside the cups and . . .

"It's really hot out here," she said, pulling his attention away from her breasts.

He cleared his throat. "Yeah. How about we get in the water?"

"Sounds like a great idea."

They turned and headed into the waves. He grabbed her hand as the water lapped at their ankles, then their knees and thighs.

"Oh this feels so good," Harmony said, as they ended up standing waist deep in it.

"Care to dive in?"

She shook her head. "No thanks. You don't even want to know what water does to my hair."

Today she wore her hair straight, though he liked it curly, too. "I'm not even going to ask."

"Good. Don't. But feel free to dive away."

"I'm going to."

He turned and dove into the next wave, coming up feeling a hell of a lot cooler, and hopefully more clearheaded.

Harmony had dipped her body up to her shoulders. How women managed to stand in an ocean with waves crashing over them and not get their hair wet was a goddamned mystery to him.

He made his way over to her and swept her up into his arms.

"Time to get wet," he said, and lifted her up.

Harmony screamed, but she was laughing as he set her body gently into the water. He still held on to her.

"Don't worry. Your hair is safe with me."

She wound her arms around him. "You do not want to see this hair all wet."

"Oh, see, now it's a challenge to see it. What happens to it? Does it stick out all over? Because mine is sticking out all over."

"Yes. It sticks out all over. It's a mess."

"I'll bet it's a sexy mess."

She shook her head. "It is not."

He let her down in the water, but she held on to him, which meant her body slid down over his.

Yeah, still torture.

"I guess if you want to see my hair wet, you'll have to get me in the shower. And to get me in the shower, you'll have to see me naked."

He frowned. "Don't tempt me."

She turned away, giving him one hell of a sexy smile. "Don't you know? I've been trying to do that all day."

She headed out of the water, her hips swaying as she walked onto the beach.

Barrett decided he should stay in. He needed to cool down some.

Get her naked. What the hell, Harmony? Was she playing some kind of game with him?

Then it hit him. Of course. She'd just gotten dumped by her

boyfriend. She needed a self-esteem boost, and he'd been nearby right after it happened.

She was rebounding. She wasn't really interested in him at all.

He knew what that was like. He'd been dumped before, and the first thing he wanted to do was lick his wounds and go right after the next available female.

That's all Harmony was doing, hitting on the next available male, which had just happened to be him.

He'd give her a pep talk, tell her she needed some time to heal after her breakup and remind her that she wasn't ready yet.

And he absolutely wasn't the right guy for her—for obvious reasons.

Then they could go back to being friends again, and this crazy sudden attraction he felt for her would go away.

Now that he had a plan, he headed out of the water.

THIRTEEN

HARMONY HAD FALLEN ASLEEP. SHE WASN'T SURE IF it was her utterly draining morning, or the rotating ceiling fans that had lulled her into a prone position on the sofa, but she opened her eyes to realize she'd conked out, cold. She picked up her phone to see she'd been out for over an hour.

She sat up and realized she wasn't the only one snoozing. Barrett was on one of the chairs, his feet propped up on the ottoman, his arms laced over his stomach. His eyes were closed and his breathing was deep and even. She took a moment to simply admire his beautiful body.

Even asleep, he looked formidable. She wanted to snap some photos of him with her phone, but that would be taking advantage without his permission, and she wouldn't do that. Instead, she leaned back, grabbed her ice water and took a long, slow sip from the straw, enjoying the eye candy. Her mind filled with visuals of stripping naked and straddling him, rubbing herself against his board shorts until he got hard.

She inhaled a deep breath, imagining him taking hold of her hips, rising up to kiss her. The kiss would be hot, passionate, and he'd fill his hands with her breasts. She could already imagine her breasts rubbing against his chest as he rose up only long enough to shed his board shorts, his cock springing up, hard and pulsing.

He'd sit again, only this time she'd slowly lower herself onto him and—

"Stop that."

She startled out of her fantasy, snapping her gaze to Barrett, who hadn't moved but his eyes were now open.

"Stop what?"

"Staring at me like that."

She swallowed past the dryness in her throat evoked by her oh-so-intense fantasy. "Like what?"

"You know like what." He pushed upright and grabbed for his water, then leaned forward to take a drink, but not before she caught sight of his erection.

He must have been awake longer than she was aware, and he'd caught her staring at him. Had her expression given away her thoughts?

Her lips curved and she leaned back against the sofa and took a long swallow of water, then set the glass down. "I have no idea what you're talking about."

"You know exactly what I'm talking about, so don't play innocent with me, Harmony. And there's something I need to talk to you about."

"Really. And what is that?"

"Your ex-boyfriend."

"What about him?"

"I think you're not over him yet, and you're only interested in me because you need a rebound."

Men were so clueless sometimes. "Uh, no."

"Really, I totally understand how that happens. You got dumped and you want to jump right back on board with a new guy. It's happened to me before."

Her lips quirked. "You got dumped and wanted to jump right back on board with a new guy?"

"Funny. No. But after a breakup, the first thing I did was get together with a new woman. Like right away. It's an ego thing. I needed to feel wanted, and there's no better way to do that than with another person. The first available person."

"Oh, so you think I latched on to you at Mama's right after Levon and I broke up, and I'm using you to rebound."

"Yes."

"No."

He let out a sigh. "Harmony."

"Barrett, I appreciate you looking out for me and all, but I can assure you I didn't select you as my rebound guy. Frankly, I could have used any random guy to rebound, if that's what I was after. I mean, look at me. It's not like I can't get men."

He stared at her for a few seconds. "Point taken."

"Do you think I'd go through this hassle of choosing you with you being so close to my brother if I didn't really like you? I'd have chosen a different guy to"—she used air quotes around her next word—"rebound."

He didn't say anything, and she knew that she had him.

"Your whole notion of me rebounding is idiotic, Barrett. I'd have to be heartbroken to rebound, and, frankly, I wasn't all that into Levon."

"Oh."

"Yeah."

"I thought you were upset that night."

"I was upset. No one likes to get dumped. We were seeing each other fairly exclusively, you know? But it wasn't love or anything."

"I see."

She could tell he didn't see at all. "I'm not a player. I don't date multiple men. Levon and I had been exclusive for about three months. But I could see the writing on the wall with him well before that night. He had some idiosyncrasies that were beginning to get on my nerves. It was only a matter of time until we broke up."

"But maybe you wanted to be the one to do the breaking up?"

"Not necessarily. Maybe I wanted it to be more of a mutual thing, where we'd sit down and have a civilized discussion about where we saw our relationship heading, and that we didn't see eye to eye on a lot of things, so we should probably go our separate ways. What I didn't expect was his it's-not-you-it's-me speech and how he didn't have time to devote to the relationship so we need to break up bullshit, which wasn't the case at all. I mean, is it too much to expect an honest conversation from a guy?"

"Of course not. But I can tell you're still harboring some hostility over him dumping you."

She stood, irritation rising. "No, I'm not hostile. To be hostile I'd have to care, and trust me, I don't. What aggravated me was his less than honest way of ending the relationship."

"Okay, I think I see your point. You wanted him to sit down with you so the two of you could mutually end your relationship with an honest discussion about why it wasn't working."

"Yes. That's it exactly."

Barrett laughed. "Babe, that's never going to happen. With any guy. First, because we're just not wired that way. If we want out of a relationship, we want out fast. So we're just going to end things, in the least messy way possible—at least that's the way we figure it out in our heads. If we have to make up bullshit reasons for it, we will, mainly to spare your feelings."

She gave him an incredulous look. "Seriously, Barrett? You're taking his side?"

"I'm not taking anyone's side. If you ask me, the man was a dick. I usually try to be as honest as possible throughout a relationship and don't set up a woman with any unrealistic expectations. And when it's over, it's over. But I can guarantee you the last damn thing I'm gonna want to do is sit down and have a long-ass conversation with a woman about why it's over. That tends to lead to accusations and recriminations and tears on the woman's part. No man wants that. It's best to just cut the cord and be done with it."

She stared at him for a few long seconds, then shook her head. "I do not understand your species. At all."

"Ditto."

He didn't seem at all upset, while she wanted to take one of the very colorful decorative pillows on the sofa and throw it right at his damn head.

Deciding she needed a break from men in general, she packed up her things in her bag. "I'm going to the room."

"Are you hungry?"

She shoved her sunscreen in the bag. "No, I'm not hungry. I'm pissed."

"Want me to go with you?"

"Oh, hell no. The last thing I want or need right now is you." She slung her bag over her shoulder. "You can hang out here, or in the water, or at the gym, but honestly, Barrett, I need some space from you for a while."

He looked confused.

"Okay. Like . . . for how long?"

She rolled her eyes. "Awhile."

She walked across the sand toward the hotel entrance, shaking her head.

Maybe Barrett was right and she needed some space to think about men in general. Because right now getting involved with any man—Barrett included—seemed like a giant waste of her time.

Men were obtuse, made no sense, and clearly did not care about women's feelings.

All men.

OKAY, SO MAYBE BARRETT HAD GONE TOO FAR IN HIS discussion with Harmony, but if he'd succeeded in pushing her away, it had been the right thing to do.

Right?

After all, that had been his intent. To make her see that she was possibly attracted to him only because she was on the rebound from her breakup with her ex-boyfriend, and she needed some time to honestly think about what it was that she wanted.

Only now she was pissed at him, and that part he didn't like.

They'd had fun today. At least after her bout with hypoglycemia this morning, she'd eaten and relaxed and they'd managed to have a good time.

Now he'd gotten her all riled up, and that part he hadn't intended.

Plus, it didn't sit well with him that she'd lumped him into the category of "all men are assholes."

He wasn't an asshole. He could be brutally honest with a woman at times, and he'd managed to piss off a few, but he'd never lied to a woman in his life and he didn't intend to start now.

But this was Harmony, and she was . . . different.

He was going to sit here awhile and let her have her space.

Then he was going to try the talking thing again, maybe this time with a touch more tact.

FOURTEEN

AFTER GOING UP TO THE ROOM AND TAKING A SHOWER that cooled her down, followed by some quiet time with a great book, Harmony found her mood improved dramatically.

She'd blown up at Barrett for no reason whatsoever. What could have been a highly enlightening conversation on the relationship differences between the sexes had turned into her throwing a tantrum because Barrett refused to see things her way.

That wasn't how she normally behaved. She was typically level-headed and saw the other person's point of view in a discussion. She might not agree with it, but she was always willing to listen.

So what the hell had gotten her so emotional?

She laid her book down and stood, walking over to the balcony to look out over the water.

She knew exactly why. Because he wasn't playing her game. He was trying to get rid of her and she didn't like it. She'd flirted with him, and to a certain extent he'd flirted back, but for the most part, he'd held his ground—rather firmly, much to her frustration.

She might think he wasn't interested except she knew better. He'd sprouted some rather impressive erections around her. Biology, sure, but a man who wasn't interested in a woman didn't get hard around her.

And he'd definitely gotten hard around her. She wasn't a naïve kid. She was a woman, and a woman knew when a man was interested.

It was just his stupid man code rearing its ugly head. And while she appreciated all that nobility crap and his dedication to her brother, she was going to have to stand firm if she wanted Barrett in her life.

Resolve firmly in place once again, she changed out of her shorts and tank top into a sundress, fixed her hair and applied makeup.

Then she left a note for Barrett and headed downstairs.

FIGURING A COUPLE OF HOURS SHOULD HAVE BEEN enough time to leave Harmony alone, Barrett made his way up to the room. When he opened the door, he peeked his head in first.

"Harmony?"

No answer. Maybe she was in the shower, so he stepped in and shut the door.

The bathroom door was open and she wasn't in the room.

Huh. He walked into the room to find a note on the pillow.

Barrett—

I'm downstairs in the bar. Why don't you clean up and come meet me?

H

Okay, so maybe she wasn't pissed at him anymore. That was a good sign. He took a quick shower and changed clothes, then headed downstairs to the bar. He saw Harmony sitting at the bar chatting with some dude. The guy wore shorts and a button-down shirt. Looked to be a vacation type. Only he had no wife or family with him. He was a big burly guy with short, spiked blond hair and lots of muscles.

Harmony laughed at something the guy said and the guy laid his hand over hers.

Okay, enough of that shit. He walked over to the bar. Harmony saw him and smiled. The dude smiled, too.

Whatever, buddy.

"Hi," Harmony said. "Barrett, this is Ted Lester. He works here at the hotel. Ted, this is Barrett Cassidy."

Barrett shook his hand. "Ted."

"Barrett. You play for the Hawks, right?"

"Yeah."

"Big fan."

"Thanks. What do you do here at the hotel, Ted?"

"I manage the bar."

Barrett had a burning urge to tell him he should go manage it. "Off duty?"

"My shift isn't starting yet."

"Ted was telling me about how much he's traveled. He's worked for hotels all over the world. Tokyo, Sydney, London, Beijing."

Barrett cocked a brow. "You must love travel."

Ted grinned. "I do."

"So what are you doing in Tampa?"

"My family lives here. Grandparents are getting older and frail. Figured I'd set down roots here for a while, put the travel on hold for a bit, ya know?"

Barrett nodded. "Yeah, I do."

Okay, so maybe Ted wasn't an asshole. The guy loved his family, and you couldn't hate on someone who wanted to be there for his grandparents.

Dammit.

"Are you two staying the night?" Ted asked.

Harmony lifted her gaze to Barrett.

"We have a room, yeah," Barrett said.

"You should eat at the Salt N Pepper Bistro. Best French restaurant in Clearwater. Amazing food."

"Thanks for the tip, Ted," Harmony said.

Ted picked up his phone. "I gotta run. I hope to see both of you here in the bar later. Great to meet you."

"You, too," Barrett said, then slid into the chair after Ted left.

"He was a really nice guy," Harmony said. "Since he's come back home, he's reconnected with one of his old girlfriends from high school. He was talking to me about her."

Okay, so Barrett really had it wrong. "He was, huh?"

"Yes. He was telling me about how they went their separate ways in college, and how she ended up back here in Tampa at the same time he did. It's like they were destined to meet up again."

"Like a freakin' fairy tale or something."

She laughed and picked up her cocktail. "Something like that."

The bartender came over and Barrett ordered a beer. "What are you drinking?"

She lifted the glass with the pink liquid. "A vodka and cranberry juice. And I had a mini snack in the room earlier when I was up there alone, so I don't want you to worry about me and food and eating. I won't be fainting on you."

"Good."

"And about earlier," she said. "I'm sorry I went off on you."

He nodded. "It's okay. I'm the one who should be sorry. I was being a dick about relationships."

"No, we were having a discussion. One where we didn't agree on a few things. And I got mad and stormed off in a very immature fashion."

"You were entitled to disagree."

"That's true. But storming off was childish. And for that I'm sorry."

"I pushed too hard and I spouted a bunch of bullshit I shouldn't have. And for that, *I'm* sorry."

Her lips curved. "We'll agree that we both acted badly. Let's forget all about it then, and start over?"

"Agreed." He grabbed her drink. "How about we get comfortable at a table. There's one by the windows with a view of the water."

"Sounds good."

They sat and had drinks and, this time, had positive conversations about his work and hers and kept relationship talk out of the equation. Barrett decided he'd back off trying to get Harmony to see that she shouldn't be with him. He intended to keep it neutral for the rest of their time together tonight. Probably safer that way.

And when Ted came over and told them he'd arranged a reservation at the French bistro he'd mentioned, Harmony grinned.

"Thanks so much, Ted."

"Yeah, thanks," Barrett said. "We appreciate it."

"Hey, I told you. I'm a big fan, and Harmony put up with me talking about my girlfriend."

"Nothing to put up with," Harmony said. "From what you told me, you and Willow seem perfect together."

"That means a lot to me. I hope the two of you enjoy your dinner tonight."

Barrett paid the bar tab and they headed out front to grab his car. It wasn't a long drive to the restaurant, which didn't look like much on the outside. But Barrett had found many a great restaurant when he traveled that looked like hell on the outside but had great food.

They made their way into the restaurant and were seated by the waitress, who dropped off menus and said she'd be right back to get their drink orders.

"What would you like to drink?" Barrett asked.

"I'm going to switch to water."

He nodded, and when their waitress came back, he ordered two waters.

"This menu looks amazing."

Harmony nodded. "I can't decide whether I want crepes or pasta or the duck."

"I want the steak."

She laughed. "Of course you do."

When their waitress came back over, Harmony ordered the duck and he ordered the steak.

"Thank you for today," she said.

"You're welcome."

"I know you probably have a million things on your to-do list, and instead, you pushed it all aside to spend the day with me."

He took a sip of water, then laid his glass on the table. "Maybe not a million."

Her lips curved. "You're a busy man."

"Gearing up to be, but not yet. I've got some free time before training camp starts."

"That's true. And I'll be hitting you up during some of that free time for house stuff."

"Yeah, I know."

"Don't sound so excited."

"I actually am. About moving in once it's finished, anyway."

"I know the waiting part is tough, and you're not all that thrilled about having to select appliances and paint and all that."

He waited while their waitress set down salads before he replied. "Not really. But I know it's part of putting the house together, so I'll deal."

"Trust that I'll take care of any part that you don't have to. I'll only come to you with the essentials."

"I'll trust you on that."

"Besides, I know how busy you're going to be once training camp starts."

"We've got a while yet. But I do plan on doing some traveling."

She dug into her salad and took a bite, followed up by a sip of her drink. "Really? Where are you going?"

"I want to head out to San Francisco to see my brother, then down to the ranch in Texas to visit my folks."

"I've never been to San Francisco. I'd love to go there sometime. Be sure to say hello to Flynn for me. How's his restaurant coming along?"

"Right now he's remodeling."

She smiled. "Remodeling. A lot like you, then."

"Yeah, sort of."

"I'd love to see what he's doing with the place."

He scooped up a forkful of salad, then looked at her. "So, come with me."

"Oh, sure. Just like that."

He shrugged. "Why not? I'll only be gone a few days. And you said you want to see San Francisco. You could come with me."

Harmony knew Barrett was just blowing smoke, that he thought being self-employed she'd never take him up on his offer. But the idea of it was tempting. She really did want to see San Francisco, and she honestly was interested in seeing what Flynn was doing with his restaurant.

"When are you going?"

"Heading out this weekend."

The timing was kind of perfect. She had nothing going on this weekend, and she had a lull in work.

It would also give them time alone. How would he react to that?

"What would you do if I said yes?"

He had finished his salad and nudged his plate to the side. "Yes to what?"

"To your invitation?"

"Oh, about San Francisco? I didn't think you'd be able to take the time off."

"So why make the offer, unless you really didn't mean it."

"Uh, sure I meant it."

"Then I accept."

He stared at her for a few minutes, then shrugged. "Okay. We'll go together."

FIFTEEN

OKAY, SO BARRETT HAD THROWN OUT THE INVITATION figuring Harmony would be too busy to take him up on it. But when he'd told her earlier today that he never said things he didn't mean, he meant what he said. He'd invited her. She'd said yes. So he was going to take her to San Francisco.

Which would likely open up a lot of questions from Flynn about Harmony and him, but he'd have to tell Flynn he and Harmony were just friends. And then hope like hell Drake never found out he'd taken his sister to San Francisco.

After dinner, they headed back to the hotel. Harmony said she was overly full from that great dinner, so she wanted to take a walk on the beach.

He had to agree with her. The food had been damn good. He made a note to find Ted later and thank him for the recommendation.

Harmony had pulled off her shoes and held them in her hand

while they walked along the edge of the surf. Even though it was dark, it was still hot outside, but being next to the water helped some.

"Someday I'll have a place right on the water," she said.

"You've got that now. Sort of."

"I have a view of the water, which I enjoy. But I mean a place right on the water. Kind of like you have, though you're not beach-front."

"You want beachfront."

"Yes. Mama used to bring us to the beach on weekends whenever she could. And I hated to leave. I'd sit and dig in the sand for hours, then play in the water until Mama insisted we leave. I fell in love with the water from an early age. It's my dream to live somewhere right on the beach, so I can get up in the morning, grab my coffee and go sit outside and watch the sun come up over the water. Then in the evening, pour a glass of wine and listen to the sound of the waves as the sun sets." She lifted her gaze to his. "I love the water, so my goal is for it to be the first thing I see in the morning and the last thing I see at night."

He brushed his shoulder against hers. "Water lover."

"You're damn right I am. And I'll work my tail off until I get what I want."

"I don't doubt that about you."

"You love the water, too, obviously, since you bought the house right on it."

"Yeah. I like to take the boat out. Mom and Dad always had us out there fishing, taking trips out on the lakes to water-ski. We'd go tubing all the time in the summers."

"See what a good match we are, Barrett?"

He laughed. "Well, we have water in common, anyway."

"Oh, I don't know. I'll bet we have a lot more than that."

She'd paused to look up at him. They were alone out here and as he looked at her mouth, her lips parted, and all he wanted to do was take a taste of her.

Bad idea.

"I don't know about you," he said, "but I'm thirsty. How about we head inside to the bar for a drink?"

Her lips curved. "I think you're trying to avoid kissing me."

Harmony was way too smart for her own good.

"So is that yes or no to the drink?"

"A drink is fine, Barrett. But before the end of tonight, you will kiss me."

They headed up the beach toward the bar. "If that's some kind of challenge, or you think you might be able to get me drunk enough, you're going to lose."

"We'll see."

Did he think walking away from her was easy? She was beautiful. Sexy. Magnetic. And the pull she had on him was strong.

But he could resist. He knew mixing it up with her would be disastrous, and would hurt not only her in the long run, but also his best friend.

He was doing the right thing by keeping his distance. And he was a strong man. He could resist temptation. Even if that temptation was as hot as Harmony.

The room was crowded when they walked through the doors. "We could sit at the bar," Barrett suggested.

Maybe they could find Ted and strike up a conversation. Keep things light and easy that way.

"No, there's a table over there in the corner," Harmony said.

Great. Nice and remote. Intimate. Just what he didn't want, but he followed her to the table and held out her chair for her to sit.

"Thanks."

"What would you like to drink?"

"Vodka and cranberry juice."

"I'll go get us drinks."

He wandered up to the bar and ordered Harmony's drink and a beer for himself. He ran into Ted.

"Hey, how was dinner?"

"Fantastic. Really appreciate the recommendation."

"You're welcome. Where are you two sitting?"

Barrett pointed out their seats.

"I'll have drinks brought over."

"Thanks." He took his money out to pay, but Ted waved him off. "Tab's on me."

"Not necessary."

"Hey, it's my pleasure. I like you two."

"Well, thanks again."

He headed back to the table. Harmony pulled her attention from the window and onto him, giving him a quizzical look as he took his seat.

"Ran into Ted. He's having the drinks sent over. And he's comping them."

She smiled. "Isn't he a nice guy?"

"Yeah."

"I'd love to meet his girlfriend. I'll bet they're perfect together."

"Really. What makes you think that?"

She shrugged. "The way he described her—their relationship. He's almost giddy about reconnecting with her, as if he almost can't believe it happened. He told me he feels really lucky that she was available at the exact moment in time that he came back home."

"That was a nice thing to say."

"Yes, it was."

A waitress brought over their drinks and set them down.

"My name is Donna. Ted said to just flag me down whenever you want a refill. Drinks are on him the rest of the night."

"Thanks, Donna," Harmony said. "There will definitely be flagging."

Donna laughed. "I'll be looking for you."

After Donna ran off, Barrett cocked a brow. "Planning on doing some drinking?"

She shrugged. "My first appointment isn't until noon tomorrow. I might indulge." She took a sip from the straw. "Besides, cranberry juice is very good for you."

He shook his head, then tilted the bottle of beer to his lips. She might be trying to play coy with him, but he could see right through her. Her intent was to get him shit-faced drunk, then take advantage of him in their room tonight.

Though the thought of it made him push back a laugh.

She was tiny. He was a big guy. It would take a lot of beers to get him shit-faced, and he had no intention of drinking that much—or letting her take advantage.

And talk about role reversal. Why was he even thinking about his "virtue" anyway? It wasn't gonna happen.

Not that he had any virtue to protect.

When he focused his attention back on Harmony, she was weaving back and forth as if she was trying to look behind him.

"What are you doing?"

"Looking for the smoke that must be coming out of your ears. I've been talking to you for like the past three minutes and your head is somewhere else. What have you been thinking so hard about?"

How not to have sex with you tonight.

"Nothing. Football. The house. The trip to San Francisco. You know how it is when your mind wanders all over different topics, right?"

"I . . . guess."

He could tell she didn't believe him.

"Sorry to be so distracted. What were you talking about?"

"I was asking you about your brothers and if any of them will be coming to the ranch when you'll be there."

"They should all be there. Tucker will be on break from baseball, and Flynn and Grant are just like me, on vacation. Plus two of my brothers are planning weddings right now, so I'm sure that'll be a hot topic of discussion."

"A lot going on in your family, isn't there?"

"Yeah. The family focus right now is on Grant and Katrina's and Tucker and Aubry's weddings."

"When are they getting married?"

"Grant and Katrina next March. Tucker and Aubry in November."

"That's so exciting for them. You must be so happy for your brothers."

"Katrina's pretty great. So are her brother and sister. Grant's built himself an awesome family. We all love them. Tucker was damn lucky to find an awesome woman in Aubry. She's fantastic."

"I've met all your brothers before, but the women sound lovely."

"Yeah, they are."

She'd finished her drink and set it aside. Miraculously, Donna appeared, whisked the empty glass away and returned within a minute with another drink for Harmony and a beer for Barrett.

"You're really good at this," Harmony said.

Donna smiled. "Thanks. It's my job to keep an eye on you two tonight."

"We'll make sure to be on our best behavior, then," Harmony said.

Donna looked from Harmony to Barrett. "Now what fun would that be?"

Harmony laughed as Donna disappeared. "Ted has good staff."

"He's doing it right. Keep the customers' glasses filled. That'll keep them in the bar."

She took a long swallow of her drink. "I don't intend to spend all night in the bar, unfortunately for Ted."

"Really. And where do you intend to go next?"

"Up to the room."

Now he was concerned. "Are you tired? Are you feeling all right?"

She gave him a tender smile. "I'm fine, Barrett. But I would like to go up to the room if that's okay with you."

He stood. "Let's go."

Barrett left a generous tip for Donna, then laid his hand on Harmony's back as she stepped in front of him.

He wasn't sure what was going on with her, but he didn't want a repeat of this morning.

When they got upstairs, he opened the door and she walked in and headed straight for the bathroom.

"I'll be right out," she said, shutting the door behind her.

Leaving all the lights off, Barrett stepped out onto the balcony and took in a breath of fresh air, listening to the sounds of the waves crashing against the shore.

When he felt a hand on his shoulder, he turned around.

And nearly swallowed his tongue.

Harmony had undressed down to her underwear. Sexy, barely there lace and silk red panties with a matching bra.

"What are you doing? Are you okay?"

"I'm more than okay, Barrett."

And when she leaned up and wrapped her hand around his neck to draw his lips to hers, all that restraint he'd held in check blew away with the Gulf breeze.

Because her mouth was on his, her body against his, and his restraint was long damn gone.

He wound his arm around her, tugged her close and crushed his lips to hers.

SIXTEEN

IT HAD BEEN A CALCULATED RISK, FOR SURE, BUT Harmony knew she had to take it. The worst that could happen was Barrett telling her no.

This didn't feel like no.

His mouth on hers, his hands on her body were a definite yes. And the groans he emitted as he kissed her made her nipples tingle and her sex quiver. She felt damp and needy and her body throbbed with anticipation. His hands roamed her body and with each stroke of his tongue against hers, she felt weak and desired and deliciously turned-on.

She'd had high expectations about him kissing her, had fantasized about it for years. First, they'd been girlish fantasies. As she'd gotten older, her fantasies about Barrett had receded, but she'd always noticed him at Mama's. He was a formidable, attractive man. What woman wouldn't dream about a man like this putting his mouth on her?

He'd exceeded all her fantasies. He had a great mouth and he knew all the right things to do with it, brushing his lips across hers, teasing her with his tongue and drawing her into a sensual web that was heady and provocative. His hard body pressed against hers, his hand roamed over her back, grabbing her butt and drawing her against his erection.

Oh, his erection. He was supremely hard as he backed her into the room and laid her down on the bed. She felt all that delicious, steely evidence rubbing against her sex when he lay on top of her, yet still held his weight off of her.

And he continued to kiss her, a dizzying array of kisses.

The man had an amazing mouth, making her wonder what else he could do with it.

And when he lifted her arms over her head and nuzzled her jaw, then licked along the side of her neck, she arched her hips, rubbing her clit against his erection.

He raised his head to look at her, his eyes dark with passion.

A very good look for him.

"Harmony."

She undulated her hips against him. "Barrett."

His breathing was harsh, and she hoped his pulse raced fast like hers. She felt out of control, breathless, and she really, really, wanted to see him naked.

"We shouldn't do this."

Not at all what she wanted to hear. Not right now, not when things were just starting to get good.

"Which part? You kissing me or you rocking your damned impressive cock against me?"

He kissed her neck, groaned, then raised up on his arms. "Any of it."

The sexy, sultry mood evaporated. "You are not going to bring up that man code thing again right now, are you?"

He slid off of her and sat on the edge of the bed. "It's more than that."

Refusing to cover herself, because she wanted him to see exactly what he was *not* having at the moment, she rolled to her side and propped herself up on her elbow. "Then what is it?"

He threaded his fingers through his hair, looking down at the floor for a few seconds before dragging in a breath. Then he turned his gaze to her. "It's just that I have so much respect for you."

That did it. She slid her legs over the side of the bed. "That is such bullshit, Barrett."

She grabbed her dress and slid into it, pulling the straps up over her shoulders, then marched into the bathroom, threw all her things into her overnight bag and zipped it up.

Barrett was still sitting on the side of the bed when she came out. She slipped on her sandals, shoved the rest of her clothes into her bag and closed it.

"What are you doing?" he asked.

"I'm leaving."

"We can talk about this."

"No. We can't. If you're too much of a coward to take what you want, then I'm sure as hell not going to throw myself at you."

She went to the door to open it, but he was right there. "You came with me, remember?"

Refusing to even look at him, she opened the door. "I did. But I'm not leaving with you."

She walked out, hearing the door close behind her as she made her way down the hall.

BARRETT STARED AT THE CLOSED DOOR IN FRONT of him.

Okay, so that hadn't gone like he'd expected.

The entire night hadn't gone like he'd expected. He sure as hell hadn't expected Harmony to greet him on the balcony in the sexiest red underwear he'd ever seen. And he hadn't planned on kissing her, or dragging her to the bed to touch her, inhale her sweet scent and think about fucking her.

He finally walked away from the door and went out onto the balcony.

Okay, so maybe he'd screwed up. He'd spent the entire day—and night—with Harmony. Everything had been going well. Maybe he'd subconsciously rented the room with this in mind.

He turned and looked back into the darkened room.

"This" being spending the night with her, having her in bed. They'd been so close.

Until he'd been the one to put on the brakes. And then to make matters worse, he'd made up a lame excuse about respecting her too much.

Not that he didn't respect her—he did. But that hadn't been the reason.

He knew it. And so did Harmony.

It was time for him to decide if he wanted to move forward with her, or forever keep his distance.

He was going to have to have an honest conversation with her.

Which could be difficult, because judging from the way she looked when she stormed out of here, it was possible she'd never speak to him again.

SEVENTEEN

THERE WAS NOTHING LIKE THROWING YOURSELF INTO your work to get your mind off your personal problems. And despite thinking she was going to have a light day, Harmony's morning had been super busy. She had had an unexpected meeting with a walk-in client to discuss the potential for new business, had fielded multiple phone calls and had met with another client to cover a new kitchen and family room makeover.

So it was well after lunch by the time she was free, and, conscious of what had happened to her yesterday, she stopped and had a great salad before heading back to the office.

Since she hadn't slept at all last night, by the end of today she was going to drive back to her town house, do a workout at the gym, then climb into a pair of shorts and a tank top and settle in on her sofa for a night of relaxation. Maybe she'd get back to that book she'd been reading yesterday, or catch a baseball game on TV.

Either way, she was already wiped out and looking forward to the end of the day. All she had left at the office was some paper-work and several e-mails.

She walked in to find Barrett having a conversation with Rosalie.

He was the absolute last thing she needed today.

"What are you doing here?" she asked.

"I need to talk to you."

Not wanting to get into it with him in front of her assistant, she nodded. "We can talk in my office."

She led him into her office, then closed the door behind him. She moved to her desk, needing to put distance between them.

"What are you doing here, Barrett?"

She was still standing. He moved to the front of her desk. "I need to talk to you."

Trying to act as if her heart wasn't pounding, she shrugged. "I think you said enough last night."

"Yeah, about that." He started to come around to her side of the desk, but she held her hand up.

"No."

He stopped.

"Harmony, I screwed up last night."

Yes, he had. Except for the kissing her and touching her part, which unfortunately she hadn't been able to get out of her head. Which was why she hadn't slept at all. "Tell me something I don't know."

He tried to come over to her, but her "come any closer and I'll cut you" expression made him pause.

"Okay, look. You . . . surprised me when you came out on the balcony in your underwear."

"That hideous, am I?"

He cocked his head to the side. "I think from the response you got from me you know better. But I guess I got into it—into you—a lot more than I expected to."

Okay, now things were getting interesting. "Go on."

"And I backed off because there were a hundred things going through my head at once. How turned-on I was. How I've known you for a long time. How I could potentially hurt you. I don't want to hurt you."

"You haven't mentioned my brother."

His lips curved. "Harmony. I had you nearly naked and underneath me. I can guarantee you I wasn't thinking about Drake at the time."

She finally smiled. "I'm glad to hear that."

He made it around the desk and smoothed his hand up her arm. "I'm sorry. I let all those thoughts take over what we were doing. And what we were doing was really good. I backed off because I honestly was afraid that if we went too far, it would hurt you."

She leaned against the desk. "Tell me why you think you'll hurt me."

"I am going to bring your brother into this. You know how protective he is of you. He's also my best friend and my teammate and the last thing I want to do is piss him off. He wouldn't like the two of us together."

She shrugged. "Drake doesn't like me with anyone. He doesn't think anyone is good enough for me."

He leveled a smile at her. "That's because he cares about you."

"No, it's because he's overprotective."

"Either way, I'm being selfish about this. The last thing I want is to get in the middle of a battle between the two of you. Or even worse, do anything to damage the friendship I've built with Drake. This has disaster written all over it, Harmony. Even you have to see that."

Maybe she did and maybe she didn't, but the last thing she wanted was her brother to interfere in her life in any way. Especially her romantic life. "I can see where you're coming from, Barrett. But I won't let Drake dictate the terms of my life." She shoved a finger at his chest. "Nor should he yours."

"Yeah, I know. But there's more than just Drake involved in this. Say you and I get all hot and heavy."

"I like the sound of that."

He gave her a sexy grin. "Yeah, me too. But then what happens if it doesn't work out? If you and I have a big blowout of a fight, or we decide we're not compatible? Can you imagine the mess that'll make? And then what happens to my friendship with your brother when he does find out that I'm the one who broke your heart?"

She appreciated that he'd thought this all out, but she wasn't one to think long-term. "That's easy. Don't break my heart."

"Harmony. I can't make that guarantee and you know that. I can't guarantee you anything other than right now."

"I know that. Which is what I'm trying to tell you. I just want today, Barrett. You and me and right now. I know there are no guarantees of tomorrow and I'm sure as hell not asking you to fall in love with me. I just got out of a relationship. I wasn't looking for a commitment or a boyfriend. I just wanted sex."

Leave it to Harmony to put it out there, straight and with no bullshit.

He didn't know why he'd been so reluctant.

Or so stupid.

"Okay."

She gave him a wary look. "Okay?"

"Yeah. We'll dive in and give it a try and see what happens."

Her lips curved. "Okay, then. So what happens next?"

"You're still coming to San Francisco with me?"

"Well, I hadn't planned to after last night."

"But I'm forgiven now, right?"

"Does that charm always work?"

"Usually."

She came up to him and dug her nails into his chest. "You'll find I'm a harder sell, Barrett Cassidy."

He wrapped his fingers around her wrists and drew her against him. "And you'll find me hard around you. Probably all the time. You said all you want is sex. That I can give you."

"That's all I want."

"Then that's what you'll get. You ready for me, Harmony?"

"Yes."

He ran his hand down her back, letting his fingers wander over the soft material of her dress.

"I want to kiss you, fuck you right now. I want to bend you over your desk, lift that pretty yellow dress you're wearing over your hips and drive into you and make you come over and over again."

He watched her lips part, her breaths increase.

"So that's how it's going to be," she said, her breath a low whisper.

"That's how it's gonna be." He moved into her, letting her feel how damn hard he was. "That's what you do to me, so don't ever think you don't turn me on. Don't ever think I don't want you."

He took a step back, saw the disappointment on her face. He knew the feeling.

"But your assistant is out there, and your blinds are open. So this isn't the right time or place. Because when I fuck you, Harmony? I'm gonna make you scream."

Now he saw the passion flare in her eyes. He wanted her more than anything right now. Dammit.

"I'm counting on it."

"Tonight."

"Just like that?"

He cocked his head to the side. "You got another date?"

"No."

"Then tonight. Your place, my place, I don't care. But tonight. I'm not waiting any longer."

She nodded. "Come on over to my place. Is seven thirty all right? I could cook—"

"I don't want dinner, Harmony. I just want you."

"All right, then. Seven thirty."

He was glad his T-shirt covered his raging hard-on as he walked out of her office, and he was also glad her assistant was on the phone as he walked by.

He climbed into his SUV and fired up the air conditioner to arctic levels.

It was going to take a lot to cool him down, especially since all he could think about was how many hours until seven thirty rolled around.

EIGHTEEN

HARMONY HAD WANTED TO CALL ALYSSA, TO TALK about and examine everything she and Barrett had been through and talked about.

But in the end, she had finished up her workday and had gone home, first stopping at the store to pick up some beer and wine. And despite Barrett's warning that he didn't plan on having anything but her tonight, she also bought a few snacks.

They might not be hungry before, but she intended to make him burn off a few calories tonight, and he might have an appetite later.

She had a light dinner, then took a shower and dried off. She felt a tingly awareness all over her body, as if every cell awaited Barrett's touch.

Kind of crazy. She'd never felt this sense of anticipation before. Barrett had been all she thought about as she'd gone through the remainder of her day today.

She lotioned her body, fixed her hair and makeup, and decided on an easy-to-remove silk sundress. She considered lighting candles in the bedroom, then decided that was a little too cheesy.

She went downstairs and thought about opening the red wine to let it breathe.

No. All he wanted was sex.

She lifted her head and stared out the doors to her balcony. Was she upset by that? She thought about it for a few seconds, then decided she wasn't.

She'd just gone through a breakup and she'd been honest with him when she'd told him she wasn't looking for a boyfriend or a relationship.

She was attracted to Barrett. All she wanted was sex, to feel desirable.

He most definitely desired her, and, for right now, that was all she needed.

When the doorbell rang her heart began to race—like teenage-girl, first-date race. Which was ridiculous. But also made her feel giddy, and what was wrong with that?

A man *should* make a woman feel like that, shouldn't he?

She went to the door and opened it. Barrett was leaning against the doorway, and when he gave her a smoldering half smile, parts of her quivered.

All the good parts, of course.

"Evening, Harmony."

"Barrett."

She held the door open for him and he stepped in. She shut and locked the door behind her, and for good measure, turned the dead bolt.

Barrett looked delicious in dark jeans and gray T-shirt. She wanted to lean into him, to run her arms over all that delicious muscle. But she resisted.

Soon.

She walked into the living room, unsure how soon he planned to throw her to the ground, lift up her skirt and shove his cock inside of her. The thought of it made her tingle.

Okay, maybe not soon enough. She turned to face him. "Would you like some wine or a beer?"

"No, I'm good. But if you need a glass of wine to relax you, go ahead."

She felt his energy. It fueled her own. "Honestly, Barrett, I'm so pent up right now I don't think it would help."

He stepped toward her and smoothed his hands up and down her arms. "Pent up?"

"Yes."

"Do I make you nervous, Harmony?"

"No. I'm never nervous around you. Not anymore. More like . . . aware of you." She laid her hands on his chest. "The way you stand, the way you cock your head to the side when you're thinking about something, your crooked smile—"

"You notice a lot."

"About you? Hard not to, you being all imposing and hot."

He laughed. "Thanks for the compliment. Now let's talk about you."

"Me? What about me?"

He tipped his finger under her chin and tilted her head back. "You have the prettiest eyes, Harmony. And the way you smile makes me catch my breath. And your mouth—damn you have a sexy mouth. Your laugh makes me turn my head whenever we're in the same room. It's like you put your entire soul into your laugh. It's genuine, and if there's one thing that makes a woman attractive to me, it's when she's real. And everything about you is real. There's no bullshit about you. I know when you say something, you mean it."

"Well, that's true." She loved that he told her what he liked about her. It made her toes curl.

And when he leaned in, his breath sailed across her cheek. He cupped the back of her neck. "Did I mention how much I like your mouth?"

Her breath caught when he kissed her and she grasped his arms, digging her nails in.

He groaned, then wrapped his arm around her back, tugging her closer, fitting his mouth firmly with hers and sliding his tongue inside to lick against hers.

She was swamped with sensation. She breathed in his crisp, clean scent, taking in how hard his body felt as he pushed her against the counter. Her nipples tingled and she pulsed with damp desire as he cupped her butt to draw her in closer to his erection.

And when he arched against her, rubbing his cock against her pussy, she wanted to lift her dress, draw down her panties and get off against him. She needed release, the kind only Barrett could give her.

She'd fantasized about this moment for years, of what it would be like to have him touch her and make her come. It was almost surreal to believe it was about to become reality.

When he pulled his mouth from hers to rain kisses along her jaw and her throat, he whispered in her ear.

"I've thought about fucking you, Harmony. I've thought about it for a long time."

She leaned back, searching his face to see if she could read that as some kind of bullshit line men laid on women.

All she saw on his face was earnest desire. "Did you?"

"Yeah. Last year at New Year's Eve at your mom's. You leaned over to get something out of the oven and your dress rode up. I wanted to come up behind you and lift your dress and touch you. Hell, if I'm being honest, I wanted to do a lot more than just touch you."

She shuddered at the visual. "Why didn't you ever say anything to me?"

He ran his hands down her rib cage and over her hips. "You know why."

She most definitely did not want the topic of Barrett's friendship with Drake to interfere in what was happening with them tonight. "Touch me now. Do whatever you want to me now. I'm here and I'm all yours."

He had a handful of her dress and bunched it, then lifted it over her hip, smoothing his hand over her butt. "I love your ass, Harmony. So soft and curvy. You're built like a woman. Did I ever tell you how much I appreciate your body?"

She was going to swoon in an embarrassing way if he kept tossing out the compliments, not to mention feeling weak in the knees from his hand on her ass. She clutched his shirt and drew his mouth to hers.

When he kissed her, it was an explosion of hot passion. Suddenly his hands were everywhere, lifting her dress, his fingers on a quest inside her underwear to grab her butt. She was out of breath as he pulled her closer to his erection.

Oh, why weren't they naked yet?

He lifted her as if she weighed nothing. She wrapped her legs around his hips and he walked up the stairs toward her bedroom.

"You don't have to carry me," she whispered against his lips.

"Faster this way." He set her down next to her bed, then untied the straps of her sundress, letting it fall to the floor. "And if I didn't get you up here right now, I was going to fuck you in the kitchen."

Her lips curved. "I would have been all right with that."

"I'll keep that in mind for round two."

She was happy to hear he was game for round two. She'd already made sure to clear her calendar for tomorrow morning. She intended to keep Barrett up all night.

But first, she needed him to shed some clothes. She lifted his shirt and he helped her out by pulling it over his head and tossing it to the side.

Now she had access to his beautiful skin. She splayed her hands over his sculpted abs, letting her fingers map a trail along his muscular torso. She slid her hands up his chest, lingering where his heart was, to feel the mad pumping.

She tilted her head back to look at his face. "You're heart's beating fast."

The wickedly sexy look in his eyes seared her. "Yeah, you do that to me. You turn me on. I like your hands on me."

Keeping her focus on his face, she let her hands drift lower, over his abs and down to his jeans, where she undid the button. His cock was hard, straining against the zipper as she drew it down.

She grasped his jeans at the hips and shoved them down to pool at his feet. He toed out of his tennis shoes and kicked them off, then stepped out of his jeans, leaving him in only his boxer briefs.

The man was so incredibly sculpted, with amazing, well-muscled thighs, strong calves, and the package—well, the package was eager to escape the briefs and she had to admit she was just as anxious to get a peek.

She met his gaze again, and he leveled his signature crooked smile on her that signaled he was happy to let her do the unveiling.

She dropped to her knees and pulled his boxer briefs down. His cock sprang up and she looked up at him and smiled, then wrapped her hands around his thick shaft.

"Oh, hell yeah," Barrett said. "Put your mouth on my cock and suck it."

His command raised goose bumps on her skin. She flicked her tongue over the wide cockhead, using her hand to stroke him. He was so hard, so impossibly thick, and when she put her mouth over the head and fit her lips over him, bringing his cock into her mouth, he shifted forward, sliding the shaft along her tongue.

"Yes, like that. Flick your tongue along the head."

He cupped the back of her head, controlling her movements. She had to admit it was such a turn-on to give him pleasure, to hear his groans and the way he spoke to her as she rolled her tongue over the shaft, pulled it out of her mouth, then engulfed him.

"Christ, that's good. Now take it in deep. I want to see your mouth filled with my cock."

She breathed in the musky scent of him, then slid her lips around his cock and pressed down, giving him suction, taking his cockhead all the way to the back of her throat.

"Fuck yeah. Like that."

When he withdrew, he bent and lifted her to stand.

"Any more of that and I'll shoot come down your throat. God, you're good at sucking me, babe."

Before she could say anything he took her mouth in a deep kiss, his hand coming around to unhook her bra. He smoothed his hand over her back, then around the front of her, sliding down to slip his fingers inside her panties.

She moaned against his mouth as he dipped his fingers along her sex.

"You're wet," he whispered against her mouth, pulling back enough to look at her. He slipped a finger inside of her. "Wet and hot."

She couldn't speak, could only gasp as he tucked another finger inside of her. "Do you feel that? Do you feel the way your pussy grabs onto my fingers?"

"Yes."

He withdrew his fingers, then pulled the straps of her bra down, tossing it onto the floor. He laid her on the bed and she wriggled onto the center. He grasped her panties and pulled them off, then joined her on the bed.

She expected him to grab a condom—she'd laid a box on her nightstand in clear view. Instead, he nestled in next to her, pulled her against him and kissed her—thoroughly, his hands roaming over her breasts, teasing her nipples with light brushes of his fingers until she writhed against him.

He pushed her onto her back and fit a nipple into his mouth, gently sucking until she thought she was going to die from the sensations that shot from her nipple to her sex. Was there anything Barrett didn't know how to do, and do perfectly? He went from one nipple to the next, gathering her breast in his hand and lavishing attention on each nipple, nipping and sucking on them until she arched against him, either needing him to do that forever because it felt so damn good, or please get to her pussy because she needed to come right now or die.

But he lifted his head and gave her that smile. "You have the softest skin," he said, before licking his way over her belly and lower. "And you smell so damn good."

He nipped at her hip bone, making her moan before spreading her legs and kissing her inner thighs. He teased her, kissing and licking just above her sex.

"Barrett."

He raised up. "Yeah, babe."

She looked down at him. "Nothing."

He teased his thumb around her clit. "Something you need?"

"You know damn well what I need."

"Yeah, I know damn well what you need. But I like playing with your pussy. You smell and taste like tart honey down here."

She was quivering all over, anticipation making her feel like a needy addict jonesing for a fix.

She was addicted all right. To the man nestled between her thighs. And when he put his mouth on her, she couldn't help the long, low moans that fell from her lips. His tongue was hot, wet and exactly what she needed as he lapped her up from her clit to her pussy. He slid his tongue inside of her, and all she could think about was that the reality of this was infinitely better than any of the fantasies she'd had about Barrett.

The man had a talented tongue and lips and knew exactly what to do to make her soar. He rolled his tongue all over her, never lingering in one spot. The sensations were indescribable, and when she came the first time, it was a shock. She cried out and shuddered uncontrollably as her orgasm crashed through her. And when Barrett licked her gently into another one not long after, she moaned and thrashed like she hadn't come in ages, even though it had only been a few minutes since the last one. This time, he had his fingers inside of her and she felt her pussy squeezing them as she climaxed.

When he climbed up next to her, she was still breathing hard.

"Twice, huh?" he asked with a supremely confident smile.

"That doesn't happen often. Or like, hardly ever."

"We're just getting started, Harmony."

She believed him. If any man could give her multiple orgasms tonight, it was this man.

Still quivering and breathing hard, she reached over onto the nightstand and grabbed a condom, handing it to him. "Suit up, Barrett. Let's see how many more you can give me."

NINETEEN

BARRETT HADN'T EXPECTED HARMONY TO BE SO responsive, so hot, so damn . . .

Sexual.

He liked a hot woman, one who could own her sexuality and have fun in bed. He had an inkling he might find that with Harmony, but until now, he'd had no idea how incredible she'd be.

And they'd barely gotten things rolling.

He tore open the condom and slid it on, then kneeled between her legs.

Damn, she was beautiful, her skin glowing like banked embers in what little light there was in the room. He grasped her hips and draped her legs over his thighs and inched the head of his cock between her pussy lips. He cupped her butt and held on to her as he eased into her, feeling every inch of her draw him in and tighten around him as he filled her. He held her like that for a few seconds, letting her get accustomed to the feel of him.

She raked her nails down his arms and lifted against him, signaling her need for more. He drew her against him as he thrust, watching as her lips fell open and she grabbed onto his arms to pull herself deeper.

He leaned over to slide his arm under her back and lift her up so she was seated on his thighs, impaling her deeper onto his cock.

"Oh, fuck yeah," he said. "I like being buried deep inside you like this." He showed her how much by thrusting up and then rocking back and forth, giving her the friction she needed.

She responded, panting against him, using her nails to dig into his shoulders, lifting, then slowly sliding down on top of him. He grasped her hips and helped her, the two of them falling into a tempo that worked for them both. Slowly at first, which sure as hell worked for him as he felt every inch of her sweet, hot pussy grabbing onto him whenever he slid back inside of her. And her answering moans told him she liked what he gave her.

"Do you feel it, Harmony?" he asked as he stilled, feeling her body quiver. "Do you feel your pussy tightening around me?"

She moaned, her gaze lifting to his. He saw the hunger in her eyes, and fed off of it, giving her a slow, easy thrust.

"Yes. I feel it. Make me come, Barrett."

He laid her on the bed and spread her legs, keeping her up on his thighs to give himself access to her. He used his fingers to tease her clit as he eased into her.

"Oh. Oh yes. Like that. That makes me come."

"Like that?" He gently stroked back and forth on the tight nub until she arched against him.

"Yes. Oh, God yes." She tightened her grip on his arms, bucking against him until she tilted her head back, cried out and squeezed his cock with the force of her orgasm.

He slid her off of him and dropped onto her body, entering her with full, deep thrusts, feeling every quake of her orgasm while he powered into her. She was so hot, so tight and coming apart around him. He couldn't hold back, and when he came, he shuddered against her, taking her mouth in a deep kiss that left him sweating and spent.

He wrapped an arm around her and held her while they both caught their breath. Finally, he released her and left to dispose of the condom in the bathroom. When he came back, Harmony had propped her pillow up against the headboard and leaned against it.

He joined her but not before leaning over to brush his lips against hers. "That was damn good."

"It was for me, too." She slid out of bed. "And now I need a drink. What would you like?"

"Ice water."

"Okay."

She was gone only a few minutes, and when she came back in she carried two glasses of water. She handed one to him, then climbed onto the bed and sat on her heels, sipping her glass of water.

He liked that she didn't run for a robe or put on clothes or hide under the covers. He admired a woman who was so confident about her body. Harmony had a right to be. She had a bangin' body, curvy in all the right places. He reached out and smoothed his hand up and down her thigh.

"You're beautiful," he said.

She took a deep breath and let it out. "Thank you." She swept her hand along his leg. "You're pretty damn hot yourself. Let me know when you've had enough rest time, so we can do it again."

He really, really liked this woman. And he was going to really, really ignore the fact she was Drake's sister.

He put his glass on the end table, then took hers and set it down next to his. He pulled Harmony across his lap and kissed her, played with her breasts and soon had her breathless and moaning as he slid his hand between her legs.

"I've had enough rest time," he said.

Her lips curved. "I figured you'd be ready to make me come again."

"And again and again, babe."

He'd give her all she needed. And more.

All damn night long.

TWENTY

HARMONY HADN'T SET AN ALARM, MAINLY BECAUSE she and Barrett had been up most of the night, but also because her body woke naturally anyway.

So when she got up to use the bathroom and grabbed her phone, she wrinkled her nose.

Seven a.m. So much for sleeping in. She was awake now, though, and as she stared down at Barrett's gorgeous naked sleeping form, she figured there was no point in waking him. She slid into a pair of shorts and a tank top and went downstairs to brew coffee.

She slid her cup under the brewer and waited, checking her e-mail on her phone. Fortunately, nothing pressing happened last night and she didn't expect anything this morning, so maybe she'd have some time to jump all over Barrett before he took off this morning.

She grabbed her now-filled cup and went to the fridge for cream, then to the sugar bowl for a teaspoon of sugar. She pulled up a chair at the table and had taken one long, glorious sip of coffee just as Barrett came down.

If she'd known he was going to show up in her kitchen shirtless and with his jeans mostly undone, she wouldn't have bothered to make a cup of coffee, because she was definitely awake now.

He gave her a sexy smile. "Good morning."

"Good morning. I tried not to wake you."

"You didn't. My body has an internal clock. It wakes itself."

She grinned. "I know that feeling."

He came around behind her and nuzzled the back of her neck, sending chill bumps all over her and making her nipples hard. "Sleep well?"

She reached behind her to wrap her hand around the back of his neck, then tilted her head back to kiss him. "What little sleep I had was good."

His eyes looked exceptionally blue and desirable this morning as he made eye contact with her. "And who was the one who insisted on one more round at three a.m.?"

She shrugged, then turned around to grab her coffee. "I'm going to say it was you."

He laughed. "Yeah, I don't think so."

"And I don't recall you complaining."

He made himself a cup of coffee, then pulled up a chair next to her at the table. "You'll never hear me complain about sex. I'm a guy. You know how we are."

"Yes, I do know how you are."

She liked their morning banter, and that he hadn't run downstairs fully dressed and ready to go out the door like so many guys she knew would do—and had done. Even Levon had been like that. He had never been one to linger, or make small talk.

"Got any appointments this morning?" Barrett asked.

She shook her head. "Not until later this afternoon. It's mostly paperwork."

"Good."

"What about you?"

"Nope. I'm free."

"That's good." He moved his chair closer and raised one of her legs, resting it on his thigh as he drank his coffee. "So we have some time this morning."

"Time for what?"

"You know, to kick back and relax. Or . . . whatever."

Her gaze drifted to his face. Hot desire was written all over it, and, coupled with the way his hand drifted up and down her leg, the warm stirrings of need quickened inside of her.

He pulled her chair closer and continued to sip his coffee. Her coffee was forgotten as his fingers inched up her thighs, sliding underneath her silk shorts to tease her bare flesh.

He arched a brow. "You dressed sparingly this morning." He cupped her sex, his fingers tapping ever so lightly over her clit.

She drew in a breath. "I was in a hurry."

"Needed that coffee fix, huh?"

"Yes."

He slid his fingers lower, parting her flesh to tuck a finger into her pussy. Warm pleasure surrounded her as he found an easy rhythm that lulled her into a sensual haze.

"What do you need now, Harmony?"

She lifted her hips, riding his finger. "I need to come."

"I know what you need. You need my hot, wet tongue on your pussy, licking you all up and down until you scream."

Just hearing his deep, gravelly voice uttering those words made her quiver in anticipation. "Yes."

He laid her foot on the floor, slid out of his chair and dropped to his knees, then drew her shorts off. He spread her legs, cupped her butt in his hands and lifted her toward his mouth.

She leaned back and watched as he slid his tongue over her pussy, avoiding her clit while he teased her lips and the top of her sex.

She reached out to grasp his hair, tugging on it. "Barrett."

His only response was to make humming noises against her. It was the sweetest torture, and when he found her clit, covered it with his lips and tongue and bathed her in hot, wet pleasure, she closed her eyes, lost in sensation. She was catapulted to another realm where only pulses of desire existed.

He dipped a finger into her, fucking her slow and easy as he danced a languorous route around her clit with his tongue, swirling it over and over the bud until she thought she'd die from the pleasure. She was lost in a sexual fog, in her own feelings, as she took a slow, beautiful ride to orgasm.

And when she climaxed, it was with a low moan, her entire body feeling every sweet pulse as she watched Barrett latch onto her clit and suck her, then gently lap around the now sensitive bud to take her down from that incredible high.

She lay limp against the chair and he reached up to tangle his hand in her hair and kiss her. She tasted herself on his mouth, an incredible aphrodisiac that fired up her desires all over again.

She pressed on his chest. "Drop your pants and sit on the chair."

His lips curved. "Yes, ma'am."

He stood and unzipped his jeans, dropping them to the floor. She grabbed his jeans to kneel on them, then nestled between his thighs as he took a seat in her kitchen chair.

"You taste damn good, Harmony," he said, sifting his fingers through her hair.

His cock was hard, and she grasped hold of it, stroking it as she looked at him. "You made me come so good, Barrett. Now I'm going to do the same to you."

She heard his deep breathing as she lifted up, then took his cock in her mouth.

"Oh yeah. Just like that. Suck it. Suck it hard and make me come."

His words enticed her, made her pussy quiver even as she took his cock deeper into the recesses of her mouth. She held the base, flicked her tongue around the tip, then engulfed him.

"Fuck. Oh, fuck yeah."

She wanted him to feel how he'd made her feel—that out-of-body experience where all she'd felt was the heady pleasure of his mouth on her. She wanted his brain to explode from the pleasure she gave him. So when he started pumping his cock into her mouth, when sweat beaded on his brow and all he could utter were one-word expletives, she knew she had him right where she wanted him—out of his mind, in the moment and concentrating on what her mouth was doing to him.

"Fuck, Harmony. Yeah. Suck it. Harder. Oh, fuck, that's gonna make me come. I'm gonna come in your mouth. You ready for it?"

She hummed against his cock and took him into the back of her throat, gently squeezing his ball sac as she rolled her mouth up and down over his shaft.

He let out a low groan, spurts of hot come splashing against her tongue. She felt his legs tremble as he rocketed through his orgasm. She held tight to his cock and swallowed what he gave her, licking him until he grew soft along her tongue.

"Christ," he finally muttered, sliding his hand along her cheek. He lifted her and pulled her onto his lap, brushing his lips against hers. "I think you blew the top of my head off. I feel dizzy."

She smiled and dragged a finger across his bottom lip. "I know the feeling."

He kissed her again, this time a deeper, soulful kiss that left her feeling a little woozy. She slid off his lap, climbed back into her silk shorts and poured them both a glass of orange juice.

Barrett put his jeans back on. "Now you need food," he said, as they sipped their juice.

"I do. I can fix us some eggs and bacon."

"How about we do that together?"

"Sure."

She didn't mind spending a little more time with him, and she sure hadn't minded the extra sex this morning, knowing it was going to be a one-time thing.

Barrett fixed eggs while she did the bacon and popped bread in the toaster. They sat down and ate together.

"I don't know about you," she said, as she scooped eggs onto her fork. "But I'm starving."

He nodded as he wolfed down his third piece of bacon. "Sex works up an appetite. You feeling okay this morning?"

She cocked her head to the side and nodded. "I'm fine. Why?"

"I hadn't thought about feeding you breakfast before we did all the fun and sexy play."

She smiled. "I'm fine to go an hour or two without eating, Barrett. I just have to be mindful about not going more than that."

"Duly noted. So when we go to San Francisco, I'll make sure to feed you early."

"San Francisco?"

"Yeah. This weekend."

"Oh." She'd totally forgotten about that.

"You're still coming, aren't you?"

"I'd . . . love to. I guess I thought . . ."

"You thought what?"

"I guess I thought now that we had sex, you'd be done with me."

Barrett frowned. "Just what kind of man do you think I am, Harmony?"

Uh-oh. "Okay, maybe I didn't phrase that right. I mean, before when you asked me, we were friends."

"And now we're not?"

This was not coming out like she intended. "No, that's not what I meant. Now we've had sex. So I assumed with you and my brother and you and me and sex, you'd want distance."

He leaned back in his chair. "Okay, now I'm confused. First, how about we not talk about you and me and sex and your brother in the same sentence ever again, okay?"

She tried not to smile at that. "Okay."

"Second, sex with you isn't a one-time thing. That's not how I saw it, anyway. Did you?"

"Well, that's not how I wanted it. I just assumed—"

"You assumed wrong. I want you. I wanted you before last night, and I wanted you this morning. I still want you. Which means I'm going to continue to want to have sex with you—a lot. If you're not okay with that, you need to tell me now."

Now she did smile. "Oh, I'm totally okay with that."

"Good." He picked up a piece of bacon. "Then we're going to San Francisco this weekend."

It wasn't exactly a declaration of love, and they weren't having a relationship. They were having sex. And according to Barrett, there was going to be a lot of it.

Since she didn't want either love or a relationship, but she sure as hell wanted more of Barrett, this arrangement worked for her.

For now. And all she wanted was "for now."

So she was going to go to San Francisco this weekend.

And have sex. A lot of it.

Awesome.

TWENTY-ONE

THE WEATHER WAS CHILLY WHEN THEY LANDED IN SAN
Francisco. But she was so happy to be here.

She'd caught up on work the past day, had met with clients and
had checked on the status of Barrett's home renovation. Everything was going smoothly and she had nothing on her list that had
to be handled right away.

She'd been up late last night sending Rosalie e-mails and a to-do
list. Rosalie was probably going to hate her. Then again, Rosalie was
competent as hell, so she'd likely have everything on the list done by
the time Harmony came back to the office on Monday.

She'd also texted Alyssa to let her know she'd be out of town.
She and Alyssa were always in touch, and she hadn't had a spare
second to fill her in on what had been going on with Barrett. She'd
tell Alyssa all about it when she got back from her trip.

But she was exhausted by the time the flight took off this morning. Barrett was reading a book on his tablet. She read a book and

enjoyed the breakfast that was served in first class, but after that she leaned her chair back and fell asleep while Barrett watched the movie. He nudged her when the plane was preparing for landing. Despite the long flight, she'd slept soundly and undisturbed. No doubt she had Barrett to thank for that.

Barrett rented a car for them, so they got into the car and he headed off to the city.

Along the way, Harmony enjoyed the spectacular view of San Francisco, from its incredibly bustling freeway system to the gorgeous bridges and stunning skyline. As they went over the Bay Bridge, she wished they could stop in the middle so she could snap some pictures. Unfortunately, that wasn't possible.

"I hope we have some time to tour the city while we're here," she said.

Barrett looked over at her and smiled. "Sure. It's a great city. Incredible architecture and history. Amazing food. We'll get out and wander around."

She looked forward to that. Before she left town she'd made a list of places she wanted to see, like Fisherman's Wharf, Pier 39, Ghirardelli Square, Haight-Ashbury, Coit Tower. She also wanted to ride on a cable car, drive down the world's crookedest street, see Golden Gate Park, Alcatraz . . .

Okay, so she had a long list and maybe they wouldn't be able to hit everything in a short weekend.

They pulled onto a street filled with beautiful, quaint houses. Barrett pulled into the driveway and Harmony gasped.

"This is it?" she asked.

Barrett turned off the engine. "This is it."

She got out and walked around the front of the most adorable Craftsman house.

"I hadn't expected Flynn to have a house, let alone one like this."

The front yard was charming, with a nice grassy area, beautiful landscaping and an adorable front porch. She walked up the steps to see two chairs and a table on the porch. The front door was painted a dark blue, the rest of the house a lighter shade of blue with pale trim. White shutters framed the picture window.

Barrett joined her. "Yeah, he liked the old place and had it remodeled, inside and out, about a year and a half ago."

"I can't wait to see inside." The interior designer in her vibrated with excitement.

Barrett rang the bell. A few seconds later, the door opened and Flynn was there.

She'd met all the Cassidy brothers because they'd all come to visit Barrett in Tampa over the years.

Flynn was definite eye candy. Tall and imposing like all the Cassidys, Flynn was built like a solid wall of muscle and had amazing arm tattoos.

So. Sexy.

He smiled at Harmony and brought her in for a hug. She had to admit, she liked all of Barrett's brothers. Besides being incredibly hot, they were all really nice guys. But her attraction had always been to Barrett.

"Barrett told me he was dragging you along," Flynn said. "I'm glad you're here."

"Me, too. Thanks for letting me come."

"Hey, I'm always happy to see you." Flynn moved away from Harmony and hugged his brother. "Good trip?"

"Long damn flight."

Flynn stood aside so they could walk in. "Tell me about it. Why do you have to live so far away?"

"Why do you?" Barrett asked, as they stepped in.

While the two brothers argued, Harmony took in the amazing

original wood floors, the open, expansive living area and the charming features of the home. It had built-in shelving on either side of the brick fireplace, and wood beams on the ceiling.

"Feel free to look around," Flynn said.

"Thanks." She moved into the kitchen, which had been completely renovated and now had black and white cabinets and a beautiful gray stone countertop. And awe-inspiring appliances that would make any chef green with envy.

She wandered into the butler's pantry, marveling at the original woodwork. Some of the features had been refinished and kept as is, while others had been modernized.

Gorgeous. Absolutely gorgeous.

"But training camp should be solid. Looking forward to seeing what the rookies have got," Flynn said, as he and Barrett wandered into the kitchen.

He looked over at her and smiled. "The verdict?"

"It's perfect. You've kept enough of the original style that you haven't lost the charm of the old house, yet you've modernized it and decorated it beautifully."

"I don't take any credit for that. I had a good designer. But there were a few things I wanted kept as is. Fortunately, the previous owners had the place carpeted, so the original wood floors were in great shape. All we had to do was refinish them."

"That's amazing."

"Yeah. But the kitchen was old and outdated, so it had to go."

"Understandable, especially if you like to cook."

Flynn grinned. "I do like to cook."

They wandered upstairs. The house had three bedrooms upstairs, as well as two bathrooms. There was also an office with a balcony.

"It's wonderful, Flynn," she said, as he led her back down the stairs. "You've managed to keep the original beauty of the home, but you've modernized the areas that needed it."

"Thanks. I like the place a lot. Come on, I'll take you across the yard to the guesthouse."

They walked out onto the back deck. He had a nice deck with a grill and plenty of seating, a fire pit in a separate gravel area, and a tiled path that led to what used to be a garage but was now a beautiful guest cottage with a small living area, bedroom and bath.

"No kitchen in here, but there's a mini fridge and drinks are stocked."

"It's perfect."

Barrett came into the cottage with their bags.

"Staying together?" Flynn asked with a raised brow.

"We are." Barrett brushed past him without another word to set their bags down in the bedroom.

She and Barrett hadn't discussed the sleeping arrangements for the trip. She wasn't sure how much of what was going on with them he wanted his brother to know about. She supposed that question had been answered, and she was glad it would be in this cottage, and not a room next door to Flynn.

Flynn turned to her. "So when did you and Barrett become a thing?"

"Mind your own business, Flynn," Barrett said. "How about a beer?"

"Sure."

She was glad Barrett had jumped in on that conversation, because she had no idea how she would have answered.

They weren't really a "thing." They weren't anything, actually, other than two people who knew each other and were having sex.

They defied a relational descriptive. They weren't dating, they weren't a couple and she absolutely would not define herself as Barrett's booty call. It was nothing like that.

It was . . . well, she had no idea what it was. And now, thanks to Barrett, she wouldn't have to label it.

She followed them back into the house.

"What would you like to drink, Harmony?" Flynn asked. "I have wine, beer, or I can make you something harder."

"Actually, it's a little early for alcohol for me."

"Never too early for alcohol," Barrett said, shooting a grin to his brother, who grinned back.

"I also have iced tea," Flynn said.

"That works."

He poured her a glass of iced tea, including slicing a lemon for her, which Harmony said wasn't necessary. Flynn ignored her and they took a seat at the table.

"Where's Tess?" Barrett asked.

Flynn shook his head. "We broke up."

"Oh, sorry man," Barrett said. "I thought things were going well between you two."

Flynn shrugged. "So did I."

Harmony wasn't going to ask. "I'm sorry, too."

"Thanks."

"I recently broke up with someone, too. It sucks."

"Oh, so Barrett is your rebound, huh?" Flynn asked with a smirk.

"Hey. Fuck off. I am not."

Flynn leaned back and took a long swallow of beer.

"Uh-huh."

"Really, he's not," Harmony said. "And you might be deflecting to get off the topic of your own breakup?"

"Ohhh, she burned you, Brother." Barrett slid a sly grin in Harmony's direction.

Flynn narrowed his gaze at Harmony. "Fine. Topics of relationships are off the table for now."

"Agreed. How's the restaurant coming along?" Barrett asked.

"Finalized the purchase of the property, gutted it, and they're already starting construction on the place."

"Have you come up with a name for your new restaurant?" Harmony asked.

"Yeah. Ninety-Two."

Barrett's lips ticked up. "Your jersey number?"

"Yup. It was my college jersey number and my pro number. So far it's been lucky for me. And this way the restaurant doesn't have my name on it."

Harmony took a sip of tea, then set her glass on the table. "Why don't you want your restaurant to bear your name?"

Flynn shrugged. "First, I don't have that big an ego. Second, I think it's better to be subtle. The food should speak for itself. I want people to come in because they like the food and the ambiance, not because they think I might be in there—which frankly, I probably won't be. My goal is to let the talented people run the place."

"But you'll have some say-so on who runs the place, such as chefs and management, right?" Harmony asked.

"Yes. I've already hired someone to manage the place, but he and I will work together on the rest of the hires. I'm no world-class chef, but I know food and I know what I want as far as people cooking for me."

"So you have some ideas on chefs?"

"I have a few ideas."

"In other words, you plan to steal from your competition?" Harmony asked.

"I didn't say that."

"But you implied it."

"Maybe." He gave her a devilish smile and put the bottle of beer to his lips, tilted it back and finished it off.

"Now I'm very curious. And I'd love to see your restaurant."

"It's mainly just a shell right now. But we'll do a drive-by. And I'm interviewing for a head chef this afternoon."

"We can take two cars," Barrett said. "I told Harmony we could take in some sights."

"Perfect. If you want to change or get ready or something, we can leave in about thirty minutes."

"I'm good with what I'm wearing," Barrett said.

Harmony had worn leggings on the plane, and she definitely wanted to freshen up and change clothes. "I'll go get ready."

"I'm going to sit here and finish this beer," Barrett said.

She smiled. "You do that."

She went over to the guesthouse, took a few minutes to unpack, then washed her face, brushed her teeth and hair and redid her makeup. She decided on a pair of black capris, a long-sleeved blouse, and slid into a pair of wedges. She also grabbed her sweater, which seemed a little ridiculous for July, but she'd already been warned about San Francisco's weather, which could be cool in the summer months.

After sliding on a bracelet and applying lip gloss, she made her way back to the main house, marveling at all the gorgeous greenery in Flynn's yard. It wasn't a huge yard, but whoever had done the landscaping had done a great job. There were a couple of trees to provide shade, some medium-sized bushes along the fence perimeter, and several flowering plants to give off color. Nothing major, but just enough to make it look homey and comfortable without being cluttered. And the fire pit was a perfect touch.

She went inside and only Flynn was in the kitchen.

"Where's Barrett?"

"He went to take a leak."

"Okay."

"Are you hungry?" Flynn asked.

"A little."

"I know this great place. You're going to love the food here."

"I can't wait."

Barrett showed up and slid his arm around her waist. "Hungry?"

She rolled her eyes. "Yes. But not starving, so you can relax about the food thing. I'm not about to faint or anything."

He smiled down at her. "Noted. But I'm hungry, so let's go eat."

They piled in their cars and drove to what Barrett told her was Hayes Valley, where Flynn had bought his restaurant. It was a charming—no—gorgeous section of San Francisco, filled with Victorian homes, but also had a vibrant fresh vibe about it. She couldn't wait to explore.

They found a place to park and got out.

"This looks like a fabulous area," Harmony said.

Flynn nodded. "I looked at a lot of places. I ate at a lot of places, talked to quite a few people who lived in those areas. This one was just it for me. Plus it's close to where I live. It has an old-city charm to it, yet modern and fresh. It just felt . . . right."

She could tell Flynn loved this area. Who wouldn't, with its tree-lined sidewalks and people milling about, wandering up and down the street and stopping in the shops. She was kind of envious of Flynn being able to live in such a beautiful city.

He took them into a restaurant called The Grove, very atmospheric with a woodsy décor. They were seated and presented with the menu.

Harmony perused it, her stomach grumbling.

"Well," she said, as she laid the menu down, "I want everything."

Flynn laughed. "I've had just about everything on the menu. Trust me, it's all good."

Since they served breakfast all day, and it was her favorite meal, she settled for the salmon omelet. Barrett decided on a turkey club and Flynn the tuna melt. They ordered drinks, which their waitress brought over right away.

"Tell me about the chef you're interviewing today," Barrett asked.

"She's from Oregon," Flynn said. "Comes highly recommended

by the manager I hired. She's looking for a fresh start. Recently divorced and has no attachments in the state she lives in, so she's free to move. Her credentials are really damn good, and if she's as good as my new manager, Ken, says she is, then I think she might fit what I'm looking for."

"You gonna make her cook for you?" Barrett asked.

"I dunno."

"You should. I would."

"I don't know if that's necessary."

Barrett shrugged. "Why not? No better way to find out if someone is as good as they say they are on paper than to put them to the test. You should invite her to the house for dinner. Have her prepare a meal for us. I mean for you."

Harmony laughed. "Nothing like putting pressure on someone, Barrett."

"It's not a horrible idea," Flynn said. "I'll talk to her this afternoon. If I feel like she could work out, I might suggest dinner."

"If that happens, be sure to text your brother," Harmony said. "I wouldn't want to miss it."

"Plus, we like food," Barrett said.

Flynn smirked. "Yeah, yeah."

The subject shifted from Flynn's restaurant to football, so Harmony sipped the tea she'd ordered and listened in as Barrett and Flynn argued various defensive strategies until their food arrived.

She not only ogled her plate, but Barrett's and Flynn's as well. "Wow."

"I told you how great it was, didn't I?" Flynn said.

Harmony dug into her salmon omelet, savoring every bite of goodness. "This is amazing. In fact, it's so good, I want to eat it twice."

All Barrett did was grunt, which she assumed meant he agreed. They all ate and made very little conversation, and when they were finished, she told Flynn he'd taken them to the best restaurant ever.

"At least until mine opens," he said with a grin.

"True. I hope to come back and have dinner at your restaurant when it opens."

"You have an invitation for opening night. Have Barrett bring you."

She shifted her glance to Barrett, figuring he'd be uncomfortable with that. But he only leveled a knowing smile at her.

Hmm.

After lunch they walked a short way to the restaurant. It was just a shell right now, but Harmony loved the location.

"It's perfect, Flynn," she said. "I can see why you chose this area."

He smiled. "Thanks. It'll be even better when there's something inside."

"That'll happen soon enough," Barrett said.

Flynn took them on a tour of the inside of the restaurant, then they parted ways and Flynn took off to run some errands before his meeting, leaving her and Barrett alone.

"What do you want to do first?" Barrett asked.

"I have no idea. I've never been here, so I'm going to rely on you to be tour guide for me."

"Okay. Let's roll on out of here."

Harmony couldn't wait to see everything—or as much of everything—that San Francisco had to offer.

TWENTY-TWO

AFTER RUNNING SOME ERRANDS, FLYNN CAME BACK to the restaurant and met with his new manager, Ken, prior to the interview with the proposed chef. And since Ken had a lot of years of restaurant management experience, they discussed some inventory items and went back and forth on the layout. Since the place was gutted right now and no walls were up, he had some time to decide on placement before he met with the architect and contractors.

Right now they had a folding table and four chairs situated in the middle of the concrete floor. All he had was a vision.

"The windows out front afford a lot of light," Ken said, "which will be great for your daytime crowd. You'll have to decide what kind of ambience you want for evenings."

"Cozy. Inviting. And we have the space out back that will provide ample seating. I'd like to do garden seating. Since we're on the corner, I think that'll attract people walking by."

Ken nodded. "Agree, and it's a good idea. Our weather permits almost year-long outside eating, and if you put heat lamps out there during cooler weather, the diehards won't mind eating out there at all."

"That's a great suggestion." He plugged that into the notes feature on his tablet so he wouldn't forget.

"When's the meeting with the architect?" Ken asked.

"Monday."

"I think you have a good idea of what you want. And he's done the walk-through with you, right?"

"Yes. We've talked at length, so he knows what I'm looking for in terms of seating space and cooking area. He said he'd have some mock-ups."

"I'm already looking forward to this place opening. And you know you didn't need to start paying me, since it's going to be at least four to six months until you're operational. I could have kept my old job."

Flynn smiled. "Trust me, I'm going to need you around, especially once football season starts gearing up and I'm on the road and busy with my job. I'm going to need you on the scene to manage the day to day, work on staffing issues and inventory, plus keep me updated."

Ken nodded. "You got it. And speaking of staffing, Amelia should be here soon."

"I'm looking forward to meeting her."

"I think you'll really like her. She impressed me during our initial interview in Portland."

A car pulled up out front and a woman got out. She was tall, slender, with long blond hair pulled into a high ponytail. She was wearing jeans that fit tight to her body, killer high heels that made her legs look miles long, and a silk blouse that ruffled in the wind outside.

Flynn couldn't believe that was Amelia, but when she pulled

the door open, it couldn't be anyone but her. He supposed he had a different picture in his mind of this accomplished chef. He figured she'd be older, though he had no idea why. This cool beautiful woman was about his age.

He and Ken stood.

"Amelia," Ken said, walking over to shake her hand. "Great to see you again."

She gave him a generous smile. "It's good to see you, too, Ken."

"And this is Flynn Cassidy."

She turned to him, giving him more of a polite smile as she held out her hand. "Amelia Lawrence."

"Nice to meet you, Amelia."

"Same here. Thank you for inviting me to interview."

"I've heard good things about you. You have an impressive résumé."

"Thank you."

They went through her background as a chef, from her education to her work experience. Flynn had already read that on her résumé, and Ken had discussed it extensively with him, but it was good to hear it from Amelia.

"Beyond the education and work experience, I've been cooking since I was a child. My mother was an avid cook and allowed me to be in the kitchen with her. Much of my love of cooking came from her. She allowed me to experiment from an early age, to try my hand at creating different dishes. It was that freedom of culinary expression that gave me my love of food and the desire to become a chef."

Flynn smiled. "I cooked a lot with my mom, too."

She arched a brow. "Really."

Not the first time he'd been met with an incredulous look like that. "You think football players spend all their time either on the field, in a club or playing football video games. But you'd be wrong. Which isn't surprising given that the media plays up that aspect of players. As far as it relates to me, the reason I'm opening up this restaurant has a lot to do with my love for food."

"I'll be honest with you. I thought you were just in it for the money and the name aspect."

"And I appreciate your honesty. But you're wrong about me."

"I wouldn't have come to work for Flynn if he was some dumb jock only in it to stick his name on a restaurant," Ken said. "That's not what I'm about, either."

Amelia nodded. "Okay. I'm glad to know that."

He got the idea she was still withholding her opinion about him. Not that he much cared. She didn't need to like him. She just needed to be a kick-ass chef.

They talked for a while about Flynn's planned setup for the restaurant, but didn't get into too many details about the menu. He wanted to wait to see if Amelia would be a good fit before they started planning it out.

"What would you think about cooking for me tonight?"

She looked around. "I wouldn't mind it, but you're not exactly set up here for a demonstration, are you?"

His lips curved. "Not yet. I was thinking about you cooking dinner at my place. My brother and his girlfriend are in town for the weekend. I was going to cook for them tonight, but since you're here, and if you're available tonight, you could come over."

"I'd be happy to."

"Great." Flynn looked over at Ken. "Ken? Are you available?"

"Sorry. Adam's brother's engagement party is tonight, so we have to go to that."

"Oh, that's right, I forgot about that. You two have a great time."

"Thanks, we will." Ken turned to Amelia. "But I have no doubt whatever you cook up will be fantastic."

They talked awhile longer about Ken's husband, Adam, whom

Amelia had met when Ken and Adam had flown up to Portland so Ken could do Amelia's initial interview.

Amelia gave Flynn her phone number and she got his along with his address. She told him she'd bring the food for tonight.

"If you text me a grocery list, I'll have the food at the house," Flynn said.

She shook her head. "If you don't mind, I'll do the shopping. It's important that I choose the ingredients myself. Plus, I need to prepare a few things in advance. So I'll bring it with me."

"Isn't that kind of inconvenient, with you staying at a hotel?"

"I'm actually staying with some people I know, so there will be a kitchen for me to do advance prep."

Flynn finally shrugged. "Up to you. You're the chef."

"Thanks."

They said their good-byes and she called for a car and left.

"What do you think?" Ken asked.

"Not sure yet. She's a little quiet. Seems . . . I don't know." He ran his fingers through his hair. "I don't know what to think about her."

"Trust me, Flynn. She's competent, she's not temperamental and she doesn't throw pots and pans around."

Flynn laughed. "You only see those types of chefs on TV."

Ken slid him a look. "You'd like to think so, but I've worked in this business a long time and those kinds of chefs do exist."

"Really."

"Yeah. And Amelia is very animated once she gets going on the subject of food. She's very particular in her kitchen and knows what she wants and how she wants things done. Which is exactly what you need in a head chef. I think once you see her cook you'll be happy."

"I hope so. We'll see what happens tonight."

"Listen, I gotta run, but I want a full report on Monday."

"I'll see you then. You and Adam have a great time tonight."

Ken grinned. "We will."

Flynn locked up the restaurant, then walked outside to stare at it. He could already envision the name, the people inside, the kind of food he wanted to serve.

He hoped like hell Amelia Lawrence was the answer to what he was looking for.

She sure was pretty. With mesmerizing, inquisitive hazel eyes that seemed to focus on him an awful lot.

Then again, maybe he was reading way too much into that.

He didn't need to focus on a pretty woman with gorgeous eyes. The last time that happened he got dumped.

He was always getting dumped.

Food? That he knew. Women? Not a damn clue.

He sure as hell didn't need a woman in his life right now.

All he needed was a talented chef.

TWENTY-THREE

BARRETT HAD TAKEN MANY TRIPS TO SAN FRANCISCO before, and had pretty much seen everything the city had to offer.

But, he had to admit, seeing it through Harmony's eyes was fun. There was nothing like playing tour guide for someone who'd never been here before.

There was no doubt San Francisco was a beautiful city, so he'd enjoyed every second of taking her to see all the sights.

They stood at the railing at the edge of Pier 39. He breathed in the crisp sea air, making him wish he were out on his boat right now doing some fishing. A large group of sea lions sunbathed on the boat docks.

"This is amazing," Harmony said. "They're so cute."

She got out her phone to take pictures.

"Well, they're noisy. And they smell."

She laughed. "They're definitely noisy. All that barking. What do you think they're talking about?"

"Probably things like 'Move over, you're in my spot.' Or 'Hey, that's my woman you're hitting on.'"

She rolled her eyes. "You're such a guy."

"Come on. Look at those two big ones yelling at each other. There's a ton of sea lion testosterone flying around."

"If you say so. And in the meantime the lady sea lions are ignoring it all, sunning themselves on the deck, oblivious to all that male posturing."

"Imagine that. Just like human women, ignoring all our best moves."

She leaned against him. "We can't make it too easy for you."

Barrett's phone buzzed. He pulled it out of his pocket and read the text message.

"It's Flynn. The interview went well and he's bringing the chef—whose name is Amelia—over to the house to cook dinner for us."

"That's great news, right? He seemed eager to hire a head chef, and if he's bringing her to the house to cook dinner, he must really like what she could bring to his restaurant."

He typed a text message back to his brother, then shoved his phone back in his pocket. "I hope so. I guess we'll find out at dinner tonight."

She slipped her hand in his. "In the meantime, how about a ride on a cable car?"

Now that was something he hadn't done yet. "Sure."

They grabbed the cable car on Hyde Street and rode the entire line and back. Barrett had to admit it was pretty fun, especially since the cable car was crowded, so they had to stand, and he had his arm around Harmony the entire time. Her body was pressed to his and though she held on to a pole, the movements of the cable car shoved her into him.

He didn't mind that at all. Neither, it appeared, did Harmony, as after a while she turned to face him, wrapping her arm around him.

"You're missing the sights."

"I don't know about that. You're a pretty hot sight."

He bent and brushed his lips across hers, wishing he could deepen the kiss and take a full taste of her. But he was mindful of their audience on the cable car, which included children, so he tabled that thought for later.

Once they hopped off the cable car, he took her hand and they headed toward his car. It was getting late and they needed to head back to Flynn's house. He shoved the bag of souvenirs Harmony had bought into the backseat and drove off.

Flynn's car was already in the driveway when he pulled in.

"I wonder if he brought Amelia with him?" Harmony asked, as they got out of the car.

"I guess we'll find out when we go inside."

She took the bag from his hand. "I'm going to stop in the cottage first to freshen up."

He tugged her against him. "You look pretty fresh to me already."

She laughed and pushed him away. "I'll be right in."

Barrett went in through the back door. Flynn wasn't in sight, so Barrett went to the fridge and grabbed a beer, went into the living room and grabbed the remote, turned on the television and scrolled through until he found the sports station, then settled in and took a couple of long swallows of beer.

"Making yourself at home, I see," Flynn said, as he came down the stairs.

"You know me."

"I do. Did you two have fun today?"

"We did. We did the whole touring thing, or at least as much as we could get done in an afternoon."

Flynn went to the refrigerator and pulled out a beer for himself, then came into the living room and took a seat on the recliner to watch sports with Barrett.

"When's Amelia coming?"

"About six."

"Great. What's she cooking?"

"No idea."

"Didn't you buy the food?"

"Nope. She said she wanted to."

"Huh. Interesting. So you're letting her foot the bill, then?"

Flynn shot him a glare. "Of course not. I'll reimburse her. What kind of an asshole do you think I am?"

Barrett's lips lifted. "You got time for me to make a list?"

"Fuck off, Barrett."

Flynn continued to stare at the TV. Barrett's lips lifted. He knew being insulted by his brother was like being given a compliment.

Harmony came through the back door. "I'm going to grab a glass of iced tea if that's okay, Flynn."

"Make yourself at home, Harmony."

"Thanks."

Barrett found himself watching Harmony as she reached up for a glass in the cabinet. He stared at her legs. She had great legs. He loved touching her, making him wish the two of them were alone so he could go into the kitchen, skim his hands over her thighs, lift her dress, bend her over . . .

Well, hell. Not the kinds of things he should be thinking when his brother was in the room.

Dammit. They should have stayed at a hotel.

When Barrett heard the word "Cassidy" on the television, he shifted his focus to the screen. "Hey, Tucker's on TV."

Flynn looked up from his phone to the TV. "He pitch another no-hitter?"

"He wishes. No, he won his game this afternoon, so he's being interviewed."

"Always bragging, isn't he?"

"Yeah. What a dick."

Harmony came in and sat on the sofa next to Barrett. "That's your brother, isn't it?"

"Yeah."

They all sat quiet and listened to Tucker talk about the game, giving credit to the five runs his team had gotten as well as the solid defense his team had put up.

"He pitched a shutout," Flynn said. "Well done."

"Yeah. He did good. Like a Cassidy should."

The sportscaster was all over him, kissing his butt, too. Barrett shook his head.

Flynn smirked. "Next thing you know they'll be interviewing Grant."

As if Flynn's remarks were telegraphed on the screen, mention was made of the Cassidy family, and there was Grant on the screen, talking about the upcoming season for the St. Louis Traders football team.

Barrett looked over at Flynn and rolled his eyes. "Notice how they only interview quarterbacks?"

Flynn nodded. "It's like the defense doesn't exist."

"Which is total bullshit because we're the ones who win the games for the teams."

"Really," Harmony said. "You do manage to score points now and then. And you keep the score close by preventing the opposing teams from scoring."

Barrett put his arm around her. "See why I like her?"

"I see that. But her brother plays defense as well, so she kind of has to root for the defensive side of the ball."

"Hey," Harmony said. "I do not. I just know where the true talent lies and where all the hard work is done."

"Hell yeah," Flynn said, lifting his bottle of beer and tapping it against Harmony's glass of tea.

"How did your interview go today, Flynn?" Harmony asked.

"It went good. Amelia has all the experience I need. We'll see how her cooking skills measure up when she gets here tonight."

"I can't wait. What's she cooking for us tonight?"

"I don't have any idea. She wouldn't let me do any of the shopping, insisting on doing it herself."

"Really. That's interesting."

"She said something about needing to prep stuff in advance and choosing the ingredients herself."

"What difference does that make?" Barrett asked.

"I have no idea."

Harmony shifted to face Flynn. "Well, you like to cook, right?"

"Yeah."

"How important is it to you to be able to choose your own food, your own ingredients?"

She watched as Flynn pondered it for a few seconds, then shrugged. "Not at all. If I walked into a kitchen where the raw ingredients were already there, I could still dig in and cook."

"Okay, then maybe it's something that's important to Amelia. It's part of her process."

"I guess so."

The doorbell rang. Flynn got up to answer it and pulled the door open.

Harmony got up as well and saw a stunning blonde standing at the door with a large roasting pan cradled in her arms.

"Here, take this," she said. "I have some other things in the car."

"Barrett," Flynn said, "come here."

"I've got this," Harmony said, taking the pan from Flynn. She took it into the kitchen and, since the pan wasn't hot, laid it on the kitchen counter.

Flynn, Barrett and Amelia walked in with several bags.

"I could have taken you shopping," Flynn said.

She waved her hand. "I didn't need you to take me shopping."

"And what's this?" Flynn asked, motioning to the pan.

"I'm soaking cedar in apple cider."

"I could have done that for you as well. Did you buy the roasting pan?"

"I did."

"I have roasting pans here."

She lifted her chin. "I have my own methods, and I didn't mind buying the pan. And if you're worried about reimbursing me for the pan, don't bother."

"Did I say I was worried about reimbursing you? And of course I intend to pay for everything. I'm the one who invited you here to cook."

She waved her hand at him. "Whatever." She turned and smiled at Harmony and Barrett. "Hi. I'm Amelia Lawrence."

Harmony held out her hand. "Harmony Evans."

"I'm Flynn's brother Barrett. Nice to meet you, Amelia."

"We're so thrilled to have you here tonight to cook for us," Harmony said, setting her glass of tea on the counter. "I was just about to refill my iced tea. Would you like a glass?"

"I'd love one, Harmony. Thank you."

She fixed the glasses of tea then handed one off to Amelia, who had already tied her hair back, put on an apron, and was busy opening all of Flynn's cabinets and pulling out pots, pans, mixers, and generally taking over his kitchen. Flynn, in the meantime, had grabbed another beer and a stool at the kitchen island.

"I think we'll get out of their way," Harmony said.

Barrett just shrugged and followed her into the living room.

"Wasn't that interesting?" she asked as she and Barrett took their seats on the sofa.

"What?"

"The sparks between your brother and Amelia."

"Really?" Barrett looked into the kitchen, where Amelia was whipping something with a whisk. "I thought it was more like her being snippy, and him being a dick."

She laughed. "That's what I mean. Sparks. It wasn't like he didn't like her. The chemistry between them is intense."

"You think so, huh?"

"I definitely think so."

"I guess you'd know about all the chemistry stuff."

She shifted her focus away from what was going on in the kitchen and onto Barrett. "Excuse me? What does that mean?"

He picked up a piece of her hair and played with it. "It means, woman, that you have loads of chemistry. It's why I can't take my eyes—or my hands—off of you."

"Oh." She smiled.

"And what did you think I meant by that? Some sexist remark?"

She laughed. "Actually, yes."

"There you go, disparaging my gender again."

"Sorry." She laid her hand on his knee. "I promise to make it up to you later. When we have some alone time."

He ran his fingers up her bare leg, making goose bumps break out on her skin.

"Have I mentioned to you how much I'm looking forward to being alone with you?"

"You have not."

"I was thinking earlier that I wished we had stayed at a hotel. Then I could have you to myself."

She liked hearing that, and she had to admit she'd had similar thoughts. "But you need to see your brother."

He let out a laugh. "I see more than enough of him. You, on the other hand, I haven't seen nearly enough of. In fact, right now, I'd like to pull you onto my lap, lift your dress and rub your pussy until you start moaning."

She shifted her gaze to the kitchen, where Flynn was acting as assistant to Amelia, who was barking orders at him. An amusing sight.

Meanwhile, Barrett was distracting her by walking his fingers ever closer to the hem of her dress. When his fingers disappeared, she inched away.

"Stop," she said, though she didn't want him to stop. Not at all.

He gave her a wickedly sexy smile. "Later."

Later couldn't come soon enough.

They ended up watching a movie on television until Flynn came into the living room to tell them dinner was going to be ready soon.

"Would you like me to set the table?" she asked.

He shook his head. "I've got that covered."

"It smells wonderful," she said.

"Yeah," Barrett said. "Whatever she's cooking up in there is making me hungry."

"You're always hungry," Flynn said.

"Okay, that's true, too."

Flynn went back into the kitchen.

"So whatever she fixed went outside on the grill," she said to Barrett. "Any thoughts?"

"Steak."

She shook her head. "Doesn't smell like steak, and she wouldn't have made a steak on the grill."

"Why not? That's where I cook mine."

She laughed. "You're not a chef."

"So you say. I'll have you know I make killer steaks."

"I'm sure you do. But I'm talking restaurant quality."

"There you go, insulting my manhood again."

She rolled her eyes and they focused on watching TV.

Flynn came in a bit later, a bottle of wine in his hand. "Dinner's ready."

Harmony stood. "I'm excited."

"I'm hungry," Barrett said, following her into the dining room, where Flynn had finished setting the table.

"This is lovely, Flynn," Harmony said, as Barrett held a chair out for her and she slid onto it.

"Thanks. Our mother made sure we knew how to set a table. If Barrett isn't doing that for you, let me know and I'll give Mom a bad report about him."

"Shut up, Flynn," Barrett said.

Harmony didn't even try to fight her smile. "Actually, he has cooked for me and he did very well. He told me you taught him everything he knows."

Flynn grinned.

"That is not what I told her at all. I said I picked up a few pointers from you."

"Which is pretty much everything," Flynn said. "Other than how to microwave hot dogs, he knew nothing before."

"You're full of it," Barrett said.

"He was telling me about his prowess in steak cooking," Harmony said.

"Oh, those charred and black things he pulls off the grill?" Flynn said. "I guess you could call those steaks."

Barrett poured wine in all the glasses. "I can out steak you any day of the week."

Amelia brought salads and set them on the plates. "Are the brothers always like this?"

"In the times I'm around them, always," Harmony said.

"Interesting."

Flynn held out a seat for Amelia, who acknowledged him with a nod.

Flynn held up his glass. "I'd just like to welcome Amelia, and thank her for cooking dinner for us tonight."

"Agreed," Barrett said. "And whatever you cook, I know I'm going to love it."

"Thank you, Amelia," Harmony said.

Amelia smiled. "Thank you all. For starters this evening, we're having a crab, apple and watercress salad with a walnut vinaigrette. I do hope you enjoy it."

They sipped their wine, then dug into the salad. Sweet and tart flavor combinations burst on Harmony's tongue, and the crab was delicious.

"This is so good, Amelia," Harmony said.

"Thank you."

Harmony looked over at Flynn, who seemed to be dissecting his salad with the tines of his fork. But he ate every bite, then looked at Amelia and nodded.

Amelia stayed mostly silent while they ate, but Harmony noticed Amelia watching all of them.

Harmony was nervous for Amelia, though she had no idea why. The salad was amazing.

Flynn and Barrett cleared the table, and Amelia went to dish up the main course. When it was presented, it was gorgeous, with salmon, onions and fennel.

"Dinner is grilled cedar plank salmon, sweet onion and caramelized fennel."

Salmon was Harmony's absolute favorite seafood, and she

couldn't wait to see how Amelia had prepared it. When she took a bite, the savory flavor filled her senses.

"This is wonderful, Amelia. How did you prepare this?"

"I marinated the cedar plank in apple cider for several hours, then used the plank on the grill to provide a smoky cider flavor to the salmon."

"It's . . . incredible."

"Thank you."

"It's amazing, Amelia," Barrett said. "I really like it."

"The fennel and onions are also amazing," Harmony said, realizing she could use the word "amazing" only so many times, but the food was fantastic.

Harmony focused mainly on her food, and carried on small talk, but she also noticed the looks shared between Amelia and Flynn. She also noticed Flynn didn't comment on the food.

She could only imagine how stressful this must be on Amelia, having her meal judged while she was in the middle of eating it.

She understood Flynn was evaluating Amelia as a prospective employee, so he was probably waiting until the end of the meal. Still, it wouldn't hurt for him to say something tasted good, would it?

And when Amelia brought out dessert, a chocolate mousse with a white chocolate truffle topping, Harmony was certain there was no way Flynn wouldn't hire her.

"I'm in love with this dessert, Amelia," Harmony said. "It's incredibly light and airy, yet the taste is decadent."

"I'm so glad you're enjoying it."

She could tell from the smile on Amelia's face that she was proud of the meal she'd served.

After Barrett ran his spoon around the empty ramekin several times, he said, "This was a kick-ass meal, Amelia. Thank you."

"You're welcome."

They all looked to Flynn, who nodded. "It was very good."

Amelia nodded back. "Thanks."

Harmony wanted to throw her shoe at Flynn. *Very good?* That was it?

"Tell me about your life in—Portland, is it?" Harmony asked.

"I'm actually in the process of selling my house and making a move here to San Francisco."

"Oh. Do you have family here?"

"No. But I've been here many times and I enjoy the vibe of the city. And of course, the food and restaurant culture here is spectacular, so this is where I want to settle."

She nodded. "I can understand why. This is my first trip out here, but I love what I've seen of the city so far."

Barrett shrugged. "It's an okay place, if you like architecture, incredible vistas, history, great music and incredible food. Otherwise . . . eh."

Amelia laughed. "I'm really looking forward to making the move here."

"And I'm looking forward to eating wherever you end up as chef," Barrett said, giving his brother a pointed look.

"I'm sure Amelia will be successful wherever she ends up," Flynn said.

"Now that Amelia fixed us this amazing meal, Flynn and I will do the cleanup," Barrett said, standing. "Harmony, why don't you and Amelia take the bottle of wine and head out onto the front porch and relax?"

"That's a great idea."

Clearly Barrett had had enough of his brother's noncommitment as well. She grabbed the bottle and her glass. Amelia followed her.

They sat in the oh-so-comfortable cushioned chairs. It was cool out tonight, so Harmony was glad she'd grabbed her sweater.

"Are you cold?" she asked Amelia, who was dressed in flowing pants and a short-sleeved silk top.

"I'm fine, thank you. This weather feels perfect to me. A lot like home."

"Did you grow up in Portland?"

"Seattle, actually. But I've lived in Portland for the past five years."

"What brought you down there?"

"My marriage. My husband—ex-husband now—moved there for work, and I followed. But I loved it there. It was a great city to live in, and I had a phenomenal job as a chef at a fantastic restaurant."

"And yet you're moving here."

Amelia stared down at the glass of wine in her hand, as if it were some kind of crystal ball that would yield her a glimpse into her future. "Time for some changes in my life."

Harmony didn't want to pry, but she figured Amelia could tell her to mind her own business if she wanted to. "I imagine the ex is the cause of those changes?"

Amelia lifted her gaze to Harmony's and smiled. "Oh. Definitely."

"Sounds to me like you need to get the hell outta town."

Amelia laughed. "I'm not fleeing or anything, but yes, I want to put some distance between myself and my ex-husband."

"You're safe though, right?"

"Yes. It's nothing like that. I just want a clean slate, and I'd like to establish new memories. Portland reminds me too much of him, and of all the promises he made to me that were never fulfilled. Does that make sense?"

"Yes. It absolutely does. Well, you've chosen a beautiful city to start over in."

"I think so, too."

"And about Flynn. I don't know why he wasn't gushing over that meal you cooked. I thought it was phenomenal."

Amelia waved her hand. "Oh, don't worry about that. I considered it part of the interview. I'm sure he'll speak to me about it later."

"So you weren't pissed? I'd have been pissed."

Amelia laughed. "Not at all. I've often had to fix a meal for prospective employers, and they very rarely comment at all while they're eating. Though I appreciate you and Barrett overcompensating on Flynn's behalf."

"I was not overcompensating. If it wasn't inappropriate, I might have kissed you. I kind of have a thing for food."

"Then I'll take that as a compliment. Thank you. I'm so glad you enjoyed it. Now tell me about you, Harmony. You said you were visiting out here. Where are you from?"

"I live in Tampa."

"Oh, a lovely city. And warm, too."

"It can get very warm. But it's my home and I love it there."

"What do you do for a living?"

"I'm an interior designer."

Amelia's eyes widened. She shifted in her chair to face her. "Seriously? What a fabulous career."

"Thank you. I love it. Right now I'm working on redesigning the new house Barrett just bought, among other things."

"I love design. I don't really have a knack for it, other than I know I like pretty things. But to be able to select the right things and appropriate colors, to put an entire room together must be the most exciting thing ever. And to top it off, you get to spend other people's money."

Harmony laughed. "I have to admit, that part is fun."

Barrett and Flynn came outside. Barrett had a beer in his hand. Flynn didn't.

"Get those dishes done?" Harmony asked.

"Yeah," Barrett said. "Amelia, we bagged up your roasting pan. We figured if you can't take it back to Portland with you, then maybe your friends will want it."

"Thank you."

"I can have it shipped up to you in Portland if you want," Flynn said.

"That's not necessary."

Flynn nodded. "Are you ready to head out?"

"Yes. I can call for a car."

"I'll drive you back to where you're staying," Flynn said. "It'll give us a chance to talk."

"All right." Amelia stood and turned to Harmony. "It was such a pleasure to meet you. I'm glad we had a chance to talk."

Harmony hugged Amelia. "Me, too. I'm going to give you my number. Let me know how it goes. How everything goes."

"I will."

They exchanged phone numbers.

"Nice to meet you, too, Barrett," Amelia said.

"Same here. Thanks for the awesome dinner."

She smiled. "You're welcome."

"I'll be back later," Flynn said.

Barrett nodded, then gave his brother a look. "Take your time."

"Yeah, well I've got some people I need to meet up with, so I'll probably be back late."

Harmony got the idea some subtle messaging had just gone on between Barrett and Flynn.

After Flynn and Amelia left, Barrett turned to her. "Finally, we're alone."

She walked into his arms and threaded her fingers into his hair. "And what do you want to do with this alone time?"

He wound his arms around her. "I'm taking you to the cottage, closing and locking the damn door and getting you naked. Then I'm going to lick you all over until you come."

She shivered at the mental images of his tongue on her. "And yet you're standing still. Get your ass moving, Barrett."

TWENTY-FOUR

BARRETT WAS ALWAYS HAPPY WITH MEETING NEW people and spending time with his family. He'd had a great day playing tourist with Harmony and having dinner with Flynn and Amelia, but now he wanted to get Harmony alone.

He led her out back and to the cottage, and, true to his word, locked the door behind him. His message to Flynn about needing alone time with Harmony had hit the mark. Not that he needed to kick Flynn out of his own house. He just didn't want his brother to come knocking on the door of the cottage.

Flynn knew what was what. He wouldn't be coming around.

Now he could focus on the gorgeous woman in front of him.

Harmony turned around and backed her way into the bedroom, kicking off her sandals and shimmying out of her dress along the way.

Today she wore light purple satin underwear, and as he made his way toward her, she pulled down the comforter and climbed onto the bed, kneeled and spread her legs, sliding her hand into her panties.

His cock went hard in an instant. Hell, he'd been semi-hard all night just being around her. There was something about listening to her talk, hearing her laugh and being close enough to touch her that drew his balls up tight and made his dick hard.

And as he drew closer to the bed, her scent filled the air around them, a sweet, musky scent that made him want to put his tongue on her clit and make her come over and over again.

He pulled his shirt off, kicked off his shoes, then shrugged out of his pants and boxer briefs.

She smiled at him. "Never saw a man get naked that fast."

"I want your skin next to mine. Now let's get you naked."

He climbed onto the bed and slid his hands around her neck, tilting her head back. Her gaze met his.

"I've wanted to kiss you all night," he said.

He started the kiss, light and easy at first. When her tongue slipped out to rim against his lips, he caught her tongue, sucked it into his mouth and pressed his lips firmly against hers.

She grabbed hold of his cock, sliding her hand over the shaft, using her thumb to circle the crest and dragging her hand down to the base. Her soft hand on him made his cock tighten, made him want to thrust into her hand over and over until he released.

But he restrained himself, because he wanted to be inside of her. He broke the kiss and trailed his fingers over her neck and collarbone, then teased the swells of her breasts, watching them rise and fall with her deep breaths. He reached behind her and unclasped her bra, pulling the straps down her arms. After freeing her breasts, he cupped them in his hands, using his thumbs to swirl over her nipples, watching them tighten to sharp points.

She moaned in response, so he gave her more, this time with

his mouth, circling one bud with his lips, flicking his tongue over it before covering it with his mouth and sucking.

"Barrett," Harmony said.

He liked hearing her say his name, especially when he had his mouth around one of her nipples. Her voice had lowered to almost a whisper, and she arched against his mouth, feeding him more of her soft flesh. He was more than happy to make her moan out his name. He intended to hear it more than once tonight.

So while he sucked back and forth on both her nipples, he slid his hand inside her panties and cupped her sex.

She whimpered when he slid his fingers inside of her, using the heel of his hand to rock against her clit. Her pussy tightened around his fingers, gripping him as he stroked her in soft, rhythmic movements.

"Yes. Oh, yes just like that. Make me come, Barrett. Make me come hard."

He lifted his mouth from her breasts, needing to see her face when she let go. "Tell me how it feels, Harmony. Tell me what you need."

She reached down to grip his wrist. "I need your fingers fucking me, in and out. Faster now, and rub my clit harder."

He loved a woman who could give direction, who knew exactly where and how she wanted it. He was happy to give it to her. It made his dick throb to watch the way she licked her lips, the way she was in tune to her own body's needs and went after it.

"That's it, babe," he said, feeling the way her body responded with moisture, the way she shook all over as she fought for her orgasm. "You gonna come on my hand?"

"Yes, yes. All over it."

He gave her everything she asked for, soaking in every whimper, every moan, and when she came, she tilted her head back and cried out, thrusting her pussy against his hand and taking his mouth in a fierce kiss that made him desperate to fuck her and fuck her hard. Her pussy gripped his fingers in an undulating vise of quivering waves until she finally settled.

But he wasn't nearly finished with her yet. He pushed her down onto the mattress, removed her panties, and grabbed a condom. He put it on and spread her legs, then drove inside of her while she was still quaking from her orgasm.

She met him with a thrust of her hips, wrapping her legs around him and raking her nails down his arms.

"That's it, Barrett," she said, rising to meet his movements. "Make me come like that again."

He reached under her to grab her butt and tilt her pelvis up so he could drive deeper into her. Touching her and having his fingers inside her only made him more eager to feel her pussy surrounding him, tightening around him as he powered into her, each time needing to be deeper, harder, until his balls filled with come and he couldn't hold back.

But he did, because he wanted her to come again.

He ground against her, giving her friction against her clit. In return, she gave him a low moan.

"I like that," she said. "Give me more."

He kept up the movement, and when her eyes widened and she tightened around his cock, he knew he had her.

"Oh. I'm coming, Barrett. Fuck me hard, I'm coming."

He was already spurting as he powered into her—her hot, dirty words the catalyst that sent him reeling. He groaned against her neck as he gathered her close and emptied into her, his body shaking with his release.

Spent, he rolled off to the side, got up to dispose of the condom, then went into the other room to grab drinks for them from the mini fridge. Harmony was propped up on the bed, looking like a dark angel, her black hair spread against the white pillows.

"You are a damn sexy naked woman, Harmony," he said, as he handed her the bottle of sparkling water.

She took a sip, then set it down on the coaster on the table next to the bed and cuddled up next to him. "I think you bring out the wild thing in me."

He put his water on the table as well, then pulled her on top of him, smoothing his hands over her naked backside. "No. The wild thing in you already existed."

She rubbed her breasts against his chest. "Then let's get wild."

There was something about her that made him want to be inside of her, to drive deep and hard until the need in him was satisfied. He shifted, sliding off the mattress, pulling Harmony to the edge of the bed.

"Roll over onto your belly."

With a wickedly sexy smile, she flipped over, grabbing a pillow to shove under her stomach. It lifted her ass in the air, and God, he loved her ass. He could stand here and stare at her smooth, sweet butt for hours, run his hands over her ample curves, maybe smack it a little.

He gave her a light tap. She wriggled and moaned, but not in complaint.

"Make you wet?" he asked.

"Put your cock inside of me and find out."

He slid on a condom, parted her legs and eased inside of her, grabbing her hips to hold on as he began to pump, giving it to her gently at first. He reached around in front of her to give her clit some action.

"Barrett. Yes. Touch me there."

She was wet, her body hot as he drove into her and rubbed her clit with slow, precise movements.

She moaned, thrusting her pussy against his hand. "Faster. Faster, so I come."

He parted the hair at the back of her neck and kissed her there. "You keep talking to me like that you're gonna make *me* come."

"That's what I want. I want you fucking me hard and making me come, then I want you to come inside me."

He shuddered, giving her neck a light bite.

"Oh, God," she said, shuddering as her pussy tightened around his cock. "I'm coming, Barrett."

She sure as hell was. He pulled back and powered into her, driving as hard as he could. He couldn't hold back his own orgasm, and lifted up, gripping her hips and thrusting, then burying himself deep as he climaxed.

He swept his hands over her ass as he came down from that incredible high. Harmony turned her head to smile at him. He gave her a playful slap on the butt, then disengaged, disposed of the condom, and grabbed his bottle of water from the nightstand before climbing into bed next to her.

Harmony slid her toes up and down along his lower leg. "I was thinking for round three we might want to try out that oh-so-comfortable sofa in the living room."

He took a couple of long swallows of water, then turned to face her. "No, what you're trying out is my stamina."

"Oh, please. You can handle four quarters of football. I'm five foot four, Barrett. I think you can handle me."

He put the cap on the bottled water, scooped his hands under her butt and lifted her off the bed. "I'll handle you all right, woman. I'll make you come until you pass out."

She laughed all the way into the living room.

TWENTY-FIVE

IF THERE WAS ONE THING BARRETT KNEW HOW TO DO, it was win. Though he wasn't sure who actually won last night, since he and Harmony had both come over and over again.

So maybe it was a win for both of them.

Right now, Harmony was facedown on the bed sound asleep, her mouth slightly open, her hair spread all over her pillow. She looked like she'd been well and thoroughly fucked.

Hell, just looking at her like that made his dick hard again.

But he intended to let her sleep. They'd been up until almost one a.m. last night and it was barely past six a.m. He figured he'd have plenty of time to get a gym workout in with Flynn and still get back before Harmony woke up.

He dressed in his workout clothes and put on his tennis shoes. He had downed a full bottle of water to hydrate, but what he really needed was caffeine.

He headed over to the main house.

He knew Flynn would be up, and he was, drinking a cup of coffee.

"Sleeping in this morning?" Flynn asked, grabbing a cup and shoving it under the brewer.

"Yeah, right." The smell of coffee was almost enough to wake him up. Almost, but not quite. When Flynn handed him the cup, he grabbed it and inhaled a deep breath of the awesome aroma before he took his first sip.

Yeah, that's what he needed.

"Ready for a workout?" Flynn asked.

Barrett held up his hand. He just needed this one cup. "In a minute."

Flynn was already geared up and stretching. "Sure. Let me waste my time while your wussy ass sips your cup o' tea."

Unconcerned, Barrett continued to drink his coffee. He sipped it slowly.

Flynn sighed. Loudly.

Finally, Flynn said, "Time's ticking, asshole."

"Fuck off. I might have a second cup."

"Yeah, you do that. And I'm leaving you."

Barrett laughed and put his cup in the sink. "I'm ready. Jesus, you're grouchy. When was the last time you got laid?"

"Too long. And don't remind me."

They headed to the gym, which fortunately had an outside track. After warming up with a fast walk, they took off on a run.

This was when Barrett really missed his brothers. No one motivated him to be better, run faster and push harder than one of his brothers. They were nothing if not competitive with each other, especially Flynn and him because they were both defensive players.

If Flynn started dragging, Barrett would kick up his pace, making Flynn keep up. The same would happen if Barrett found himself slowing. Because there was no way in hell either one of them would lag behind.

As a result, their three-mile run was done in damn good time. They slowed to a cooldown mile to catch their breath, then headed into the gym.

They warmed up with light weights, then went to the heavier ones, spotting each other. Within an hour, Barrett was soaked in sweat and his arms and legs felt like overcooked spaghetti.

He'd already drunk a gallon of water and still felt drained, so he went to the beverage bar and grabbed an electrolyte drink.

"Wimping out on me?" Flynn asked, ordering the same thing for himself.

"Yup. You go ahead and do several more sets, though. I'll spot you."

"Nah, that's okay. I'll quit now so you don't feel like a big baby."

"Sure. Thanks." Barrett knew damn well Flynn was as wrung out as he was but would never admit it. As the oldest Cassidy brother, Flynn would be the last one to admit defeat. He always saw himself as the leader of the pack of brothers, which was bullshit. They were all strong, but if Flynn needed to feel that way, Barrett would never let on that he knew Flynn was just as tired as Barrett was.

Flynn drove them back to the house.

"Hungry?" Flynn asked.

"Yeah."

"You gonna wake Harmony?"

"I'll wake her when breakfast is ready. We were up kind of late."

"Doin' what? Watching old movies on TV?"

Barrett grinned. "Something like that."

They got out pans along with bread, potatoes, eggs and bacon and started working side by side.

"So what happened with Tess?" Barrett asked as he started peeling potatoes.

Flynn took the potatoes after Barrett peeled them and sliced them into small chunks, then heated the pan to fry them.

"Not sure exactly. Things were going great for a while. We saw each other a lot. She loved football and came to the games. Then all of a sudden, it became a lot more about having her picture taken whenever she was with me. And she was more interested in the limelight and being at the clubs and the VIP spots, and less about doing things with me that didn't involve spotlight stuff, ya know?"

Barrett grimaced. He knew the type. "Yeah, I know."

"So I thought, okay, let's try hanging out alone more often. She was disappointed. I told her being in the spotlight wasn't my thing, and if that's what she was interested in, it wasn't what I was about. Suddenly she stopped being available. Her replies to my texts became more infrequent. I asked her what was wrong and she told me nothing, but you know when something's up."

"Yeah."

"And then I saw a picture of her on social media with some basketball player."

"Sports groupie, for sure. I'm sorry, Flynn."

Flynn shrugged. "Not the first time it's happened."

"Yeah, it happened to me before, too, but it sure as hell sucks."

"It does. I liked her. I thought she was genuine. I guess I was wrong."

Flynn turned the sizzling potatoes over, then added chopped onions to the skillet.

"Smells good already."

Flynn smiled. "We haven't even started yet."

Once the potatoes were done, Flynn poured the potatoes onto a plate and covered them, then got out the package of bacon and put the strips in the already hot pan while Barrett opened the carton of eggs and took a pan out to cook them.

"So what now?" Barrett asked.

"What about now?"

"Anything on the woman front?"

Flynn let out a snort. "Hell no. I've got the restaurant and training camp coming up, and that's all I'm focusing on. I think I've had enough of women and relationships for a while."

"Can't say I blame you for that."

But Barrett felt bad. Even though Barrett gave his brother a hard time, Flynn was a good guy. He knew his brother was ready to settle down. But man, Flynn was having a hard time finding the right woman.

Barrett knew she was out there somewhere.

Flynn flipped the bacon over while Barrett poured the eggs into the pan, then tossed the bread into the toaster. "How did things go with Amelia last night?"

"I offered her the job."

Barrett grinned. "Awesome. Did she accept?"

"She said she'd get back to me."

Barrett laughed. "Keeping you on the line about that, is she?"

"I guess."

"Maybe she doesn't like you."

Flynn pinned him with a glare. "How the hell could she not like me? I'm fucking amazing."

Barrett snorted. "Sure you are."

The back door opened and Harmony walked in. She wore a tight-fitting T-shirt and those pants that only went past her knees, but hugged her body, showing off her curves.

Since his brother was in the room, Barrett would try not to notice how hot she looked.

"You didn't wake me."

"I was up early. Flynn and I went to the gym."

She went to grab a cup to make coffee. "And now you're fixing breakfast? I don't know how some women haven't swept in and married the hell out of both of you."

Flynn grinned, then set the cooked bacon onto a plate. "I don't know, either, considering how amazing we are. Well, I'm amazing. Barrett's still a work in progress."

"Kiss my ass, Flynn," Barrett said.

Harmony laughed, then fixed herself a cup of coffee. "Anything I can do to help?"

"Nope," Flynn said. "Take a seat."

"I'll do that."

Flynn went to the refrigerator and grabbed cantaloupe, strawberries, honeydew melon and a pineapple, then started slicing them up while Barrett finished the toast.

"Grab some fresh oranges out of the fridge," Flynn said to Barrett. "The juicer is in that cabinet."

Barrett arched a brow. "Going all out, are we?"

"We are."

Shaking his head, Barrett grabbed the juicer from the bottom cabinet, plugged it in, got the oranges out and sliced them in half, then juiced them.

Harmony had washed her hands and sliced oranges, handing them to him to move the process along.

"This is some fancy machine, Flynn," Harmony said. "Most of us just buy orange juice in the container."

"It's better fresh."

Harmony lifted her gaze to Barrett, who shook his head. "He's all healthy and shit. What can you do?"

Harmony laughed and took the pitcher of fresh juice to the table, then got out plates and utensils.

Flynn brought the plate of bacon to the table. "I'm not all that healthy. We're having bacon and fried potatoes with breakfast."

"But the fresh fruit and juice counteract the effects," Barrett said.

"Oh, they do, do they?" Harmony asked.

"Yeah. I read it somewhere. Plus, we burned off about two thousand calories already this morning."

"You'd like to think that," Flynn said, taking a seat at the table.

They dug in and ate. When Barrett took a drink of the juice, he had to admit it was damn good. "Okay, Flynn, you win. The fresh juice is better."

"I can't believe you admitted that."

"Hey, I'm evolving."

"Barrett's right," Harmony said. "The fresh juice is incredible. You should put a juice bar in your restaurant."

"I don't know about a juice bar, since we won't be open for breakfast, at least not initially. But my plan is to use only fresh, organically grown and locally sourced ingredients. So we'll see how it goes."

"I can't wait to see the menu," Harmony said. "Or at least look it up online."

"I told you that you'll have to come back for the grand opening and taste everything."

"Sure. Or, we'll see how it goes, I guess."

Flynn looked from her to Barrett. "You mean providing my brother doesn't fuck up things between the two of you?"

"Hey," Barrett said. "And mind your own business."

"Whatever. So are you heading to the ranch this weekend?" Flynn asked.

"Yeah."

Harmony swallowed, then turned to Barrett. "What's going on at your parents' place?"

"Our parents have invested in a new blues club that's having their opening weekend in Austin. So we're all flying in to hang out with the parents and go to the club. Tucker's off because it's the midseason break, so even he'll be around."

She smiled at him. "That sounds fun."

"You should bring Harmony," Flynn said. "Hell, you should bring her entire family, Barrett. They've come to the ranch before, haven't you?"

She shook her head. "My mom and my brother have been there, but I was on a college trip the last time they came out, so I missed it."

"Then you definitely have to come. Doesn't she, Barrett?"

Barrett had no idea how to respond to that. Bringing Harmony's family would be innocuous enough, except he'd want to be alone with Harmony, and if Drake was there . . .

"What?" Flynn asked.

"My brother doesn't know Barrett and I are seeing each other. And Barrett doesn't want him to know."

"Ohhh," Flynn said, giving his brother the once-over. "So, uh, what's the big deal?"

He knew he was going to end up having this conversation with Flynn. "Drake and I are teammates. He's protective of Harmony. How do you think he'd react if he found out Harmony and I were seeing each other?"

Flynn shrugged. "No way to know unless you tell him."

Barrett shook his head. "No way. We're getting ready to head into training camp, then preseason. The last thing Drake and I need is tension between us. We need a solid defense."

Flynn rolled his eyes. "I think you're underestimating him."

"And I think you're underestimating his potential reaction. I've seen him around Harmony. He's never approved of the guys she dates."

Harmony laughed. "This is true."

"Yeah, but none of those guys have been you."

"Not gonna happen."

Harmony got up and took her plate to the sink, then started doing dishes.

"Hey, leave those," Flynn said.

"Nope. You two cooked. I'll clean up."

Barrett finished his plate, then took it over to the sink, helping Harmony dry the pots and pans.

When she finished with the dishes, she turned to him. "I'm going to go take a shower."

"Okay."

After she left, Barrett joined Flynn in the living room.

"I think you're off the mark with Drake," Flynn said.

"And I think you should butt out on this. This thing with Harmony and me is brand-new. We aren't sure where we stand with each other. It might not even work out. And what if that happens? How do you think Drake would feel then if we break up? He and I have been friends a lot of years. I was reluctant to even start anything up with Harmony for this very reason."

"Oh, so she forced you into it?" Flynn asked with a smirk.

"No. Dammit, Flynn, this is complicated. Which is another reason I'd just as soon leave Drake out of it."

Flynn raised his hands. "Hey, I get it. I'm just giving you shit. What you do in your personal life is your business. But just be careful, okay. I like Harmony. I kind of think you're okay, too. I'd really hate for either of you to get hurt."

"I don't want to hurt her. But let the two of us navigate this in our own way. And that means leaving Drake out of it."

"Your choice. But I think it's going to blow up in your face."

"Maybe. I just intend to take this thing day by day and we'll see how it goes."

Flynn gave him a dubious smile. "You do that, Brother."

"I've gotta shower. I promised Harmony a full day of sight-seeing."

"Okay. Tonight we'll head into the city for dinner, since I know you two have an early flight tomorrow morning."

"That sounds perfect."

"Sure wish you could stay longer. I kind of didn't hate having you around this weekend."

"I didn't hate it, either." It was times like this that he missed his brothers, though he'd never admit that to any of them. "But I'll see you again next weekend. And hey, the restaurant is coming along."

"It is. Next time you come out it'll be more than just an empty shell. And I'll have an actual staff."

Barrett smiled. "You have Ken."

"I do. Fortunately, he'll drive the wheel for me while football season gears up. And when I'm in town, I'll get to watch the inside of the restaurant take form."

"Yeah, kind of like my house. I'm anxious to get back home to see how things are going there."

"We didn't get to talk about that. I'm sure you're anxious about it."

"Not really. I have a great contractor, and Harmony's actually handling it all. She's an interior designer."

Flynn's brows rose. "Is that right? Very cool, man."

"Yeah. So hopefully I can just pop in, check progress and not have to stress the minor details."

"Perfect for both of us, since it's about time to get our heads in the game again."

"I can't wait."

Flynn grinned. "Me, neither."

"All right. I'm off to take a shower."

"Yeah, me too."

He headed out to find Harmony. She was in the bathroom, fixing her hair.

"I'm going to shower, then we'll head out for more fun today."

She smiled. "I'm looking forward to it."

He pulled off his shirt, then leaned against the bathroom counter. "Flynn said dinner in the city tonight."

"Sounds perfect. I wish we had a longer weekend to spend here."

"Me, too. You should take more time off work."

She laughed. "I should. I'd love to come back when I have longer to explore. It's a beautiful city and I feel like we just scratched the surface."

"We'll come back."

She turned to face him. "Will we?"

She was wearing a towel. He wanted to pull that towel off of her, bend her over the counter and sink into her. But she was clean, and he was sweaty and needed a shower. So instead, he traced the swell of her breasts with the tip of his finger.

"Maybe we will. In the meantime, what do you think about you and your family coming out to the ranch next weekend?"

She looked at him, and he read the uncertainty in her eyes. "I don't know. Kind of iffy with Drake being there. I really don't know his schedule. Mama would love to go. She hasn't been to the ranch in years and she told me how much she enjoyed spending time with your mother."

"They did have a great time together."

"I guess we'll ask them."

"So you're free?"

"I'm free next weekend."

"Then we'll plan it and see what happens."

She gave him a smile, one filled with promise. "I guess we'll see what happens."

He stripped out of his clothes and turned on the shower, then turned back to face her. "Oh, and Harmony?"

"Yes?"

"I can get you alone on the ranch, away from your brother. So we'll have some time together next weekend."

She moved up to him and brushed her lips across his. "I'm counting on it."

TWENTY-SIX

HARMONY HAD BEEN WORKING NONSTOP ALL WEEK. She always loved being busy. Busy was great for business. But she hadn't had a break all week.

She'd picked up two new clients, so she'd had consults with both of them. One wanted a complete main floor redesign. The other was doing a top to bottom renovation with a redesign. Both were going to be large projects, which would be awesome.

She'd been by Barrett's house and the renovation was coming along nicely. Jeff and his team were right on track, as she knew they'd be. She'd also met with Barrett to go over more choices in furniture and other design items. Not fun for him, but the renovation was moving along and she needed to start making purchases for his new house, since he wanted everything new in there.

Tonight, though, she was meeting Alyssa for early drinks before dinner at Mama's house. They needed to catch up and she wanted some alone time with her best friend.

She hightailed it over to the bar, happy to see Alyssa's car was already in the parking lot. Alyssa was always either early or right on time, one of the things she loved about her. She found her at a booth in the back.

Tossing her purse next to her, she took a seat.

"Girl, you look wiped," Alyssa said. "And I already ordered sangrias for us."

"That sounds incredibly good."

"I thought you might like one."

The waitress showed up and placed the pitcher and glasses in front of them, then poured.

"Any appetizers?" the waitress asked.

"No, I think this will do for now," Alyssa said. "Unless you want something, Harm?"

Harmony shook her head. "I'm good. Thanks."

"I feel like it's been ages since we last talked," Alyssa said. "What's been going on?"

"I'm sorry. That's my fault. Between work and . . . other things, I've just been buried."

"I'm glad work's busy for you."

"It is. Two new clients this week alone."

"That's fantastic."

"Thanks. And they're big clients, too, but I'm going to have to schedule those out, or maybe think about either hiring an assistant or promoting Rosalie beyond her current duties as an in-house assistant, because it's getting to the point where I don't think I can handle everything myself."

Alyssa took a sip of her drink. "Is Rosalie ready for that?"

Harmony nodded. "She has the design skills, and she handles more than just office responsibilities. I just need to look at finances to see if I can afford to hire extra help to replace Rosalie in the office."

"These are good problems, honey," Alyssa said. "But growth is nothing if not painful. I know all about that. It hurt me financially at the start to add the manicure and pedicure staff to the hair salon, but they've brought in additional business, so in the end I'm making more money."

"I know. But you know me. I'm a bit of a control freak, so there's also that part of me that doesn't want to let go."

Alyssa smiled. "Yes, I do know that about you. But you can't grow if you don't let go, you know?"

"Yes. I already have a note in my book to have a sit-down with Rosalie tomorrow and talk to her about increasing her responsibilities."

"She'll go crazy. I know she will."

Harmony grinned. "I know she will, too. She's wanted to have her own clients since I hired her right out of design school."

"Okay, so that's the work part," Alyssa said. "Now tell me all about this 'other.'"

She hadn't had a spare minute to talk to Alyssa about Barrett. Last weekend she'd texted her about being out of town on business. In other words, she'd lied, but everything going on with Barrett had happened so fast she hadn't had time to talk to her about it. And she really wanted to do it in person.

"So you know last weekend I said I was out of town on business?"

Alyssa stirred the fruit in her glass. "Yes."

"I wasn't out of town on business."

Alyssa looked up from her glass. "Okay. And what were you doing?"

"I was in San Francisco. With Barrett Cassidy."

The shock and surprise were evident on her best friend's face. "Get the hell out. You were not."

"I was."

"You're seeing Barrett?"

"I am."

"Damn, girl. Since when?"

"Since . . . very recently. It's all new and we're not sure where it's going, but so far, it's going good."

"Harmony. You've been hot for him since college."

She couldn't help the smile on her face. "I know. But he's very reluctant about it."

Alyssa frowned. "Why? Oh, because of Drake. What does Drake think about it?"

"He doesn't know. And right now, Barrett doesn't want him to know. He really wants to keep it a secret."

"I can't say I agree with that. More importantly, how do you feel about it?"

She shrugged. "I'd prefer to see him out in the open, but I respect his feelings about it. He loves my brother. They're best friends. He's afraid Drake will disapprove."

Alyssa let out a short laugh. "Of course he'll disapprove. He always does. He always has. No guy will ever be good enough for you in Drake's eyes."

"This is true. But I mean, it's Barrett. Drake loves Barrett."

"Drake loves Barrett as Drake's best friend. As your lover? No. Not only no, but oh hell no."

Harmony could see Alyssa's point. "Which I think is where Barrett's head is at. He and I are just getting to know each other on an intimate level. We really don't want Drake poking his nose into that part of our business."

"I can see that. You're entitled to your privacy while you two figure it all out." Alyssa took a swallow of wine. "Oh, and how intimate is it?"

Harmony laughed. "Pretty damned intimate."

"Is he as hot and sexy as he looks?"

Now it was Harmony's turn to take a long swallow of her sangria, as a rush of sexual memories slammed her. "Oh, yes."

"Honey, it's written all over your face."

She fanned herself with her napkin. "I can't help it. The man is passionate."

"Now you're making me jealous."

Harmony reached across the table. "Don't be jealous. There's an awesome and hot man out there for you somewhere."

"I know there is, and I'll find him, but, honestly, I'm not in a hurry. My business keeps me busy. Though it doesn't give me countless orgasms, and from the satisfied look on your face, I'd say you've had quite a few lately."

Harmony laughed. "This is true."

They finished off their wine and Alyssa followed her to Mama's house. As they parked outside, Alyssa put her arm through Harmony's.

"So, this might be awkward tonight. Barrett's going to be here, isn't he?"

"We talked on the phone last night and he said he was going to be." She turned to Alyssa. "Oh, and one more thing I forgot to mention. Barrett has asked Mama and Drake and me to come down to his family's ranch in Texas this weekend. His parents have invested in a blues club that's opening in Austin, which is near their ranch, and all Barrett's brothers will be there as well."

"So . . . meet the parents time already?"

"I don't think it's like that."

They headed toward the door and Alyssa gave her a knowing look. "But maybe it is."

Maybe it was. But she didn't think so. It was just an invite to the ranch for some fun. She knew Barrett and two of his other brothers were getting ready to start the football season, and they all wouldn't have much time to get together with family, so this was an opportunity.

That he'd invited her family was just about him being nice, and didn't mean anything more than that.

As soon as they walked in the house, the familiar chaotic noises of family and friends greeted her. She went to find her mother, who was seated at the dining room table with Harmony's two aunts.

She kissed her mother's cheek. "Hi, Mama. Hi, Aunties."

"Hello, Harmony. I haven't seen much of you lately."

She set her purse on the table and sat in the chair her Aunt Michelle had just vacated. "I know. Work has been really busy."

Her mother squeezed her hand. "Not too busy, I hope."

"It's hectic for sure, but nothing I can't manage. How are you doing?"

"I'm fine, honey. Making ribs for dinner tonight."

Harmony laughed. "If I'd known that, I'd have gone home to change out of this white dress."

Mama patted her hand. "That's okay. We'll get you a bib."

"And won't she look so cute in that?" Drake asked, leaning over to kiss Mama on the cheek.

"Shut up, Drake. I'm not wearing a bib."

"It's your dress," Drake said, winking at her before wandering off to join his friends.

Harmony took a quick peek, saw Barrett in the group, then turned away before anyone could notice her looking at him.

"So tell me about work and what's got you so busy?" Mama asked.

Harmony filled her mother in on work, then excused herself to go grab a glass of iced tea. Alyssa joined her.

"Your man is looking fine tonight," Alyssa said.

She chanced a look. Alyssa was right. Barrett wore a tight-fitting dark T-shirt and relaxed faded jeans, and all she wanted to do was go over to him and kiss him, then put her hands all over him.

So. Frustrating.

Their gazes met, and he slanted a brief smile in her direction before turning his attention back to Drake and the other guys.

"I saw that look," Alyssa said.

Harmony turned to her. "So did I."

"I swear, it's like the temperature in the house just rose ten degrees. I might go up in flames just being in the same room with the two of you."

Harmony laughed. "Shut up, Alyssa."

She made her way around to say hello to friends and relatives. Somehow, she and Barrett ended up in the kitchen together.

"Hey," she said, wishing she could touch him.

"How's it going?"

"Good. Stopped by your house today."

He nodded. "I was there the other day. They've made a lot of progress. Walls are in place and drywall and flooring is in. I can see how the place is going to look now."

"I really like how it's taking shape. You'll be surprised how fast they finish it. Before long I'll be putting the final decorating touches on it. In fact, you need to make the final decision on paint because they're waiting on that."

"Yeah, I know."

Drake came over and draped his arms around both of them. "You two over here talking pillow colors?"

"You know it's my favorite topic," Barrett said.

"How's the place coming along?" Drake asked.

"Good. You need to come by and take a look."

Drake stepped back. "What? And miss the big reveal? I'll wait for the open house. The one that comes with beer."

Barrett laughed. "Okay."

"In the meantime, Mama said dinner's ready."

They sat and ate and, as usual, Mama and her aunts had set out a feast—way more food than Harmony could eat in one sitting.

She'd grabbed a dish towel and tucked it into the neck of her dress. This was one of her favorite dresses, and no way was she going to get barbecue sauce on it.

"You should put one of your mama's robes on," her Aunt Paula said.

"Yes, because that would be even more attractive than that towel you're wearing." Alyssa gave her the side eye.

"Oh, I'm fine with this, thank you."

"The bib looks great," Barrett said. "I especially like the red and blue birds."

That's because the red and blue birds were spread across her breasts, but she was not going to say that out loud. "Thanks, Barrett. I thought the color scheme was ideal."

After dinner, the guys did dishes, which was the norm.

Harmony and Alyssa took glasses of iced tea out to the back porch. A storm was brewing. It was cloudy and the wind had picked up, but she was grateful for the breeze and the sudden drop in temperature.

They were soon joined by Mama and the aunts, and then all the guys.

"I want to thank you for the invite to your family's ranch," Mama said to Barrett.

"My mother said to tell you she's made up your favorite guest room. And that they just picked some corn the other day."

"I do love fresh, farm-raised corn on the cob. Is that handsome ranch hand still working there?"

"My Uncle Elijah?" Barrett asked with a grin. "Yes, he's still there."

"I look forward to seeing that man again."

Drake shook his head. "Do I need to watch out for you and Barrett's uncle?"

Mama pointed her finger at Drake. "No, you need to mind your own business."

Harmony laughed. "Oooh, she told you."

"I guess she did."

The wind started to get violent, so everyone moved inside. The aunts left, then some of the guys.

"I should go," Alyssa said. "I have to make a stop at the hair-supply store before I head home."

Harmony hugged her. "Looks like the storm is going to get bad. You be safe driving home."

"I will. You, too."

Harmony said good-bye to her mother, who made her promise to call as soon as she got home, then told her brother she'd see him in Texas, since he was heading down there tomorrow morning and she wouldn't fly out until tomorrow night.

She headed out, with Barrett right behind her. She could see lightning out in the distance. Hopefully she'd beat the storm home.

She got into her car, and as she hit the highway, she noticed Barrett's car behind her. Not unusual, since they lived in the same direction, but as she got closer to home, his car stayed behind hers.

She smiled, and was grateful to have him stay behind her because the downpour started several miles from home. It was a hard rain, with heavy wind, thunder and lightning. She pulled into her garage, leaving the door open when Barrett pulled into her driveway. He made a quick dash into the garage, but he had gotten wet.

She shut the garage door.

"Crazy storm out there. Thanks for following me."

He shook water droplets from his hair. "I needed to be sure you got home okay."

They walked inside. "Which reminds me, I need to call my mom. There are towels in the downstairs bathroom you can use to dry off."

"Okay."

He disappeared and she fished her phone out of her purse, made a quick call to her mother to let her know she was home and safe, then laid her phone on the counter.

Barrett came out of the bathroom with a small towel, rubbing it over his face and hair.

A sharp crack of thunder made her jump.

Barrett laid the towel down and came over to her, sliding his arms around her to tug her against him. "Scared of the storm?"

"Not really. Just surprised by the thunder."

"It's okay. I'll keep you safe."

"How about you take my mind off of it?"

His lips curved. "I can do that. You know, when we were at your mom's tonight, it took all my willpower to keep my hands off of you."

"Is that right?"

"Yes." He smoothed his hands down her arms, then turned her around to face her kitchen counter. "I kept thinking of being behind you over the kitchen counter, lifting that pretty white dress and fucking you."

Her stomach tumbled, the need she'd held in check all night releasing in a full-blown shudder when he drew the zipper down on her dress, then reached inside to cup her breasts. Even with her bra on, her nipples responded, tingling and hardening against his questing fingers.

Every time with Barrett was like this, her desire for him as fast and frenzied as the lightning outside. He bent her over the counter and pressed his lips to her neck.

"Whenever I'm around you all I can think about is being inside of you. You make me hungry, Harmony. You make me hard."

He lifted her dress over her hips, drew her panties down around her ankles. She kicked off her heels and wriggled her panties off while she heard the tearing of a condom package. He pushed her thighs apart and nudged his cock to the entrance of her pussy, reaching around to rub her clit with his hand.

Her anticipation had put her nearly there. With a few strokes of his hand she climaxed. Tingling pleasure shot through her with an unexpected rush of delight. She cried out when he pushed inside of her, the waves of her orgasm continuing to pulse inside of her while he drove into her.

"Fuck," he said. "You're still coming."

She came again when he fucked her harder and faster, making her grab onto the counter for support. When he climaxed, he wrapped an arm around her waist and shuddered against her, thrusting his cock in deeply, his groan a delight to her frenzied senses.

He laid his chest against her back and she felt the wild beating of his heart, felt the perspiration of his skin as his thighs rested against hers.

"You're sweaty," she whispered.

"The things you do to me."

She closed her eyes. He had no idea what he was doing to her, the way he made her feel, the responses he evoked in her.

It had never been like this for her. Not with any man before. She'd had great sex before, for sure. But with Barrett, it was as if every time was so incredibly powerful it laid her out, made her feel as if he were irrevocably weaving a spell over her.

He pulled out, then turned her around, framing her face with his hands to kiss her so tenderly it brought tears to her eyes. She fought them back, fighting the emotion.

This was just sex. Hot, rocking, crazy sex. Nothing more.

It couldn't be more because she knew that's what it was for Barrett.

She wasn't going to get emotionally involved with him.

When he disentangled, he said, "I think I need a shower."

They went upstairs and she pinned her hair up and joined him in the shower for a quick rinse off. She changed into a pair of shorts and a tank top, then fixed them both a glass of iced tea.

"Stay tonight?" she asked. "Storm's still raging out there."

She thought he'd object, but he just nodded. "Yeah, I'd like that."

They cuddled up on the sofa together. He gathered her close and she laid her head against his chest and he rubbed his fingers up and down her arm. She wondered if maybe it was too late to fight the emotional attachment she had to him.

If so, she was in deep, and it was starting to worry her.

TWENTY-SEVEN

HARMONY HAD NEVER BEEN TO THE DOUBLE C RANCH,
but had heard stories about it from her mother and from Drake.
She'd heard it was sizable, that Barrett's parents owned it. Barrett's
father, Easton Cassidy, was a football legend, a retired quarterback
who'd forged a dynasty of amazing sports stars.

Barrett, Flynn and their brother Grant played football. Tucker,
Barrett's twin brother, was a pitcher and the only member of the
family to play baseball.

Of course there was also Mia, the youngest Cassidy sibling and
the only daughter. She was in postgraduate school and not the
least bit interested in sports.

Barrett's mother, Lydia, was a former attorney who now helped
Easton run the ranch as well as various family foundations. According to Harmony's mother, the woman was formidable but also one
of the nicest people her mother had ever met. She was one of the

reasons Harmony's mom had decided to go back to school, get her degree and was now a financial analyst.

Harmony had a lot to thank Lydia Cassidy for.

Drake and Barrett had flown in earlier in the day, but since both she and her mother had to work on Friday, they hadn't been able to fly out until later in the day. Barrett had told her he'd have a car waiting for them at the airport in Austin, and true to his word, as soon as they arrived there was a sign with her name on it and someone had helped them with their luggage and directed them to a nicely air-conditioned SUV.

It turned out the guy wasn't with a car service but was one of the ranch hands who'd been sent to pick them up.

It was about a fifty-mile drive from Austin to the Double C ranch. They went from city to country and when they hit the gates of the ranch, Harmony was in awe at the sheer amount of land they passed through.

The main house was massive, surrounded by tall trees and barking dogs and a lot of cars.

"Is there a party tonight?" Harmony asked.

"I don't know, honey. Knowing the Cassidys, probably. They do like to entertain. But they also have a big family."

Her mother climbed out of the car, greeted all the barking dogs, and left her to climb up the stairs and hug a petite, slender, gorgeous woman with light brown hair. She wore a maxi skirt and a tank top and sandals and looked like a mature fashion model.

Harmony made her way to the porch—after greeting all the dogs, of course.

"Go. Shoo," the woman said to the dogs, who scattered on command. "Sorry. They're all super friendly. Hello, Harmony, and welcome to the ranch. I'm Lydia Cassidy."

It was hard to believe this beautiful woman was the mother of five children. Harmony held out her hand. "It's very nice to meet you, Mrs. Cassidy."

Lydia smiled. "Call me Lydia. We're very informal here. And it's hot outside. Let's go in where it's cooler."

They walked inside and, as a designer, Harmony took in everything, from the gorgeous wood floors to the incredible, state-of-the-art kitchen. She'd already had a glimpse of the amazing, obviously handmade dining room table they'd passed by on the way. It was all done in a very homey, country way that also felt modern and was incredibly beautiful. The décor was amazing and spot on.

"Your home is lovely," Harmony said.

"Thank you. I made some lemonade. Would you like some?"

"I'd love some," Harmony's mother said.

"I would, too, thank you."

"Me, too, Mom."

Harmony turned to see a beautiful, dark-haired young woman walk in, wearing shorts and a sleeveless cotton shirt. She looked to be in her early twenties, but Harmony instantly caught the resemblance between her and Barrett.

She held out her hand. "I'm Mia."

"Harmony Evans. Nice to meet you, Mia."

"Hello again, Mia," Harmony's mother said.

"It's nice to see you again, Diane. I hope the flight wasn't awful for you two. Personally, I hate flying, but sometimes it's an evil necessity."

Harmony laughed. "That's true. Barrett told me you're in college?"

"Yes. I'm doing postgraduate work at the University of Texas. I'm working on my MBA."

"Good for you."

"Thank you. Right now I'm enjoying the summer off before classes start up again."

"Oh, Drake and Barrett detoured to the university with Easton," Lydia said. "He wanted to show them off to his alma mater. They'll be here later."

"Okay," her mother said.

"Tucker—that's Barrett's twin—should be arriving soon. Flynn is already here. He's out in the barn."

She wanted to mention she had already seen Flynn last week, but of course she couldn't say that without revealing she'd gone to San Francisco with Barrett.

"I heard you've been harvesting the corn crop," her mother said to Lydia.

Lydia grinned. "Yes. Oh, and you should see the tomatoes this year, Diane. It's been hot, but we've been lucky with the rain. The garden is thriving. Would you like to see it?"

"You know I would."

"We'll be right back," Lydia said.

"You two have fun with that," Mia said, sliding onto a barstool at the island next to Harmony.

After they left, Mia turned to her. "Mom has a thing about her garden, and is willing to show it off to anyone remotely interested in vegetables."

Harmony laughed. "My mother loves her garden as well, though she doesn't exactly have a ranch-sized one."

"Those two will likely spend an hour in that hot sun, waxing poetic about various tomato varieties. Me, I don't get the appeal."

"Neither do I. So tell me about school. What will you do with your MBA?"

"I'd like to eventually get my PhD. With a concentration in managing the sports business arena."

Harmony's eyes widened. "Wow. That's ambitious. Planning to start your own dynasty someday, or possibly buy a team of your own?"

Mia laughed. "Not sure about that, but the whole sports thing has been ingrained in me for so long I think it's rubbed off. And I love management. I'm not sure where I'm headed with it, but it fascinates me. I may end up studying the dynamics and psychology of sports at some point."

Uh, wow. Talk about ambition. "I'm absolutely fascinated by your career trajectory."

"Thank you. Me, too. What do you do, Harmony?"

"I'm an interior designer."

Now Mia's eyes widened. "Get out of town. Seriously?"

"Seriously."

"You must love that."

"I do."

"Would you mind awfully if I picked your brain? I moved into an apartment in Austin last semester, and it's bare bones. I have some ideas, but I could use some advice."

"Of course. It's my favorite thing to do."

"Great. I have some pics of the place on my laptop. Hang on."

Harmony grinned as Mia dashed out of the room. She returned a few minutes later with her laptop, then scooted her barstool closer.

"You sure this isn't an imposition?"

"Of course not. I love design."

"Awesome. Anyway it's a one bedroom, very open and industrial."

She brought up the photos and handed them off to Harmony, who perused them, her mind sparking ideas right away.

"The space is so light and spacious. And you're right about the industrial feel. But the windows—you must love all those windows."

"I do. It was the biggest selling point for me on the place. A lot of my college years were spent in tight, dark spaces. This open, airy feel is so freeing. Plus, the balcony space."

"I totally agree. You could set up a desk with study space over here, which affords your best use of natural light. Sofa here, a couple of tables here. A conversation area here."

Within twenty minutes she had sketched out furniture placement and had provided several design links for Mia to consider, from accessories to pillows to furniture.

"This is awesome," Mia said. "Thank you so much."

"You're welcome. It's a great space. All you need are a few key pieces of furniture and some accessories to set it off, and it'll be perfect."

She heard male voices—a lot of them.

"And it was so quiet while it lasted," Mia said, winking. "The boys are home."

Lydia and her mother came through the back door at the same time as a horde of people walked into the kitchen.

"What, did you all show up at the same time?" Lydia asked.

"Seems that way," Barrett said, eyeing Harmony and giving her a big smile.

She felt a burst of butterflies flitting around her stomach. Ridiculous, but there they were.

Flynn was there, and Grant and Tucker with their respective fiancées and families. Flynn gave her a grin that told her their secret was safe with him.

There was also an older man who looked just like his sons.

"Okay," Lydia said, "introductions all around since I don't know who has met whom yet."

She met Grant's fiancée, Katrina Korsova, whom she recognized because she was a world-renowned fashion model. She also met Katrina's younger siblings Anya and Leo.

Tucker introduced his new fiancée, Aubry, who Harmony learned was a doctor.

Then she met Lydia's husband, Easton, who shook her hand. "Last time Diane was here with Drake she raved all about you."

Harmony looked over at her mother, who beamed a smile at

her. "Mama does like to do that. And it's very nice to meet you, Easton. I've heard amazing things about you."

Easton grinned. "I like the amazing part."

She also met Easton's brothers, Eddie and Eldon, and their wives. And then there was Elijah.

Oh, Elijah was quite handsome. She could see why her mother had mentioned him.

Drake came over to hug them.

"Hope you two had a good flight."

"We did," her mother said. "I've already been out back with Lydia checking out her garden. Makes me want to expand mine."

Drake shook his head. "Of course you do. Do I need to buy you a bigger house?"

"I don't know. Maybe I need to move to Texas."

"Bite your tongue, Mama," Harmony said. "We'd miss you too much."

Her mother patted her cheek. "You know I'm just joking, honey. Home is Tampa. Always has been, always will be."

"Unless I get traded to Houston," Drake said.

"Now you bite your tongue," Barrett said. "Nobody wants to get traded to Houston."

Everyone laughed.

Lydia grabbed a clipboard off the kitchen counter.

"Tucker, you and Aubry will be in the cottage. Grant, you, Katrina and the kids will stay in the eastern guesthouse because it has three bedrooms. Barrett and Flynn will be in the downstairs guest room. Diane, you and Harmony in the upstairs room to the left because it has its own bathroom."

Harmony's mother smiled. "Thank you, Lydia. You know that's my favorite room."

Barrett's mother gave her a smile. "I remembered that. Drake, you'll be right next door to them."

She saw the look Barrett gave her. The one that said they were going to have to fight for alone time.

"Shall we go settle our luggage upstairs?" her mother asked.

She dragged her gaze away from Barrett and smiled at Mama. "Yes. Let's do that."

GREAT. BARRETT COULDN'T IMAGINE HOW HE'D BE able to sneak any time with Harmony with Drake in the room right next to hers, and her sharing a room with her mother. Plus, Barrett would have to share a room with Flynn, who gave him a knowing smirk.

Asshole.

He'd figure it out somehow. Because he wasn't going to spend a weekend on the ranch and not be with her.

He wandered into the kitchen, grabbed a beer and stepped out onto the front porch. Tucker was out there with a beer in his hand.

Sometimes it was like radar with him and his twin. They always gravitated toward each other. They'd fought like wild animals when they were kids, but they'd always had each other's backs.

"Saw the game the other night," Barrett said, as he pulled up a chair next to Tucker. "You didn't suck when they finally felt sorry for you and let you pitch."

Tucker's lips curved. "Thanks."

"Where's Aubry?"

"She and Mom and Mia went over to the cottage to unpack the luggage, which I think translates to girl talk about the weddings."

"So in other words, you weren't invited."

"Yup." Tucker took a long swallow of beer.

"I can't believe you're getting married, man. You and Grant."

"Yeah, sometimes I can't believe it, either. It's happened pretty fast, at least for Aubry and me. But we just decided we wanted to make it happen, and neither of our lives is going to slow down or get simpler, so why wait?"

"Grant and Katrina's is coming up next March and then you and Aubry's next November."

"Yeah. Mom's loving it, though. Marrying off two of her sons in the same year. She's in heaven right now. Aubry said she sends her links all the time."

"Well, you know, it'll probably be a while before Mia's in the wedding zone. At least as far as I know. So Mom has had to wait for one of us to decide to settle down."

"Aubry's having fun with both of the moms helping her with wedding stuff. She's busy as hell with her residency. She can use all the help she can get."

"I'm sure she can."

Tucker turned to him. "What about you? Any weddings on the horizon?"

Barrett laughed. "No."

"Come on, man. Time to jump in, find a woman and commit."

Was it? He hadn't yet found a woman he was interested in committing to.

But just then Harmony walked outside.

"Hey. Have you seen Drake?"

Barrett shook his head.

"He's out at the barn with Grant and my dad," Tucker said. "Dad bought some classic car that he's showing off to them."

"Okay. Thanks, Tucker."

"Is there something you need, Harmony?" Barrett asked.

She gave him a sweet smile. "No. I'm good. But thanks, Barrett."

"Okay."

Harmony disappeared inside.

"Oh . . . I see," Tucker said, his lips lifting.

Barrett frowned. "You see nothing. Especially with those glasses you wear."

"I see just fine. And speaking of just fine . . . Harmony definitely is."

Barrett looked around, but no one was in sight. He cradled his beer in both hands and stared straight ahead. "Nothing to see, Tucker."

"I'm not blind, man. I'm also good with keeping secrets. Is it a secret?"

Damn his twin brother for ferreting out what was going on between him and Harmony with one look. "I don't want Drake to know. Not right now. It's complicated. He and I are best friends and Drake's protective of Harmony. Like . . . way overprotective. I don't know how to explain it well. I just feel it could put a wedge in our friendship."

"I get it. You need to figure out if what you and Harmony have is real before you get into it with her brother."

Tucker was the first one who truly understood. "Yeah."

"I won't say anything. Didn't see anything. Don't know anything."

He grinned. "Thanks."

Tucker stood. "Come on, let's go ogle Dad's new hot rod and pretend it isn't some midlife crisis he's having."

Barrett laughed. "Sure."

TWENTY-EIGHT

HARMONY QUICKLY DISCOVERED THAT DINNER AT THE Cassidys' was a lot like dinner at Mama's house. Noisy, crowded, everyone talking over each other, and absolutely awesome.

She'd made fast friends with Mia, Aubry and Katrina, so the three of them sat together and talked about everything from business to medicine to fashion and design while they ate. She almost forgot about Barrett, who sat at the other end of the table with his brothers and Drake.

Almost. But not quite, since she couldn't help but occasionally drag her attention away from the girl talk and catch a glimpse of the hot man at the other end of the table. Every now and then he'd look up at the same time, their gazes would collide and there'd be a quick smile between them. Careful not to call attention to each other, she'd look away.

But those butterflies in her stomach? Still there.

Her mother, on the other hand, was sitting next to Easton's brother, Elijah. Not that she could blame Mama. Elijah was a fine-looking man, a few years older than her mother, ruggedly built and, according to her mother, divorced for many years now. He lived on the ranch and from the way he looked at her mother, who was also a very attractive woman, the two of them shared some serious chemistry. Elijah sure was being solicitous to Mama right now.

It made her wonder what went down between the two of them the last time Mama visited the ranch.

She made a mental note to ask Drake about that.

"Lydia, tell me about the blues club," her mother asked.

"It's actually one that closed about a year ago. Easton and I loved driving up there and listening to all the bands. We hated that it closed, so we found a few other investors, and we're reopening it."

Easton laid his fork down and took a sip of tea. "Yeah, we liked that old place. It had been in business a lot of years. Many famous folks played there along with some young acts getting their start. Hated seeing it shut down."

Lydia nodded. "So, we're hoping to breathe some new life into it."

"I'm so excited," Harmony's mother said. "Blues is my favorite music."

"Mine, too," Elijah said, giving Harmony's mother a smile.

Harmony looked down the table at Drake, who just shook his head and smiled.

Well. This weekend should be interesting.

After dinner, which had consisted of barbecued chicken, corn on the cob, green beans, potato salad, fresh bread and sweet carrots, everyone piled into the kitchen. Leftovers were put away and dishes were done in record time. That was always the advantage of having a big crowd, especially when all hands were there to pitch in and help.

After, everyone dispersed. The women congregated in the living room, so Harmony followed along.

The discussion was on weddings, and she was eager to sit and listen to Katrina and Aubry talk wedding plans.

"The church in Austin is booked, and the reception venue is as well," Katrina said. "I have the guest list in order. It doesn't appear to be shaping up to be small."

Lydia laughed. "That doesn't surprise me. Between family and our friends and yours and Grant's friends, plus all the media attention the wedding will have, it's bound to be quite the event."

Katrina wrinkled her nose. "I'm hoping to keep media to a minimum, or not at all. This is a family-and-friends-only event, not something I want on the cover of the tabloids."

Lydia nodded and jotted something down in her notebook. "We'll talk about security, make sure it's beefed up for both the church and the reception."

"Thank you, Lydia."

"How about you, Aubry?" Lydia asked.

"We have the church and the reception. That's about it. Oh, and I've picked out my dress."

Katrina's eyes widened. "You have? We haven't gone dress shopping yet."

"Well, I haven't tried it on, but I have something in mind. I saw it online and fell in love with it."

"Now you know we all want to see it," Lydia said.

She shook her head. "I'll wait until we hit the store. It's going to be a surprise."

"Tease," Mia said.

"I know. I can't help it. But I think you're all going to love it. I hope you all love it."

Lydia smiled. "I'm sure we will. Have you booked an appointment for the dress yet?"

She shook her head. "Not yet. But I'll be sure to let you all know so you're available."

What fun it must be to plan a wedding. It wasn't something Harmony had thought much about, mainly because she'd never been deeply enough in love to think about marriage. At least specifically.

Sure, she'd always thought she might get married someday. And she occasionally pondered the thought someday she'd fall in love and live happily ever after, but she didn't read bridal magazines or keep a pin board with wedding venues or favorite cakes or anything like that.

Whenever it happened, then she'd design the hell out of her wedding. Until then, she was mostly a live day by day kind of woman.

But listening to Katrina and Aubry talk flowers and cakes and invitations and the like sure was fun.

After a while, she got up and wandered the house, taking in all the beautiful old furniture, the antiques and the old photos of generations of Cassidys.

She refilled her tea and walked outside. It wasn't quite dark yet, but the sun was setting, a bright orange glow mixing with the straight blues and oranges streaking along the horizon.

So gorgeous.

She was alone out here—except for the dogs, who excitedly greeted her.

"Hey, kids." She bent to scratch all their ears, then stepped down off the porch to wander the path that led from the house to the barn.

She lived in the city, in a town house, where one wall butted up against her neighbors. She was used to constant traffic and loud noises. Out here it was peaceful and so quiet she could hear everything from birds to crickets to the wind rustling through the trees.

It was something she'd never experienced before. A quiet calm settled over her, a peacefulness that fell over her like a warm, serene blanket. She let it flow through her as she continued to stroll along the property, content to just breathe in the scents of hay and animals and fresh, unpolluted air.

She'd made her way past the first barn to another when she heard footsteps behind her. She wasn't concerned, figuring it was either one of the ranch hands or one of the Cassidys.

"Lost?"

Her lips curved as Barrett came up beside her. "Intentionally lost."

He led her off the path, where they walked a distance toward the second barn. It was dark in there, but he didn't turn on the light.

No sounds came from within but she inhaled the smell of hay.

"Agricultural lesson?" she asked.

He took her glass and set it down, then backed her against the wall of one of the stalls where horses were obviously housed. "No. Biology."

His mouth came down on hers, hard. She wound her arms around his neck and when he lifted her, she wrapped her legs around him, feeling the hard thrust of his cock against her.

She was damp, her breasts tingly and tender and her entire body pulsing with need.

Barrett kissed her neck, his tongue sliding along her throat as he lowered her to the ground. "I hate not being able to touch you. Damn if it isn't the hardest thing I've ever had to do."

He lifted up her shirt and leaned down to kiss her stomach, rising to pull the cups of her bra over her breasts. His lips closed over one of her nipples and sucked. She bit down on her lip to keep from crying out.

"Barrett." His name fell from her lips in a whisper. She was trying to be careful because she didn't know who was out wandering. But when he continued to lick and suck her breasts, and then slipped his hand into the waistband of her pants to cup her sex, she no longer cared.

Being so close to him but not close enough had been torture, and also a turn-on. It had been like a touchless foreplay, and she was more than ready for him.

"Yes. Touch me. Make me come."

He met her gaze and rubbed her, sliding a finger inside of her as he rubbed his thumb over her clit.

She kept eye contact with him as she gasped. "I'm going to come. I'm going to come."

"Oh, fuck yeah," he said, fucking her pussy with his finger.

When she came, she shuddered hard, waves of pure ecstasy washing over her until she fell limp against him. She bit into his shoulder while he continued to use his fingers to pump into her.

Then he pulled his fingers from her and reached down to draw her pants and underwear off. He laid them over the gate.

He pulled a condom out of his pocket, unzipped his pants and put it on, then kicked her legs apart and slid his cock inside of her.

"Ohhh, yes," she said, as he cupped her butt to draw her closer to him.

"I love being buried inside of you, Harmony. Goddamn if it's not the only fucking thing I can think about. The way your pussy squeezes my cock when I'm in you, those sounds you make when I bury myself deep. You drive me crazy."

His words drove her over the edge, the way he pulled back then thrust deeper, grinding his pelvis against her clit. She could feel the tension building, the quivering, spiraling need inside of her ready to explode again.

She dug her nails into his back. "Just like that, Barrett. Harder."

He groaned against her neck, then plunged into her, giving her what she needed to come. And when she did, she couldn't hold back the wild cry. Barrett absorbed it with his mouth, kissing her with a depth of passion that sent her careening ever deeper into the throes of her orgasm. He went with her, groaning against her lips as he shuddered against her.

They both finally stilled and he broke the kiss, looking down at her. Sweat dripped down the side of his face, his expression dead-on serious.

"What am I going to do with you, Harmony?"

The words hovered on the tip of her lips: *Love me.*

Where did that come from? She'd never say that to him.

The trouble was, in this moment, she felt it. And God, she wanted him to feel the same.

Dangerous waters.

Instead, she grinned and swiped the sweat from his brow. "I could think of several things you could do with me."

He finally let out a short laugh and disengaged. They got dressed and he led her into the tiny bathroom in the barn to clean up a little.

He splashed cold water on his face.

"Good thing it's still hot outside, which will explain all this sweat," he said.

She smoothed her hair and righted her clothing. "Good thing you didn't lay me down in all that hay. It might have taken hours to get it all out of my hair."

He turned and pulled her into his arms. "That sounds like a challenge. I'm up for it if you are."

She laughed and shoved at him. "I think we've been gone long enough."

"Okay. You go on and head back. I'll be around after you."

She didn't want to rock the boat, but felt it should be mentioned. "You know, we wouldn't have to do all this skulking around if you'd just tell Drake we're seeing each other."

He shook his head. "Not right now, Harmony. Not long after we get back, training camp starts. I don't need to be at odds with my teammate, let alone my best friend."

She wasn't sure she accepted that, but a part of her understood it. "I guess."

He rubbed his hands up and down her arm. "Listen, if it were anyone else, then yeah. But you know how Drake gets about you seeing someone."

Now that part she did understand. "Yes, I do know how he gets. He's a little unreasonable about me and dating."

Barrett arched a brow. "A little?"

She laughed. "Okay, a lot. We'll keep it on the down low for now. But not forever."

He tipped her chin with his fingers, then brushed his lips across hers. "No, not forever."

Harmony walked out of the barn and Barrett stood there, his body still burning for her.

Yeah, he wanted things out in the open.

But he also knew Drake. Drake was as overprotective as a brother could be. He'd been around Drake when Harmony started to date someone. He was like a private investigator, needing to know the guy's background. And no matter who the guy was, he wasn't good enough. And God forbid the dude did something to hurt Harmony.

Yeah, he'd seen Drake's reaction when Harmony and a boyfriend broke up. He wanted no part of that.

No. The season was gearing up and it was important he and Drake both be on their game. Putting Barrett and Harmony's relationship in the middle of all that would spell disaster. He'd just let things play out the way they were for now. See how things went for a while. And then, down the road, if he and Harmony were still going strong, he'd break it to Drake.

Because Barrett had been in and out of relationships before. He knew how those things went. Some lasted. Some didn't.

Right now it was good. He hoped it stayed good. But he just didn't trust that it always would. And he wasn't about to put his years-long friendship on the line unless it stayed good between Harmony and him.

Maybe it was shitty of him to think that way.

In fact, as he started the walk back to the house, the thought of not seeing Harmony again caused an ache in his gut.

That should tell him something. So maybe he was in denial.

But denial was a good place for him right now.

And if that put him firmly in asshole territory, he supposed he'd have to live there for a while.

TWENTY-NINE

ON SATURDAY, MIA SURPRISED HARMONY BY ASKING her to go into Austin early in the day.

"I thought we'd go shopping, have some lunch, then meet everyone at the hotel later," Mia said.

"I'd love to."

Harmony was all about shopping.

Lydia had already told her they were going to stay at a hotel in Austin that night, since they'd be out late and it was too far to drive back to the ranch. So she packed her bag and grabbed her dress for tonight, then piled into the car with Mia and they headed to Austin.

"I needed to get away from the ranch," Mia said, as she pulled onto the highway. "I love my family, but once everyone gets there, it can be too much family togetherness. Know what I mean?"

Harmony laughed. "I know exactly what you mean. And I only have one brother. I don't know how you do it with four."

"It's easier now that Grant and Tucker are engaged. And with

Katrina having siblings, I've gotten to know Anya very well. So at least when the boys come to visit, they're bringing women with them."

Harmony smiled. "I'm sure that helps. We have a regular Thursday-night dinner at my mother's house. Drake has dragged football players—sometimes the entire defensive team—into our house ever since high school."

Mia glanced over at her. "Oh, how fun for you. More testosterone in the house."

"I'm sure you can relate, but, no thanks."

Mia nodded. "Exactly how I feel."

Then again, Harmony was currently seeing a football player—and Mia's brother. Which she wasn't about to mention to Mia.

They chatted nonstop on the drive to Austin, about everything from boys to fashion. Since she had no sisters growing up, it was fun for Harmony to be in the car with Mia. They were fairly close in age, only a few years separating them, so it was a joy to have someone to talk to. She found they had similar tastes in everything from fashion to music to television.

When they got to the mall, they wandered in and out of stores. Mia was a shopper just like her. They both liked to take their time and browse. Harmony picked up a hot red lip gloss with Barrett in mind, and could already imagine driving him wild when she wore it tonight.

"I need lingerie," Mia said, as they walked along the mall.

Harmony's brows rose. "Do tell."

Mia grinned. "Oh, I don't think I'll tell."

"Oh, come on. I promise not to tell any of your brothers about the hot guy you're buying lingerie for."

"I'm not sure it's a relationship kind of thing. More like a hookup kind of thing. You know how college is." She finished with a shrug.

"Those can be fun. All the excitement with none of the messy commitment and hurt feelings."

"Exactly."

Harmony hooked her arm in Mia's. "Then let's go lingerie shopping for your mystery man."

Mia laughed. "Yes. Let's."

Once they were done shopping, they stopped at a place called the Blue Dahlia Bistro.

"You're going to love it here," Mia said. "The food is incredible."

They settled in and Harmony sipped the most amazing pomegranate tea while she perused the menu.

"So tell me about school," Harmony said. "You must really love being there."

"It's a great university. I'll finish up my MBA within the next year. I'm looking at a few universities for my PhD, so it looks like I'll probably be moving out of state for that."

"Farther away from home, huh? Are you ready for that?"

"Actually, yes." Mia took a sip from her glass of tea, then set it down on the table. "I'm all about the adventure. And chances are I'll likely end up living somewhere near one of my brothers, since they're spread out around the country. Family tends to be close by, no matter what."

"Oh, I hadn't thought of that. Any idea where you'd like to get your PhD?"

"I'm looking very hard at Stanford right now and keeping my fingers crossed that I can work something out there. Plus I'd love to live in California. And, Flynn is there."

She grinned. "Flynn is a great guy."

"You've met him before?"

Oops. "Yes. All of your brothers have visited Barrett in Tampa before, and since Barrett and my brother are best friends, they've all ended up at my mother's house for dinner."

"Oh, of course."

She was so glad to have had that excuse. And at least it was the truth.

"Frankly, I'm anxious to get out on my own," Mia said. "College has been great, but I'm ready to branch out. Even if I don't start the PhD program right away, I'm ready to move on and start working."

"I'm excited for you. There's nothing like using what you know and starting a career."

"Exactly. It was important to me to at least get my MBA, but now I'm ready to do something with all this education."

"I think you'll do great things."

"Thanks."

Lunch was amazing. Harmony had the chicken salad tartine with nuts and cranberries, which was delicious. She was so full—they both were—that they decided to decline dessert.

They had a few hours to kill before the event tonight, so they headed to the hotel. Not only did they have individual rooms, but Lydia had booked a massive suite at the Four Seasons. It had two bedrooms and three bathrooms, perfect for all the women to get ready together, which Lydia said would be a lot more fun—and easier, in case someone needed help with a zipper or their hair. And there was plenty of room for all of them to move around, plus a balcony with a breathtaking view of the lake.

Harmony and her mother would share a room, so she met up with her mother in the lobby when everyone else showed up. They all checked into their individual rooms first.

"I . . . might not be staying here tonight," her mother said, as they unpacked.

Harmony noted the slightly nervous tone in her mother's voice. It was like role reversal, with Harmony taking on the parental role. She turned to face her mother.

"Mama. Really? You and Elijah?"

Her mother straightened, didn't even look embarrassed. "Yes. Me and Elijah."

Harmony laughed. "Go get you some, Mama. And have a great time."

"I intend to, honey. Believe me."

She couldn't be more thrilled that her mother was having some fun. Whether it was temporary fun or something more, it was none of her business. Her mother was a grown woman and could do whatever she wanted.

Harmony and her mother packed their dress clothes for tonight and put their makeup and hair products into bags, then went upstairs to the presidential suite. They laid their bags down and headed out onto the balcony, while Lydia ordered up drinks from room service. She'd told them they had time to sit back, chat and relax before tonight's event.

Harmony wasn't sure she'd ever felt more pampered, especially when room service showed up with champagne, wine, sparkling water and iced tea.

It was definitely enticing. Though it was early, she couldn't resist a glass of champagne. She was looking forward to partying tonight.

They all sat and chatted together about everything from men to sex to careers, politics and religion. They all had different backgrounds and belief systems, were of different ages and in various stages of their lives, and yet the conversation stayed respectful. Harmony had never thoroughly enjoyed herself more than in this company of women.

She also loved that her mother and Lydia really seemed to hit it off. She supposed as mothers of football players and career women, they had a lot in common, because she'd eavesdropped on their conversations and the topic frequently focused on their children, which didn't surprise Harmony at all.

Soon it was time to start getting ready, and Lydia started

directing everyone to various rooms and bathrooms, no doubt to avoid utter chaos. When it was her turn, Harmony freshened up, redid her hair and makeup and brushed her teeth, then dashed into her assigned bedroom to get dressed. She ran into Aubry in the same room, so they helped each other with zipping their dresses.

Aubry was wearing a killer slinky red dress.

"Tucker is going to go crazy when he sees you in this dress," Harmony said, as she pulled the zipper up.

Aubry gave her a grin over her shoulder. "I certainly hope so."

Harmony stepped into her dress.

"Men will be ogling you all night. This silver sequined number makes your skin simply shine, Harmony," Aubry said.

Harmony loved the compliment. "Thank you. I bought this dress at the beginning of summer and haven't had an opportunity to wear it yet. I'm really excited about tonight."

"Me, too," Aubry said, slipping into her heels. "Let's go make men's tongues fall out of their mouths."

Harmony laughed and she and Aubry grabbed their clutch bags and left the bedroom.

Frankly, everyone looked stunning, including her mother, who wore a copper-colored dress that clung to her curves and showed off her cleavage.

"Mama. You are so freakin' hot."

"Thank you, honey. So are you."

It turned out the men were meeting them at the hotel, so when there was a knock on the door, all the guys piled in.

They all looked amazing in suits and ties, and Harmony simply could not take her eyes off of Barrett, who wore a dark suit, white shirt and a beautiful silver and black tie.

She knew she was supposed to play it cool, but at this moment, she simply couldn't. Everyone else was milling about and throwing out compliments, so she wandered over to him.

He leaned in and whispered in her ear. "Goddamn, Harmony. You look so fucking beautiful. How am I supposed to get through the night not touching you when you look like that?"

Her heart clenched. She reached out to brush off an imaginary speck from his jacket. "Thank you. You look amazing."

Her brother came over, and as usual, the man had an impeccable sense of style. He wore a black suit, dark blue shirt and a white tie. The man was stylin'.

He kissed her cheek. "Hey, gorgeous."

She grinned and patted his chest. "Hey yourself, hot stuff. Have you seen Mama?"

"Yeah. She's angling for a rendezvous tonight. Elijah about swallowed his tongue when he saw her."

She laughed. "I'm sure that was the reaction she was looking for. And what about you?"

Drake adjusted his tie. "Playing the options, like always."

She shook her head. "Do I need to play protector for you?"

He put his arm around her shoulders. "Not a chance, baby sister. I'm freewheeling and checking out the action. You keep an eye on Mama."

"Ha. She already told me to step clear of her action."

"Then I guess you're on your own."

Just the way she wanted it. Hopefully Drake would find some beautiful woman to hit on, and who would capture his attention, and she could find some alone time with Barrett.

Though with his entire family in attendance at the club opening tonight, the chances of that were pretty slim.

"The limos are here," Lydia said. "We need to head downstairs."

They all piled into two limos. And for some reason, she ended up next to Barrett. She was tucked into the corner, with him next to her, for the ride over. Flynn was on his other side, and Tucker and Aubry sat across from them.

Drake and Mama ended up in the other limo.

Perfect.

Especially when Barrett slid his fingers under her thigh. She breathed deeply, trying to act as if his touch didn't affect her, when all she really wanted to do was inch her fingers next to his.

Thrilling, but also frustrating.

There were spotlights in front of Just the Blues, along with a red carpet and photographers and media crews.

"Wow," she said, then turned to Barrett. "Did you know it was going to be all this?"

He laughed. "No. But leave it to Easton Cassidy to cause a ruckus."

They waited until Barrett's parents got out of the limo, then they followed.

Harmony had never been involved in anything like this before. She'd seen Drake on TV surrounded by the media, but she'd never personally experienced it.

Lights flashed in her eyes, and she was more than happy to cede the spotlight to Barrett's parents, who talked about the reopening of the club. Lydia and Easton handled it gracefully and with much enthusiasm, talking about the club's past and hopeful future.

"We're proud to be a part of the reopening," Easton said. "There are so many fantastic blues bands and artists here in Austin, and elsewhere, and since Lydia and I are such fans, we were saddened when the original club closed. When our partner, DeMartin Lewis, offered us the opportunity to invest with him, we jumped at the chance to breathe new life into this club and encourage the talent who would walk through these doors.

"We hope you'll all join us in welcoming the opening of Just the Blues and supporting the artists who play here."

There was a round of applause from the audience behind the ropes. Easton and Lydia made their way inside. Grant stopped for an interview, as did Tucker. Then Barrett stopped to speak.

Harmony brushed past him but someone stuck a microphone in her face.

"Are you Barrett's date for the evening?"

She smiled. "No. I'm Drake Evans's sister, Harmony."

"Oh. And what brings you here tonight, Harmony?"

She played it cool. "I'm a friend of the Cassidy family, and a big supporter of the blues."

Since she wasn't famous and didn't give them any gossip fodder, the media moved on to someone else, allowing her to step inside the cool, dark club.

It was beautiful inside. Dark and moody, like a blues club should be. There was ample seating with tables spread all around, but still plenty of dance floor space and a large stage. There were bars at either corner, and she headed toward one of them.

Aubry was there, taking a glass of champagne the bartender handed her.

"I'll have what she's having," Harmony said.

"Well, that was intense outside," Aubry said, then took a long swallow of champagne.

"I'll say. Have you ever had to deal with media?"

Aubry nodded. "My father owns the St. Louis Rivers baseball team, so I've been involved in the media spotlight a time or two. Not my favorite thing."

Harmony's eyes widened. "I don't know why I didn't make that connection, Aubry, since Tucker plays for them."

Aubry laughed. "No reason that you should."

Harmony looked around, watching everyone spill in from outside. It was going to be crowded in here tonight. She hoped the club was a rousing success.

"I guess we should find everyone—and our table," Aubry said. "Lydia told me we have a couple reserved tables up front."

"Okay."

The guys had found the bar, and she and Aubry spotted the other women at their tables. Harmony set her clutch down at a chair, then looked around for her mother.

A band had already started playing, something soft and appropriately bluesy.

And her mother was off in a dark corner, cozying up to Elijah, who also looked handsome in his suit, a perfect complement to her mother. Her mother was smiling, leaning against Elijah, and looking extremely happy.

She intended to leave her mother be, since it appeared as if she was in good hands. At least she hoped so. Drake was relaxing at the bar with Barrett, and didn't seem to be interested in what Mama was doing, and if Drake's radar wasn't up about Elijah, then Harmony shouldn't worry about him, either.

She took her seat and chatted with Mia about college, boys and what it was like growing up with overprotective brothers. That was something they definitely had in common.

"What was it like trying to date?" Harmony asked.

Mia rolled her eyes. "In high school? Impossible. Of course some of my brothers were off to college by then, but it's like they had radar, or maybe Mom reported to them, because whenever I tried to date a guy, I'd get text messages and phone calls asking probing questions about the boy. And talk about intimidation. Trying to have a relationship was nearly impossible. It was bad enough that Dad was intimidating as hell, but try bringing a boy to a family barbecue in the summer when all four of your brothers are giving him death looks."

Harmony nodded. "I'm familiar with the death look. I think my brother, Drake, has a patent on it."

Mia shook her head. "I doubt that, because my brothers had

perfected the art of getting a guy to run for the hills before I could even get a first kiss, let alone get laid. I was starting to fear I'd die a virgin."

Harmony laughed. "But then you escaped to college."

"Yes. Getting away from my family is the best thing that's ever happened to me. I mean, I love them, but I needed some space to figure out who I was away from the shadow of all those Cassidy males."

"Honey, I'm still trying to get away from my brother. I haven't succeeded yet."

"So he's still overprotective of you?"

"You have no idea. For some reason he still thinks he can decide what man is best for me. Though for Drake, it's like I'm forever sixteen and incapable of making rational decisions where men are concerned."

Mia wrinkled her nose. "Ugh. Brothers."

Harmony lifted her glass. "I'll drink to that."

They laughed, then the other women joined them. After a while the guys joined the table. Harmony ended up sitting with Drake on one side of her and Barrett on the other. Talk about frustrating. But she forgot all about that once the music started up, as bands and artists played.

Soon, she was lost in the strains of beautiful blues music, with occasional jazz thrown in. People got up and danced, and even her brother found himself a beautiful woman to dance with. So did Flynn.

Barrett held his hand out to her. "Dance, gorgeous?"

She smiled. "I'd love to."

They walked out to the dance floor, and Barrett pulled her against him, keeping a respectable distance as they glided around the floor together. Since the club was packed, at least they weren't dancing next to her brother.

Not that he'd notice, since Drake's entire focus was on his dance partner.

Perfect.

And when Barrett danced her to the back terrace, then out the door, she welcomed the slide of his hand down the bare skin of her back and the way he'd maneuvered her away from the prying eyes of her family and his.

He pressed her up against the cement wall of the terrace.

"I need this one minute alone with you. Just one kiss."

It was dark and intimate on the terrace. Thick vines covered the arbor and a nice breeze had kicked up, though it did nothing to cool down her need for Barrett, which raged like an out-of-control wildfire. Barrett's lips rubbed over hers, a delicious temptation that made her grasp the lapels of his suit jacket to tug him closer.

He groaned against her lips, then pulled back.

"If I don't stop now, I won't stop at all."

She fought to catch her breath and smoothed her hands down her dress. "Why stop at all? Just tell my brother we're together."

"In front of your family? In front of mine? Tonight? No."

She knew it was her emotions talking, but damn, this was frustrating. And irritating. "Fine."

She turned and walked inside, grabbed another glass of champagne, then wandered around.

She was stopped by a very fine-looking black man. He was tall, with dark, mesmerizing eyes, short cropped hair with a fade on each side, and one hell of a sexy smile.

"Hello there, beautiful. And what's your name?"

"Harmony."

"Nice to meet you, Harmony. You're here with our patrons, the Cassidys."

He was very observant. "Yes, I am."

"I've had my eye on you all night. Hard not to watch a beautiful woman grace our club."

She was flattered. "Thank you. And if I recall correctly, you're Luther Kent, one of the musicians playing here tonight."

He smiled. "You have a good memory."

She laughed. "I have a very good memory for outstanding singers."

"Thank you, Harmony. I hope you're enjoying yourself."

"I am. Are you from Austin?"

"New Orleans, originally, but I've been settled in Austin for a couple of years now. And you?"

"I live in Tampa, actually. I'm here visiting with the Cassidys."

His brows lifted. "They are fine patrons of the blues."

"So I've discovered."

"In fact, the group coming out now plays some smooth music. Would you care to dance?"

Luther seemed a little inebriated, but she was just annoyed enough with Barrett, who refused to claim her as his, that she set her champagne down on a nearby table and said, "I'd love to."

Luther took her hand in his and pulled her onto the dance floor, drawing her against the solid warmth of his body.

She let herself fall into the music, trying like hell to feel something—anything—for this fine-looking man.

Unfortunately, her body and soul were wrapped up in someone else. But she refused to give any thought to Barrett, instead tilting her head back to smile at Luther, who used his exceptional voice to softly sing the rhythmic strains of the instrumental being played onstage.

A woman might swoon at being courted in this manner, if a woman wasn't pining away for some other man.

Which was ridiculous, because Barrett hadn't asked her for any exclusivity.

So instead, she nestled in closer to Luther, who then let his hand slide down a little closer to her butt.

She corrected his erroneous assumption by lifting his hand back where it belonged—on her waist.

He gave her a smile, then pulled her closer.

The one thing she loved to do was dance, so when the next song played, he kept her on the dance floor. She didn't mind that at all, even though his hands drifted into forbidden territory again.

"A little too familiar there, Luther," she said, removing his hand from her rear—again.

His gaze gleamed hot. "Well, it's a fine ass, Harmony."

Some men. Always testing those boundaries. She stepped away. "Thanks for the dance."

She walked away, but didn't get more than two steps when she heard the raised voice of her brother. And he was arguing with Luther.

Oh, shit.

She turned and headed back there.

"You have no right to put your hands on her."

Luther had his hands raised. "We were just dancin', man."

"With your hands on my sister's ass."

Harmony stepped between them. "Drake. We are guests here. Remember that."

"I don't give a—"

Barrett stepped in. "Hey, Drake, how about we all cool down and step outside for a minute."

By then, Grant, Tucker and Flynn had walked up as well. And while Barrett walked Drake away, Barrett's brothers were having a conversation with Luther, all the while leading him toward the front door.

"Are you all right?" Lydia asked, a look of concern on her face.

"Honestly, I'm fine. He took a few liberties with his hands, but I was handling it."

Lydia sighed. "He's very talented, but new, according to DeMartin. And he'll no longer be welcome to play here."

Now Harmony felt awful. "Oh, don't do that on my account."

Lydia put her arm around Harmony. "It's not on your account. We will never accept a man putting his hands on a woman like that. It's unacceptable behavior for the club. He's gone, honey."

Harmony nodded. "All right."

She felt awful for being the cause of this disturbance.

Barrett and Drake came back inside. Drake came over to her. "Are you all right?"

She directed her irritation to her brother, though in a very restrained fashion. "I'm fine. I *was* fine, and I can handle myself without you constantly treating me like I'm some kind of idiot who doesn't know her way around men."

Drake grasped her shoulders. "He put his hands on you."

She shrugged off his grasp. "Lots of men have put their hands on me. Some I accept, some I don't. Stop treating me like a child you have to monitor, Drake."

She turned and walked away from him, stepping outside on the terrace. She wished she could go home right now.

She was tired of men—all men. Every single one of the men in her life pissed her off.

Barrett walked out and he was the last damn man she needed to see right now.

He leaned against the wall with her, but didn't say anything.

Finally, she did. "Okay. I get it. My brother is a ridiculous hot-head and I understand why you don't want him to know about us."

Barrett pushed off the wall, moving in front of her. "Harmony, you realize that's not why I came out here. I wanted to go over there and beat the shit out of that guy for putting his hands on you. So I'm no better than your brother, I guess."

That made her feel marginally better. "But you didn't. And your reaction came from a different place. So you were jealous?"

"Hell yes I was jealous, Harmony. I don't want anyone's hands on you but mine."

She rubbed her temple where a headache was forming. "Well, isn't this just the shit?"

"Yeah."

"Would you take me back to the hotel? I have a killer headache."

"Yup. Let me tell my parents—and your brother."

"Thanks."

She didn't want to be rude, so she found Lydia and Easton and thanked them for an amazing evening and said she had a headache and wanted to go back to the hotel.

"I'm so sorry about this," Lydia said, grasping her hands. "We'll see you back at the ranch tomorrow morning for breakfast."

She hugged Lydia. "Thank you so much for today and for tonight. I really had a wonderful time."

She also found her mother, who was sitting at the table having an in-depth chat with Elijah. Fortunately, Mama had missed the chaos between her and Drake.

"Are you all right, baby?"

"Just a dustup, Mama. Nothing more. And Drake being a hothead."

Her mother shook her head. "That boy. I'll talk to him."

"No. Don't. I dealt with it already."

Her mother hugged her, then Barrett came to claim her. They got into a car and headed over to the hotel. She was quiet and looked out the window, reflecting on what had happened. She was a mix of emotions—embarrassment, anger and frustration.

"You can just drop me off," she said once they reached the hotel.

He grabbed her hand, forcing her to look at him. "Not a chance in hell of that happening."

He helped her out of the car, then inside the hotel.

Barrett walked her to the elevators and she pushed the button, then turned to him. "I've got this."

He gave her a look. "I'm taking you upstairs."

She really just wanted to be alone, but Barrett was currently glued to her side, his hand at her back, and he appeared to be going nowhere, which, okay, was a comfort to her hurt feelings.

So maybe she didn't want to be alone as much as she thought.

When he pushed the button that was not her floor, she gave him a look.

"I'm taking you to my room. I already texted Flynn and told him to take a hike tonight. He'll get another room."

"Great. Someone else I've inconvenienced tonight."

He laughed. "First, you didn't inconvenience anyone. Second, Flynn's a big boy. He can handle it."

She sighed, and her head pounded even worse.

When they got to the room, he got out his key card, slipped it in the door lock, then pushed the door open, holding it so she could walk in. She flipped the light on and Barrett closed the door behind them.

The room was really nice. It had a living room and a bedroom with two beds and a nice, oversized balcony.

Barrett came up behind her, laying his fingers on her shoulders. "Tell me what you need."

She took a deep breath and let it out. "Right now all I want is to put on my pajamas, crawl into bed and eat ice cream."

Not a romantic thing to say, but it was how she felt.

"Sure. Let's do that."

She swiveled to face him. "You brought your jammies?"

His lips curved. "No. But I could go for some ice cream. You order up what you want. Give me your key and tell me what you want from your room."

She couldn't believe he'd be down for that, but she couldn't deny the idea appealed. "Okay."

After he left, she kicked off her heels and sat on the bed, then called down to room service and asked for ice cream. When they asked her what flavor, she realized she hadn't asked Barrett what kind he liked, so she ordered several different kinds, from vanilla to chocolate to strawberry with all the fixings. And a couple hot fudge sundaes with whipped cream, along with a bottle of champagne.

Because champagne went well with ice cream. At least that was her thought process right now.

There was a knock at the door and she went to open it. It was Barrett, with her bag.

He laid the bag down. She opened it and grabbed her pajamas. She turned to Barrett.

"Unzip, please."

"Gladly." The brush of his hands along her bare skin as he pulled her zipper down brought about an awareness that she didn't think she'd feel in her present mood. Though it shouldn't surprise her that his touch could evoke sensations of desire in her. He'd always had that effect.

She dashed into the bathroom, washed the makeup off her face, changed into the blue cotton shorts and white tank top and put the dress on the hanger, then came out of the bathroom and hung her dress in his closet.

Barrett had changed out of his suit and into a pair of gray sweats and a white T-shirt. He was on the sofa, remote in his hand.

He patted the spot next to him on the sofa. "Come on."

She came over and sat, pulling her legs up on the sofa.

He handed her the remote. "Pick something to watch."

"What if I want to watch a girl movie?"

He arched a brow. "What's a girl movie?"

"Something romantic."

"You think guys don't like romance?"

She shrugged, staring at the TV as she flipped through channels. "Right now I don't think I know anything about men."

"I don't know about other guys, but I can tell you about me. I like sports, of course. Hot women, like you. Good food, good conversation and honesty."

"Oh, you like honesty?"

"Okay, you really want to get into this thing with Drake tonight?"

"No. I don't. I already told you I get why you don't want to tell him about us. My brother is an overprotective pain in my ass. And the fact that he's your best friend just makes what you and I have together . . ."

She didn't finish. She couldn't.

"Complicated?"

She let out a huff, still scrolling through channels without even looking at them. "Understatement."

He took the remote from her hands and muted the sound. "Look at me."

She did.

"I know what we have is complicated. It's complicated as hell and I'm sorry about that. I wish it could be easy for us, but right now it isn't. Your brother is a hothead and he's protective about you. In some ways that's a good thing. I'll talk to him about us."

This was new. "You will?"

"Yes."

"When?"

"Soon. Let's get through training camp and I'll . . . find the right moment. You need to trust me to know when that right moment will be."

"Okay."

There was a knock on the door.

"I'll get that," Barrett said.

The room service waiter came in bearing a tray filled with all kinds of ice creams and toppings, not to mention the hot fudge sundaes and the champagne. When he left, Barrett slid a look in her direction.

She shrugged. "I might have gotten carried away. The ice cream mind is a dangerous thing."

One side of his mouth pulled up in a half smile. "So it seems. Let's dig in and see what kind of damage we can do."

She went for the hot fudge sundae first, while Barrett mixed scoops of chocolate and vanilla ice cream in a bowl, then sprinkled in some M&M's.

Harmony picked up the remote and found something they might both like—an action movie mixed in with a little romance.

Barrett leaned back with his bowl. "This looks like a good one."

They ate and watched the movie. After Barrett finished his ice cream, he popped open the champagne and poured it into two glasses. Harmony was cold after eating the ice cream, so she grabbed a blanket from the bedroom and laid it over both of them.

They sipped champagne and argued about the movie.

"This is ridiculous," she said. "She has to know he's only using her to get the information he needs."

"But you can tell he cares about her and he feels really guilty about it."

"Oh, and that makes it okay?"

"In the movie world, yes. Plus, you know she'll make him pay for it in the end. They'll end up married and he'll spend the next forty years apologizing for lying to her about being a spy and not coming clean about who he was in the first place."

She laughed. "Probably."

At the end, there was a happily ever after—with a twist. It turned out the heroine was also a spy, and she'd been playing the hero as well.

"Okay, that surprised me," Barrett said. "Did you pick up on her being a spy?"

Harmony shook her head. "Not at all. So maybe she'll be the one continuing to apologize for the next forty years."

He laughed. "Or maybe they'll end up even."

"Could be."

Barrett gathered up their bowls and laid them on the tray, then wheeled it out to the hallway and called room service to pick it up.

"Tired yet?" he asked as he refilled her glass.

"Not yet. I think I'm still riding that sugar high from the ice cream."

"We could get dressed and take a walk."

She picked up her phone. "It's after midnight. How about we step out on the balcony instead?"

"Sure."

He opened the slider and they walked outside. It was warm, but that breeze she'd felt earlier at the club was still present. There were two chairs out here, but all she wanted to do was stand, lean against the railing and look at the lights of the city.

"Beautiful out here."

Barrett came up behind her, wrapping his arms around her. "Yeah."

She leaned against him and put her hands on his forearms. "Nothing like your ranch, though. It must have been amazing to grow up with all that space."

"We didn't spend all our growing-up years there, but the time we had sure was fun. Lots of space to run around and get dirty."

She laughed. "I imagine that for boys it was a great deal of fun. Plus riding horses, driving the trucks around all that land."

"Mucking out stalls, working cattle . . . it wasn't exactly all play all the time. Dad made us work, too. Nothing fun comes without hard work attached."

"A lesson we all have to learn."

They both went quiet, until he leaned his head against hers.

"I'm sorry about everything tonight."

"Not your fault that one guy thought he had the right to put his hands on me, and that my brother can't seem to keep himself out of my business. I had it handled."

"I know you did. And you were walking away when Drake decided to get involved."

She looked out over the clear night sky. "I wish I understood Drake's motivations."

"I have a younger sister, Harmony. I do understand the need to protect. But I also trust Mia to handle herself. We all know she can, and that she wouldn't hesitate to call on any of us if she needed to. It doesn't mean we don't keep a watchful eye on her, or that we don't worry she won't make the right choices."

"Right."

"But the difference between Drake and me is that he's felt that pressure to be your protector because you didn't have a father in your life to do the job. So maybe he feels the need to always be there for you, even if you might not want him to be. He's having a hard time letting go of the little girl who needed him all those years ago."

She had long ago pushed the past aside. Maybe Barrett was right and Drake hadn't yet let go of their past. "You might be right about that. I give him such a hard time about being overprotective, but maybe I don't understand where he's coming from."

She needed to spend some time talking with Drake, to come to an understanding with him.

But not right now. Not when she was so angry with him.

Barrett moved his hands over her shoulders, massaging away the tension from the night.

This was what she needed to focus on. She and Barrett were finally alone, and she needed to make good use of their time. She focused on the movements of his hands on her body, the way he used his fingers to expertly find the knots in her shoulders and melt away all the stress.

She tilted her head forward. "Mmm, that feels good. I like your hands on me."

He smoothed his hands over her shoulders, pressing in, then releasing as he made his way down her arms to the very tips of her fingers before gliding back up again.

Who knew that Barrett touching her fingers, elbows and shoulders could be so sensual?

"More."

"Where do you want me?" he asked.

She let out a soft laugh. "That's a loaded question."

He came around to face her, then backed her up against the wall of the terrace. His warm breath sailed across her cheek.

"Here?" he asked, his lips brushing hers so lightly it felt like the caress of a feather.

She drew in a breath. "Yes."

"Or here." His tongue left a blazing trail across her neck, making her shiver despite the heat and humidity that still clung to the night.

She grasped his shoulders, letting him know by digging in her nails that she very much liked the direction he was going.

He pushed the strap of her top down and let his teeth graze that tender spot between her neck and shoulder. "Maybe here."

She was shaking now, anticipating where he'd go next.

"Please."

He lifted his head, his gaze full of heat and promise. "You never have to beg, baby. I'll give you exactly what you need."

He pulled up one of the chairs to sit, then lifted her shirt and put his mouth on her nipple.

She gasped at the heat and suction of his mouth, at the way his tongue flicked against the crest. Sensation exploded, making her sex quiver. She was on fire for him, and despite being outside where someone might see them, she didn't care. They were on a secluded balcony with high sides, so they were afforded privacy, at least from the prying eyes of neighboring guests.

Someone watching from afar? Now that was beyond her control, and beyond her ability to care, as Barrett kissed his way down her stomach, then pulled her shorts down and put his mouth on her sex.

She let out a low moan as he licked the length of her.

"You taste so damn good," he said, pulling away only long enough to make eye contact with her, then laid his tongue on her clit and made her tremble, as a blast of heated sensation ignited her.

She couldn't help herself. She arched her hips against him, feeding her pussy to him, delighted in the way he lapped her up, as she cried out with her orgasm.

"Yes. Oh, yes, yes," she said, her entire body shaking as she came over and over again. Maybe it was the tension release, but it was more likely Barrett's talented mouth doing delicious things to her body that made her feel like she could come like this for ten minutes, at least, quivering all over with tingling pleasure; and she didn't want it to stop.

So when he rose, she said, "Get a condom."

He smiled, then went inside, coming back out seconds later.

She had already arranged one of the chairs the way she wanted it.

"Drop your pants," she said. "Sit."

His lips curved. He pulled his pants off, his hard cock springing up. He put a condom on.

"I like that cock of yours, baby," she said.

"Fuck me, Harmony," he said. "Climb on and fuck my cock."

She straddled him, easing down over his cock inch by inch. She raked her nails down his arms, needing to feel him buried deep.

"Is that what you need?" he asked, his eyes fixed on hers.

"Oh, yes. You know I do."

She began to move, rocking back and forth, shards of fiery pleasure exploding within her with each movement.

Barrett grasped her hips and rolled her toward him. "God, I love being buried deep inside of you. My cock swells and I just want to give you all my come."

She grasped his shoulders and lifted, then slid back down on him, teasing him with her pussy, feeling him grow impossibly harder every time she seated herself fully on top of him. And when she rolled against him, she felt the tightening, the quivering tension of impending release.

"Damn, Harmony," Barrett said. "You gonna come again?"

She dug her nails into him. "Yes. Make me come, Barrett."

He wrapped an arm around her and put his lips on hers, thrusting his tongue in her mouth to mimic the movements of his cock. She spiraled out of control, her body undulating against him as she came with a rush of unending bursts of pleasure.

He groaned against her lips and drove harder and faster into her with his release, his body shuddering against her. She held tight to him as she rode out an orgasm that left her shaking in its wake.

Spent, she tried to catch her breath as she ran her hands up and down Barrett's body.

He finally stood, cupping his hands under her butt, and carried her into the room.

He took them into the bedroom and laid her down on the bed, left to dispose of the condom, then came back to lie down next to her.

"You make my legs shake," he said, stroking her arm.

"You make me crazy. Do you realize we just had sex outside?"

He laughed. "You liked it. I could tell by the number of times you came."

"You're right about that. But you make me lose all sense of time and place."

He trailed a finger along her collarbone. "That's not a bad thing, is it?"

"No, it's not."

He spent some time running his fingers over her body, from her face to her neck. She yawned, then closed her eyes and finally turned over, nestling her butt in Barrett's crotch.

She didn't remember him fetching the blanket from the other room, but he turned out the light and pulled the cover over them, and he was still touching her when she fell asleep.

THIRTY

BARRETT HAD ORDERED A POT OF COFFEE EARLY IN the morning. He leaned against the wall between the living room and the bedroom watching Harmony sleep, something he was getting used to doing.

There was something about watching the way she slept that got to him. She had such a sweet innocence about her when she was sleeping that made his heart clench, and made him want to see that look on her face every morning.

For the rest of his life.

He blinked, then his mouth went dry.

The one thing he'd never once thought about was the rest of his life and what that looked like, or who he'd spend it with.

But lately, he'd been doing more and more thinking about his future. And those thoughts included Harmony.

She just . . . fit.

Then again, maybe he was crazy and just in lust with her.

Because she was always going to be Drake's sister. And after Drake overreacted last night to some random asshole putting his hands on Harmony, how was he going to respond when he found out about Barrett and Harmony being together?

Hell, Barrett knew Drake. He'd lose it. That wasn't a conversation he was keen to have with his best friend anytime soon.

Yet eventually, he'd have to have it.

Unless he and Harmony broke up. Then he and Drake would never have to have that conversation.

You are not that much of a coward, are you, Cassidy?

That was a question he didn't want to ponder this morning.

Barrett's phone buzzed on the bedside table. He picked it up and walked into the living room.

"Hey, Dad."

"We're getting ready to head back to the ranch. You and Flynn up?"

He had no idea where Flynn was. "Yup."

"Okay. We'll meet you back at home."

"You got it. See you in a bit."

He clicked off and went into the bedroom. Harmony was up, sitting on the side of the bed. "Your parents?"

"Yeah. The convoy is ready to head back to the ranch."

"And I need to get back to my room before my mother gets there."

"Okay."

He laid his coffee cup down and went to her, pulling her into his arms for a kiss. When he drew away, he said, "I should have woken you up this morning by sliding my cock into you."

She smoothed her hands over his chest, then backed away. "Yes, you should have. Because now I have to go."

He rubbed his body against hers, and his erection was, as it always was around Harmony, instantaneous. "Dammit."

She pulled him toward her, toward the bed, and lay down on it. "Though you could probably make me come in about a minute."

He loved that she was always up for sex, that her sex drive matched his. He dropped his sweats and grabbed a condom, then drew her shorts down, spread her legs and slid inside of her. She always felt like hot silk, drawing him in, making him want to stay there forever.

But the clock was ticking and right now they needed to get out, fast, so he rocked against her, making her moan, giving her what she needed to get off. He lifted her tank top and sucked her nipples, taking her there faster. And when her pussy tightened around him, he was taut, tense and ready to go off. He just had to wait for Harmony.

She squirmed under him, fighting for her orgasm. He lifted up and rubbed his thumb over her clit.

"Oh, yes," she said, lifting toward his fingers. He swept them over her sex, giving her the friction she needed to climax.

"This what you need, baby?" he asked, sliding into her as he rubbed her.

"Yes. I need to come. Give me that cock."

She widened her legs and he drove in deep, grinding against her. Her eyes widened and she cried out with her orgasm. That was all he needed as he dropped down on top of her, thrusting hard and shuddering against her as her pussy spasmed around him. The first spurt was an explosion that rocketed out of him, making him arch his back and convulse all the way through his climax.

"Christ," was all he could manage as he came down from that exceptional high.

He gripped Harmony's hips, wanting to stay like this with her—connected to her—for the entire day.

But they didn't have the entire day. They disengaged, she grabbed her clothes, gave him a quick kiss and dashed out the door, leaving him to pack up. He texted Flynn, who told him he'd meet him downstairs in the lobby.

He was showered, checked out and at the SUV within twenty minutes. There were definite advantages to being a guy.

Flynn was leaning against the SUV, along with Drake, Tucker and Aubry. It looked like Harmony and her mother had gotten in one of the other cars.

"Waiting on you, man," Flynn said. "What the hell? Did you have to blow dry your hair?"

"You know me and my hair." That was all he was going to say, but as the rest of them crowded into the SUV, he pulled Flynn aside. "Thanks for last night."

"Not a problem. But you owe me one."

"I do."

It took them about an hour to get back to the ranch. The other cars were already there. Barrett grabbed his bag and took it up to the room he was sharing with Flynn. He left the bag on the bed, and went in search of something cold to drink.

Mom was in the kitchen, making iced tea.

He grabbed a muffin from the bag on the counter and downed it in two bites.

"Hungry?" she asked with a laugh.

"A little," he managed after he swallowed.

"Thirsty, too?"

"Now I am."

"Why don't you cut up some lemons? I'm almost finished here."

He got out the cutting board, pulled two lemons out of the fridge and grabbed the knife. By the time he'd sliced them, his mother had the tea poured into two large pitchers.

"Where is everyone?"

She leaned her hip against the counter. "Your dad is out back with the guys working on that old car of his. The women are all over at the house where Katrina is staying. She just got photo proofs from her last shoot, so they're over there ogling."

"I see." He went to the cabinet and got two glasses down, pouring one for his mother and one for him.

"Thank you," she said.

"Great party last night, Mom."

She smiled. "I thought so. How's Harmony this morning?"

He tried not to cough as he took a long swallow of iced tea. "I didn't see her this morning. She rode back in another car."

"Son, I'm not as blind to things as you'd like to think I am. And I have a pretty good idea who slept where last night."

He pulled up a chair at the island. "Oh, you do, huh?"

"Yes. You also didn't come back to the party last night, and you're not one to miss a good time, unless there was something that held you at the hotel. Like Harmony."

Leave it to his mother to know what was what. "Okay."

"So how long has this been going on?"

"Awhile."

"I like her, Barrett."

"I like her, too."

"The fact that she's Drake's sister, though. He obviously doesn't know what's going on between the two of you."

The lawyer in his mother had never dissipated. She was still adept at ferreting out the truth, even when it wasn't stated. "No, he doesn't."

She sat quietly for a few minutes, sipping her tea, no doubt deep in thought, because that was his mother. "Is that going to be a problem between you and Drake?"

"I don't know yet. Maybe. I hope not. I don't really know how things with Harmony and me are going to play out, which is why I haven't mentioned it to Drake yet. Or his mother. We're trying to keep things just between the two of us for now."

"So you're keeping this secret from everyone." Her mother gave him that look, the one he'd gotten hundreds of times as a kid when he'd done something bad. The one that used to make him *really* uncomfortable.

"Yeah."

"Are you sure that's a good idea? Secrets have a tendency to explode in your face at the worst possible time, Barrett."

"I've got this under control, Mom."

Again, that look. "I don't want you to get hurt. I don't want Harmony to get hurt."

Not the first time he'd heard that. "Just trust me to do what's right."

"How does Harmony feel about all of this?"

He could have lied to his mother, but she always knew when he did that. "She's not totally on board with the idea. She'd much prefer we were out in the open, but after Drake's display last night, she's agreeable with waiting for the right time to tell him. To tell everyone."

"And when do you think this supposed perfect time will be?"

"We're about to start training camp. I don't want to piss him off right now."

"Do you really think telling Drake you're dating his sister is going to make him mad?"

"Yes. He's very overprotective of Harmony. He always has been. You know what it was like for them as kids. No father around, and Drake felt like he had to step up and help out Mama Diane, act as father figure as well as older brother to Harmony. He hasn't yet come to grips with the fact she's a woman."

"So maybe Harmony needs to be the one to talk to him."

"She's tried. I'm hardly the first guy she's dated. Believe me, I've seen his overreaction before. And I don't want to drive a wedge in my friendship with him. He and I are tight as teammates as well as friends. This isn't the time to rock the boat."

"Is that friendship or fear talking?"

Leave it to his mother to dig deep. "Maybe a little of both."

She went quiet again, sipped her tea, occasionally looked over at him, then finally sighed. "You're an adult and I'm going to assume you and Harmony know what you're doing. But be careful. I'd hate to see you lose both your best friend and the woman you care about."

"Thanks, Mom. I'll be careful."

He ended up hanging out in the kitchen with his mother to help her prepare lunch. Mia wandered in, as well as the rest of the women, and suddenly conversation turned to Katrina's photos, which she shared with Barrett's mother. Then his father came in, so he hightailed it out of there to follow his dad and his uncles out to the barn to check out the horses.

He'd escaped one of his mother's famous inquisitions, coming away mainly unscathed.

But she'd raised some valid concerns, just as his brothers had. He knew he was going to have to talk to Drake sometime.

That time just wasn't now. And he damn well didn't have any idea when the right time would be.

But he would figure it out.

They all ate a great lunch. Barrett kept his distance from Harmony, though their gazes occasionally collided, and he couldn't help but pin her with a smile. He tried to keep it innocuous, but it was getting harder and harder to do that. She looked sexy as hell in her yellow sundress, and all he could think about was her skin, and how he felt when he touched her.

After lunch he went outside on the porch with Drake.

"I'm sorry about last night," Drake said. "You know I would never do anything to embarrass you or your family."

"It's okay."

"It's not okay. I apologized to your parents last night and again this morning. My mama was not happy with me."

His lips curved. "Which means you got an earful."

Drake smiled. "Like you would not believe, man. Her lectures are lengthy—and loud."

"Been there a few times myself. I feel your pain. But don't worry about it. You were looking out for Harmony."

Drake took a long swallow of his beer. "Like always."

"But I have to tell you, Drake—she can look out for herself just fine."

"Part of me knows that, and the other part of me just feels like I'm always going to have to watch out for her. No matter how independent she is, no matter how grown-up she is, I can't just walk away from her and let her go. She's my baby sister and I'd die if someone hurt her."

How was he supposed to respond to that? "I know. But cut her a little slack, you know? She makes good choices."

"Does she? What about Levon? What about David? What about Jamal? None of those losers treated her right."

"Well, maybe someday the right guy will come along, and you'll have to give her credit for choosing the right man."

Drake grinned. "Maybe I should choose a man for her."

"Oh right. And who would that be?"

Drake took a long pull of his beer. "Hell if I know. I don't think any man is good enough for her."

"Not even me?"

Drake laughed. "Especially not you."

Well, shit.

THIRTY-ONE

WITH VACATION AT AN END, IT WAS TIME FOR WORK TO begin.

Barrett had reported for training camp a week ago. Rookies had already been there two weeks prior. He remembered what that nightmare was like his rookie season. An entire month of not only not knowing what the hell he was doing, but grueling, daylong practices and meetings until his head spun.

He was glad he at least knew the playbook, unlike the rookies. Now it was more a case of meetings with their defensive coach, shaking off the dust and getting his body and mind ready for the season.

Truth told, he'd been geared up and ready for months now. He and Drake and many of the defensive players did workouts together at least three times a week, working with a trainer to keep them in shape during the off-season.

He'd never felt better, and never more prepared for a season.

He and Drake stood on the field now. They weren't in pads today, which meant they couldn't lay down hits, but they could run the defensive drills, check out what their team looked like this year.

From man-to-man to zone coverage, they'd looked solid the past week going through every play. Running through daily films, they had looked good. Rookie pickups had been excellent, and they caught on fast. Preseason play was coming soon, and Barrett wasn't sure he'd ever been as confident in the defense as he was this year.

Today they were running drills with the offense. No full contact, which was typical for some days at training camp, but they'd at least get the running and the plays in, to know where they were supposed to be. Good practice for their quarterbacks and receivers, too, since, in Barrett's opinion, they'd be playing against one of the best defenses in the league.

He went toe-to-toe with their wide receiver Trevor Shay on a long pass from JW Zeman, their quarterback. Barrett stayed in step and batted the pass away.

"Fuck me," Shay said, as they ran it off.

"Sucking a little wind there, Shay?" Barrett asked.

Trevor laughed. "Bite me, Cassidy. I'll burn you on the next one."

"We'll see."

Shay burned him on the next one.

"Asshole," Barrett said, as Trevor trotted back with the ball in his hand and a grin on his face.

"Wanna see me do it again?"

"Fuck off, Shay."

Trevor laughed.

They trotted back to the line, and this time Drake dropped back in zone coverage, Zeman threw the pass and Drake covered it for an incomplete pass.

At the break, they were called in for a meeting with Allen Quarles, their defensive coordinator. They went over the plays from the previous day and watched films, then had lunch and had some free time.

Barrett met up with Drake at the lounge area.

"Feeling good?" Drake asked.

"Like lightning in a bottle."

Drake grinned. "Yeah, me too. Ready for camp to be done. First preseason game next week. We have a practice game against Miami tomorrow. I can't wait."

"Me, either. Defense is solid and I think we're going to kick ass this season."

"We're going to kick Pittsburgh's ass in game one, that's for sure.

"At home. I'm ready to hear the crowd noise."

As they made their way back outside, Drake slapped him on the back. "Gonna be loud."

"And we're gonna give them a win, start the season off right and kick some ass."

"Hell yeah, brother."

This was what Barrett loved about football season, about his friendship with Drake. They were in sync, they were ready to play, and together, they could do anything.

Including kick some serious ass.

Now was the time for football season.

THIRTY-TWO

HARMONY WAS NERVOUS AS SHE STOOD IN BARRETT'S house waiting for him to show up. The transformation had been tremendous.

She'd spent the past week putting the finishing touches on his house. She and Barrett had shopped together and though he'd told her he really hated shopping, he'd given her free rein to pick and choose everything from living room furniture to nearly everything in the bedrooms. He told her he was going to rent out his condo furnished, so everything in this house was going to be new.

She'd never had more fun shopping. He'd probably had a lot less fun, but he'd been a great sport about it. They'd spent many nights after his long days of practice at furniture showrooms.

But, at least to her, it had all been worth it. As she walked around, she could see him occupying the spaces.

Walls were in place, drywall and paint had been completed, as had flooring and the entire kitchen.

The house didn't look at all the same as it had when she'd first walked in all those weeks ago. Of course, that didn't surprise her in the least. Jeff and his team were miracle workers. And she was happy with her design choices. With all the new furniture in place, from artwork to pillows to the flowers on the kitchen table, this home had her personal touch all over the place. But she'd also kept in mind who Barrett was, and she hoped she knew him well enough by now to know his likes and his dislikes, and who he was as a person. That always reflected on her design choices. Barrett was a man—definitely all man. Nothing frilly or fancy for him. But she also wanted the home to be aesthetically pleasing.

She hoped Barrett approved.

She heard his car pull up in the driveway, so she smoothed her hands over her dress, fluffed her hair, then went to the front door and opened it.

She stepped outside, smiling at him as she pulled the door shut behind her.

He cocked his head to the side. "It's not ready?"

"It's absolutely ready."

"Then why are we outside?"

"I'm just . . . delaying."

"Because . . ."

"I'm a little nervous, Barrett."

His brows raised. "You? Nervous? This is a first. Come on, gorgeous, show me what you've done."

"Before we go in, I want you to know if there's anything— anything at all—that you don't like, we can change it. It won't hurt my feelings at all."

He reached around her and turned the knob, then brushed his lips across hers. "I'm sure it's going to be great. Let's go take a look."

Since he'd pushed the door open, she had no choice but to take a deep breath and follow him inside. She closed the door and stood at the entry, waiting for him to take his first look at the remodeled living room.

It was now open and expansive, the once formal living area now not so formal. They'd redone the fireplace so it was more modern with stone, and a TV was mounted above it. Two sofas sat across from each other, with plenty of seating for guests. The room now had French doors that led out to the sunroom. Barrett didn't say anything, just walked through the doors and into the sunroom.

Biting her bottom lip, Harmony followed him.

"Wow," he finally said. "I like this room."

She grinned. "I thought you might."

The sunroom had been created to provide a play area when the weather wasn't so great outside. There was a bar set off to the side, a TV mounted on the wall, tables and chairs at both ends, along with a pool table that would double as a Ping-Pong table. It was a true entertainment area. And beyond the sunroom was the backyard.

"I love the yard," Barrett said, as he stepped through the door.

"I do, too," she said, moving next to him. "I think the landscaper did a great job with planting tall trees and bushes near the hot tub and against the house and surrounding the pool to afford privacy, but still providing enough of an opening so you'll be able to see the water from the family room."

He nodded. "It's perfect."

So far, so good.

They went back in through the sunroom and French doors, then continued through the living room and into the dining room, where there was a large solid wood table big enough to fit the entire Cassidy family and then some.

Barrett swept his fingertips along the table as they walked by.

"I remember choosing this table. I really like it. My dad will like it. And my mom will love these chairs with the pattern on the cushions." He turned to her. "But it's not fussy, so I like it, too."

Her lips curved. Score another one for the dining room.

They made their way into the kitchen, which was one of Harmony's favorite rooms.

Now she saw Barrett really smile. "Yeah, this is totally different, isn't it?"

"Yes. I love the gray granite countertops and the dark wood cabinetry," she said. "Plus, the appliances are all killer. I would love to cook at that six-burner stove."

"I think putting the wine fridge in here was a good idea," he said, opening it up and grinning at the wine stock. "I'm glad you fought me for it."

"I think you'll be happy it's here."

"I'm happy the whole thing is here. It was such a big kitchen, but man it was ugly before. Now it's awesome. I really like the island with all the seating. Good place to throw a party."

She laughed. "Barrett, your entire house is a good place to throw a party now."

"True. I guess I'll have to have one, then."

"I guess you will. Are you ready to head upstairs?"

He nodded, and she followed him upstairs. Two of the three spare bedrooms had been redone with tile floors that looked like wood, as was the rest of the house. It would be perfect for the weather and people coming in with wet feet from the pool. For the spare bedrooms, Barrett had decided on queen beds. The other bedroom had been turned into an office for Barrett. He'd chosen the one with a view of the water, and they'd decided on built-in furniture that fit the room, but left the closet intact so that at any point he could convert the room back into a bedroom.

In the master bedroom, there was plenty of space for a nice, king-sized bed, and still room for two chairs and a sitting area.

"Wow," he said, noting the light coming in. "Widening and lengthening the windows made all the difference. Now with the French doors leading out to the deck, there's an amazing amount of light in this room. And I'm glad we went with the shutters. Like you, I want it dark in here when I sleep."

"I'm so glad you like it." She was beyond happy, actually. He hadn't once mentioned anything about the décor or the renovation that he disliked.

And when he walked into the master bathroom, he took a deep breath, then let it out. "You were so right about this shower, Harmony. I'm going to love this."

"I agree. I'm actually kind of jealous of that steam shower, Barrett. Steam, multiple showerheads, single spray or multifunction, multiple jets . . ."

"I love when you talk dirty."

She laughed.

He put his arm around her and tugged her against him. "Do you think you won't be using it? Or any other room in this house? It's not like I've been using you for design skills, and now that the house is done I intend to dump you."

Her heart leaped. "So, I don't have to worry about being kicked to the curb now that you're moving in here?"

He laughed. "No. I already have thoughts of dragging you into that oversized shower with me."

He pulled her toward the shower, but she placed her hands very firmly on his chest. "Oh, no. No shower for me. I have a client appointment this afternoon."

He bent and nuzzled her neck, making chill bumps break out on her skin. "Cancel it."

She clutched his shoulders, her body pulsing with sudden need. "So what you're saying is that a walk-through of your new place was a turn-on?"

"No. Walking next to you while you're wearing that hot dress is a turn-on."

He kissed her and she fell into the taste of him, the way his mouth always worked a dizzying array of magic on her senses. She'd been pent up this week, focused on nothing but work. So had Barrett, and they hadn't spent any time together. She missed his mouth on her, the way he always touched her when he kissed her, the way he made her melt all over.

He swept his hands over her dress, then lifted it, cupping her butt. He picked her up and carried her to the bed, laying her down on it.

"What do you say we christen this nice new house the proper way?"

Her lips curved. "Appointment, Barrett."

He bent and licked the curve of her breasts. "I'd rather not make an appointment with you for sex, Harmony. How about I make you come instead?"

The business side of her wanted to object, but then he lifted her dress, drew down her panties and planted his mouth on her sex. The business side of her dissolved in a puddle. Now, she was simply a woman who craved the release her man could give her.

She fisted the comforter in her hands, disregarding the care she'd taken in smoothing out every possible wrinkle. At this moment she only cared about his mouth, his lips and his tongue, and the way he glided smoothly along her clit and pussy, making her clench and lift against him as she catapulted her way toward orgasm.

And when it hit, she arched and cried out, her entire body

shaking from the cataclysm of her climax that had been denied for too long.

Barrett stood, grabbed a condom out of his pocket and unzipped his pants. He pulled her to the edge of the bed and slid inside of her in one smooth motion.

Still quaking with aftershocks of that incredible orgasm, her pussy vibrated around his cock.

Barrett leaned over the bed, bracing his hands on either side of her. His soft gaze penetrated her as he stilled his movements, making her quiver with unexpected emotion.

"When I'm inside you like this, I feel like I never want to let go of you. I could stay like this forever."

She blinked back the tears that welled in her eyes, unsure of what to say in response.

She was in love with him, and the emotion tore at her. With Barrett buried deep inside of her, she knew with one hundred percent certainty that he was the only man for her, and always would be.

But she didn't know if what he was talking about was love, or just sex. So she wasn't going to tell him how she felt.

He began to move within her, easing in and out of her so slowly it was unbearable in the sweetest, most torturous way. She felt every inch of him, and when he pushed in all the way, burying himself deep and grinding against her to rub his body against her clit, she moaned.

"I love those sounds you make," he said. "They make my cock even harder. They make me want to fuck you hard and come in you."

She met his gaze, giving him a slight tilt of her lips. "Wasn't this supposed to be a quickie?"

He grinned down at her. "Yeah, but I can't seem to do it fast when I'm with you. I want to linger, to feel you for as long as I can. To watch you when you come."

He brushed his fingers lightly over her clit, making her gasp. "Yes. Make me come again, Barrett."

"I want you to remember this first time at my house, Harmony. Remember this first time in my bed. No man will ever make you come like this."

She already knew that. His voice was embedded in her heart, his body was enmeshed with hers. There was no one else for her. There could be no one else for her, because she loved him. And as he moved within her and used his fingers to take her to the very height of reason, she fell, his name spilling from her lips as she came.

He dropped down over her and kissed her, pistoning his cock faster and faster, prolonging her climax and making her moan against his lips. And when he groaned with his orgasm, it only heightened hers more.

After they caught their breath, he kissed her, a deep, soul-shattering kiss that made her tremble. He broke the kiss and met her gaze. "Sorry for the lack of a quickie."

She smiled. "I don't think you're sorry at all."

He held out his hand and lifted her off the bed. "You're right. I'm not."

She dashed into the bathroom to clean up, then straightened her dress, which fortunately would de-wrinkle in the Tampa humidity.

They went downstairs, where, unfortunately, there was nothing to drink. She'd stop somewhere before her next appointment and grab something cold.

"So you really like the house?" she asked.

"I really love the house. I'll move in over the next couple of days. I'm already packed."

"I'm so glad."

He pulled her into his arms and kissed her, this time a long, lingering kiss that was warm and tender and made her want to cancel her appointments for the rest of the day so she could stay with him.

But she had a job to do. So she pulled away. "I've gotta go."

"Yeah, me too. You're coming to the game Sunday afternoon, right?"

"Of course. Mama and I wouldn't miss it. And I expect you to slay the opponent."

He grinned. "I intend to."

She wanted to say the words. They hovered on the tip of her tongue. But she didn't.

"I'll see you later, Barrett."

"Okay."

BARRETT HEADED BACK TO HIS CONDO. HE'D SPENT the past few days packing up the things he was going to take over to the house.

He was just about finished taping up all the boxes. As he looked over the condo, he realized he was not going to miss it. Especially after seeing the renovated new house.

Harmony had done a great job. From the art on the walls to the sheets on the bed, it was perfect, and just as he wanted it.

Now he just had to convince her to move in with him.

She was independent, and it was one of the things he loved about her. So she might not go for it.

First things first, though. He'd have to have that long-put-off conversation with Drake. Once that was out of the way, he could move forward with Harmony.

He wanted her in his life. In his bed. In his future.

He was in love with her. He didn't want to spend any more nights without her.

He just had to get through this first preseason game, and have that talk with Drake.

And then he'd have a big conversation with Harmony about their future.

THIRTY-THREE

IT WAS THE FIRST PRESEASON GAME. BARRETT ALWAYS felt like he'd waited forever for the season to start. Now it was here, and he was damn ready for it.

Drake gave him a crooked smile as they dressed for the game. "Defense is gonna dominate today."

"You know it."

"Then we're gonna take the season."

Barrett was pumped, and he felt the adrenaline rush from his teammates.

They gathered for a team meeting and their coach gave them a pep talk, told them what to watch out for in terms of the other team's defense and offense. Then it was time to take the field.

About damn time. Barrett had all this pent-up energy, and he was ready to expend it on some offensive players.

He had a feeling this was going to be a good game. And it was going to end in their favor.

As they waited in the tunnel, he thought about his family, always behind him. The Cassidys were a dynasty. Barrett was proud to be a part of that dynasty.

Tucker had been the first one to text him this morning to wish him luck, and then added: *Not that you need it.*

He'd smiled. Coming from Tucker, that had been one hell of a compliment, since they mostly insulted each other. But when it came to the sports they played, they always had each other's backs when it was game time.

Flynn had his own first game today. San Francisco was playing Detroit on the road. Flynn had texted him last night and told him he'd better win and not besmirch the family name. That had made him laugh. He'd wished Flynn luck, too, and told him they were both going to kick ass.

Grant wouldn't play until Monday night, a home game in St. Louis. Grant had texted him this morning as well. He told him he'd be watching the game on TV and he'd better not fuck up.

He loved his brothers. Pains in the asses, all of them, but he loved them all.

His parents had called him this morning to wish him luck. His little sister, Mia, had also called, kept the call short and said she'd be watching the game from one of the sports bars in her college town in Texas.

Harmony had called him first thing this morning. She'd had a late client meeting, so they hadn't seen each other last night, and he had to be game ready anyway. But she'd called him, wished him luck and told him she'd be rooting for him and for Drake and the entire team.

Then she'd paused, as if there was something else she wanted to say. He'd waited, but then she said good luck again and she'd see him later.

He wondered what she had on her mind, but he put it aside. Game day was the only thing he needed to have on his mind today.

He was pumped and ready as he waited in the tunnel.

"Man, it seems like forever since we were in uniform," Drake said.

"Right? I hate off-season. I'm ready for this shit to get real."

"I'm down with you, brother," Drake said, the two of them bumping fists.

The other guys around them slapped hands with them.

Their teammates were pumped up. They were all ready to get this season started.

First home game always gave Barrett goose bumps. Crowd noise was escalating as they were announced and ran out of the tunnel to the raucous cheers from the full stadium. It fueled his momentum as he and his teammates took the field.

Now it was time to get down to business.

After the coin toss, Tampa had the ball first, which meant Barrett would have to wait to take the field.

"Man, I hate this," Drake said. "I mean, yeah, good for Zeman and crew. Let's put some points up. But . . . ya know?"

Barrett read and fed off Drake's anxiety and nodded. "I know, man. I know."

They both paced the sidelines, watching the offense get started. Zeman marched his offense down the field. Running game got off the ground and Zeman connected on several short and long passes.

Receivers looked good. Backs looked solid. Offense ended up scoring seven on a short run from the six-yard line.

Outstanding.

Now it was their turn to show their stuff.

After the kickoff, Pittsburgh had a short ten-yard return. Tampa's defense took the field.

They assumed a run and lined up for man coverage.

It was a run. Barrett hustled in to help with the tackles, and Tampa's linebackers made the tackle after only three yards.

In the huddle, Barrett said, "He's going to pass. I think he's going to throw up a long one. Drake and I will go deep."

He told the corners to play their receivers and the linebackers they needed to push hard on their blocks.

They got into position and at the snap, Barrett did what he'd been trained to do—he read the quarterback.

Gregson—Pittsburgh's quarterback—dropped back and looked right, then threw long.

Barrett dug in and went after the receiver and the ball, knocking it out of the receiver's hands just before the catch.

Incomplete.

The crowd roared its approval.

Pittsburgh went three and out without a first down, so they had to punt and Tampa got the ball back.

He and Drake made their way back to the sideline. Drake bumped fists with him.

"That's how it's done," Drake said.

Barrett nodded.

That had been satisfying. Now they just had to keep on doing it.

Tampa didn't score on their offensive series. On the next defensive series, Gregson threw on first down, this time caught by their tight end for a short gain. Tampa's cornerback was right there on the tackle.

Pittsburgh managed to march down the field and got a couple of rushing first downs, but Tampa's defense held them. Five minutes in, Tampa was still up seven to nothing.

Defense was looking solid. They had to keep Pittsburgh out of the end zone.

Barrett was going to make sure the defense made that happen.

* * *

HARMONY CAME DOWN THE STAIRS, JUGGLING DRINKS and snacks while simultaneously trying to watch the game. She scooted her way past the other patrons in her row, finally taking her seat next to Mama.

"Did I miss anything?" she asked, as she handed off a soda and hot dog to her mother.

"Drake batted down a pass," Mama said, setting the hot dog in her lap. "Then Pittsburgh ran for eight yards and a first down."

"Well, darn. Okay. But still no score, so that's good."

"Yeah."

Harmony took a sip of her soda and set it in the cup holder, and was about to pick up her hot dog when Pittsburgh's quarterback threw a pass. When Drake stepped in front of the receiver and intercepted the pass, she screamed.

So did Mama. So did the entire stadium. Drake took off in the opposite direction, heading for the goal line.

She held tight to her mother's hand, hollering Drake's name and mainly screaming as she watched her brother outrun the other team all the way into the end zone.

"Yes!" she yelled. "Oh, my God, yes!"

She finally caught her breath and sat down when their kicker came out to kick the extra point.

"That was amazing." She turned and grinned at her mother, who grinned back like any proud mother would.

"It definitely was."

They were seated in the family section, where they always sat, so Tina, one of the player's wives, turned around and grasped Mama's hand. "Oh, Diane, you must be so proud of Drake. We were all screaming."

Mama laughed. "I was screaming, for sure."

"Defense looks killer," Tina said. "I know we're still in the first quarter of the first preseason game, but I think we're going to kick some serious butt this year."

"I hope so," Harmony said.

And it seemed like defense was pretty impressive, at least so far. At the end of the first quarter, Tampa was up fourteen to nothing. Most of the starters would come out and second stringers and rookies would get a chance to play now.

She finally relaxed her shoulders. "I feel like I've been holding my breath the entire first quarter. I think I'll spend the rest of the game just breathing."

Mama grabbed her hand and squeezed. "It's all going to be okay. Our boys look great. They're gonna win this one, baby."

She hoped so. She knew how much football meant to Drake. He'd worked so hard all his life to provide for her and for Mama. And he'd made a success of himself. He looked so damn good out there.

So did Barrett, though she'd never say that to her mother. Or anyone else, for that matter.

Maybe Alyssa. She confided everything to her best friend, but Alyssa had an out-of-town trip today, so she couldn't make the game.

Which meant Harmony had to ogle Barrett in silence.

He looked fine today out there in his uniform, which was stretched tight over his gorgeous muscles. The man was truly ripped and it was all she could do to concentrate on the game.

Everyone in the family boxes thought she was there to cheer on her brother. Which she was, of course. But she couldn't help but let her focus drift to Barrett. He was fast and strong and the way he'd barreled into the opposing players made her clench in ways that turned her on.

And she knew that in the preseason they weren't going to press as hard as they would once the regular season started. This was more like a practice game.

Still, Barrett had looked hot. Formidable. Exciting.

Of course, everything about him excited her. All the time. Every day.

She should be used to it by now.

But getting turned-on by Barrett was not a typical response at a football game. Then again, her reactions to Barrett had never been typical. From the first time they'd been alone together, he'd lit the torch on her passions.

It had been an out-of-control wildfire ever since.

"Girl, you are miles away," her mother said.

She'd been thinking about tonight, when she'd see Barrett.

"Sorry. Work is on my mind."

"Well, get your head out of work and onto this game."

"Yes, ma'am."

She had to focus. So she did. On the gorgeous man she was in love with.

And someday very soon everyone would know Barrett was hers.

THEY'D WON THE GAME. EVEN BETTER, DEFENSE HAD held Pittsburgh at the goal line twice, leaving them without a score, even though first string had been out of the game after the first quarter. Their backup players had done well.

Barrett was as pumped up postgame as he'd been before. They all were.

But they also knew this was just the first game. The first preseason game. They had three more preseason, then sixteen regular season games to prove themselves.

Which they would. Barrett had a good feeling about this season.

"Okay, gather round," Coach George McGill said.

They moved to the center of the locker room.

"This was a good start. I'm proud of all of you. We'll set up on Tuesday with game films and practice. Until then, enjoy your time off. You earned it. We're going to take this season and we're gonna take it hard. Now bring it in."

They put hands in and yelled their victory call of "Hawks!"

Barrett showered and went to his locker to get dressed.

"Man, that was a good game," Drake said, raking his fingers through his dark, curly hair.

"Hell yes it was."

"Feel like celebrating tonight?"

Shit. "Uh, I've got something to do."

Drake grinned at him. "Got a date?"

He absolutely had a date. "More like a prior obligation, unfortunately."

Drake nodded. "Okay. Catch up with you later, then. I'm going to grab some of the boys and have a nice, juicy steak."

"Steak sounds good. You celebrate for me, too, okay?"

"You know it." He slapped hands with his best friend.

His best friend. The one he'd just lied to.

He was going to try really hard not to think about that when he was alone with Harmony tonight.

He went back to his house to change clothes. He'd texted Harmony about picking her up at her place. Then they'd go out to dinner. He fielded a few calls while he was home, including one from his parents. Mainly his dad wanted to rehash the game with him. He was always up for talking about the game, so he spent some time on the phone talking to both parents. Mom told him how proud she was, and Dad went over specific plays and high-lighted how he could have done better.

That always made him laugh. He knew his dad was proud because that was always the last thing he said before he hung up.

"Damn fine game, Barrett," his dad said, right before "I love you."

He had a great father. Someday he'd do the same thing with his kids.

Someday. When he had kids.

As he was changing clothes, his phone rang again.

It was his brother Grant.

"Shitty game," Grant said.

He laughed. "Yeah. Pretty awful, huh?"

"Seriously, your team looks good this season. Not as good as mine, though. Sucks for you."

His lips curved. "We'll see about that, won't we?"

"We will. Too bad we don't play each other this season."

"That is too bad. I'd hate to have to intercept all those passes you throw."

"Yeah, you wish. Nobody intercepts me."

Barrett rolled his eyes. "I seem to recall that game last season against Baltimore where you threw three interceptions—"

"You're such a dick, Barrett."

Barrett laughed, then heard a click and looked at his phone.

Grant had hung up on him.

He laughed again and threw his phone on the bed so he could finish changing clothes.

After he got ready, he got in his SUV. He stopped at a flower shop and picked up something for Harmony.

When she opened the door, her eyes widened.

"You got me an orchid?"

He smiled. "I thought about a bouquet of flowers, but you're special. And beautiful. And when I saw the orchid I thought of you."

She laid her hand over her heart. "Barrett. This is lovely. Thank you." She leaned in and kissed him.

Obviously he'd chosen well. "I'm glad you like it. I realized I'd never brought you flowers."

She took the orchid and laid it on her kitchen counter, then turned to face him. "You realize I've never had the expectation that you would bring me flowers. Or anything else for that matter."

"I know that." He stepped over to her and swept his hand down her hair. "But I do want you to know that I think about you, even when I'm not with you."

She breathed in deeply, then let it out. "That is the best thing a woman could ever hear from a man."

He smiled, then brushed his lips across hers. "Good to know."

"And if I wasn't absolutely starving, I'd show you how much I appreciate the gesture. However, hunger wins."

"Damn. Okay, let's get food."

He'd made a reservation at Eddie V's, one of his top five restaurants in the city. He already knew he wouldn't run into Drake here, since he knew where Drake would go to get his favorite steak.

They went inside and were seated at a table in the corner. They ordered drinks and their waiter brought the menu.

"You played so well tonight," she said. "You and the team must be so happy with how the game went."

"Thanks. We're just starting out, since it's the first game and we didn't get a lot of playing time. We have a few tweaks to make, but overall, it went well."

"On the road next week?"

"Yeah. We're in Dallas."

"I'll miss you when you're gone."

He loved the sincerity in her tone, and he knew she really

meant it. "I'll miss you, too. But we'll still see plenty of each other before I have to leave town."

She looked up from her menu. "And by that you mean we'll be naked."

He grinned. "I'm always hopeful for that part."

She laughed.

He looked over the menu. "Appetizer?"

Harmony looked up from the menu. "Yes. Absolutely."

He laughed. "You are hungry."

She smiled. "Yes. Absolutely."

Their waiter came over and they placed their orders, including the appetizer.

"Those batter-fried oysters can't come soon enough," she said.

He'd noticed he was getting looks from a group of college-age guys a few tables away, and when one of them got up and came over, he knew they were probably fans.

"Barrett Cassidy, right?"

"Yes."

"I'm really sorry to bother you, but would it be possible to get a picture with you?"

"Sure. Bring your friends over and we'll do a group shot."

"Awesome. It's my birthday and my buddies and I went to the game to celebrate. Great game, by the way."

"Thanks. And happy birthday."

The kid motioned for his friends to come over, and he took a selfie with them. Then he shook their hands.

"Thanks a lot, Mr. Cassidy," the kid said.

"You're welcome."

The kid snapped one more photo, this time of Barrett and Harmony, before hurrying back to his table.

Barrett frowned, paused.

"Barrett," Harmony said.

"He needs to delete that photo."

"Why? You invited him to take the picture."

"Not the one of you and me together."

"Awww, it was sweet of him. And for God's sake, sit down. Unless you intend to go sing the 'Happy Birthday' song to the kid."

Barrett sat, but he still wasn't happy about that photo. He turned to Harmony. "What if that kid puts that picture of us up on social media?"

Harmony slanted a very unhappy look in his direction. "What? Are you ashamed to be seen with me in public?"

"You know better than that. But stuff like that tends to get widely circulated."

"Oh, I see. And you haven't told my brother about us yet, so now you're worried."

"Yeah."

She took a sip of the wine the waiter had poured for her and just stared at Barrett.

"What?" he finally asked.

"Don't you think it's time we go public with our relationship? Because I'm damn tired of being your dirty little secret."

He reached for her hand. She snatched it away. He pulled it back and held it with both of his. "First, you have never been my dirty little secret and you never will be. I am proud to have you by my side and you know damn well the reasons we haven't had our relationship out in the open."

"Okay, fine. I might have overreacted."

Barrett picked up his glass of Jack and Coke and took two deep swallows. "Second, yes, I know. That conversation with Drake is long overdue."

"I'm not going to argue that point. And once you talk to Drake, then maybe you can stop worrying about you and me being seen together. Providing you intend to talk to my brother."

"I intend to talk to your brother."

"And when might that conversation occur?"

"I'll talk to him this week. I'll find the right time, get him alone and I'll tell him you and I are together."

"I'm glad to hear that. Because I want to tell everyone that you and I are in a relationship. Providing that's what we are."

His lips curved. "That's definitely what we are, babe."

She smiled back at him, and Barrett relaxed.

But Harmony was right. He was overdue to have that conversation with Drake, because the last thing he wanted was for Drake to hear about Harmony and him from someone else.

Dinner ended up being better than he imagined. He'd had the New York strip and lobster, and Harmony had the Chilean sea bass. He'd had a taste of her fish, which was melt in your mouth good and she'd tried some of his steak and lobster.

And now he was full and ready to get out of here. He signaled for the waiter, signed the check, and led Harmony out the door to the SUV.

"I'm so full," she said. "Thank you for dinner. It was amazing."

"You're welcome."

"We should go dancing or something. I feel like I need to work off a few thousand calories."

He looked over at her in her black silk dress. "Your body is gorgeous. And I have another idea."

"You do?"

"Yes."

"Care to share said idea?"

"Not yet."

He drove them back to his place and pulled his SUV in the garage, then went over to help her out.

"This is your idea?"

"Oh, it gets better."

He held the door for her while she walked in, then shut it behind him.

"How's everything in the house working out for you?" she asked as she laid her bag on the kitchen counter.

"The house is better than I could have ever imagined." He pressed a kiss to her bare shoulder. "You're incredible."

"Thank you."

He led her into the family room. "Do you want a glass of wine?"

"Sure."

He pulled a bottle of pinot gris out of the wine fridge, opened it and poured two glasses, carrying them over to the sofa where Harmony sat. He handed her a glass.

"Thank you."

He pulled the table closer, where the new checkerboard set sat. He knew she'd put it on the coffee table as a decoration piece. But it had been giving him ideas ever since he moved in.

"Have I mentioned how much I love this checkerboard?"

She arched a brow. "You do? It's a décor item I thought would fit the theme of the room."

"It does. And now we're going to play."

"We are? How fun. I used to love to play checkers. Though I haven't played in years."

He set his wineglass down on the end table. "But this is my own special form of the game. I like to call it Naked Checkers."

She laughed. "Naked Checkers?"

"Yes. Every time one of us jumps the other's checker, the loser has to remove something they're wearing."

Her lips curved in that sexy smile that never failed to make his dick twitch.

"Oh, I see. So basically it's strip checkers."

"Sort of. But with a twist."

"A twist?"

"Yes. After the article is removed, the other player gets to kiss, lick or suck any body part of their partner's they want to."

Harmony gave him a hot smile. "Ooh. This game just got interesting, Mr. Cassidy."

"I thought you might think so, Miss Evans. Are you ready?"

"Bring it. And hold on to your boxer briefs, because I'm about to strip you down."

"You'd like to think that, but I'm very competitive, Harmony. And I want to get you naked and lick you all over."

She lowered her chin, her eyes dark with promise and desire. "I'm not sure if the object of this game is to win or to lose."

He laughed. "I guess we'll find out, won't we?"

She nodded. "Let's do this."

They started the game, each of them strategic in their movements. But he captured her checker first.

"Okay, Harmony. You're up."

"So I am." She stood, and removed her silver bracelet, laying it on the end table.

He frowned. "I call foul on that."

She shrugged. "You only indicated I had to remove something I was wearing."

He sighed. "Okay, if that's how you wanna play it."

He got up, went over to her and grasped her shoulders. He pulled her close and licked her neck.

She moaned, and he went back to his side of the sofa.

She looked at him and said, "But it gave me goose bumps."

"Sorry. Part of the game."

"I'm not sure I like this game."

He grinned and they continued the game. He jumped another of her checkers, so she took off an earring.

"You're going to make me wish I wore jewelry."

She laughed. He leaned over and kissed her, a long, lingering kiss that made him want to pull her onto his lap and explore her with his hands. But those weren't the rules, so he had to pull back.

"Dammit, Barrett," she said, licking her lips.

Their moves continued, and she jumped one of his checkers. He took off a shoe, wriggling his toes at her.

She waggled her brows at him. "Incredibly sexy, Barrett."

"Just tempting you."

"Speaking of temptation." She got up and came over, sat on his lap and whispered in his ear. "You're driving me crazy."

Then she licked the shell of his ear. Chill bumps broke out on his skin and his cock rose up hard and fast.

Before he could grasp her, she'd moved off his lap and back to her spot on the sofa.

"Who made up this stupid game?" he asked.

She smirked. "You did."

The game wore on and Harmony lost her other earring, and both shoes.

He'd kissed her feet and licked her ear as well, figuring payback was good.

She frowned when he went back to his side of the sofa. "This is the worst game ever."

But he read the desire in her eyes, and his cock was painfully hard.

"At least you didn't wear a necklace tonight," he said. "Now you're out of jewelry and shoes."

"Yes. Whatever will I do next? Providing, of course, that I actually lose any more checkers."

"Oh, you will."

Except he lost the next two, which meant his other shoe, and his shirt.

"Shame you didn't wear socks tonight," she said. "Or jewelry of any kind."

"Yeah, I'm not a jewelry kind of guy."

She reached out and raked her nails lightly down his bare chest. "I'm fine with that. And you're running out of clothes."

When he'd lost his shoe, she'd kissed him, a long, passionate kiss that made his balls ache. After his shirt, she licked and sucked his nipple, making his cock feel like it was going to explode.

He was fast running out of patience when one of his checkers made it to the opposite side of the board.

"Crown me," he said with a wide grin. "And then take something off."

She did, and then she stood, sliding her hands under her dress and pulling the sexiest underwear he'd ever seen down her legs. It was black and sheer and barely a scrap of material and oh, fuck, he was going to come just looking at her take off her panties.

She dangled them in her fingers before dropping them on the table.

"Oh, fuck this game," he said, then dropped to his knees in front of her, lifted her dress and put his mouth on her pussy. He licked and sucked and breathed in her sweet, tart honey flavor like a man starving. He couldn't get enough of her.

"Oh, God, Barrett, yes," she said, resting her hand on his head. "Make me come. Make me scream."

There was nothing that got him off more than having his face buried in Harmony's sweet pussy, feeling her writhe and listening to her moan. She tasted like salty honey and his cock was so hard he wanted to take it out of his pants and stroke it while he licked her. He ached to be inside of her, where he always wanted to be. But right now, he wanted to make her come, wanted her out of her mind with an orgasm.

He slid a finger inside of her, then two, feeling her pussy squeeze around his fingers as she bucked against him.

"Dammit, Barrett. That's going to make me come."

He lifted his gaze to hers, to see her looking down at him. She had her dress bunched in her hands to hold it up so she could watch. Damn if that wasn't the hottest thing ever.

He wrapped one hand around her ass to bring her closer to his mouth, used the other to pump into her as he sucked her clit.

"Oh yes. Suck my clit. Make me come."

With a loud cry, she burst, coming all over his face. He licked her up, giving her what she cried out for as she bucked against him. Her pussy continued to spasm against his fingers. He needed to feel that on his cock.

He sent the checkerboard and all its pieces flying onto the area rug under the coffee table. He laid her down on the coffee table and unzipped his pants, pulling out his cock.

He leaned over her.

"Suck me. I need your mouth on my cock."

She grasped his shaft and opened her mouth. He fed her his cock, nearly dying at the feel of her hot mouth surrounding him. Just watching the slide of his shaft in between her sweetly painted lips was enough to make him want to jettison come all over her tongue. But he held back, because he wanted to be between her legs, spurting come into her pussy when he came.

Reluctantly he pulled his cock from between her lips, shuddering as he watched his hot, wet dick release from her mouth. He grabbed a condom, put it on, then picked Harmony up from the table. With her in his arms, he sat on the sofa, letting her straddle him.

"Now fuck us both and make us come."

Her eyes glittering with passion, she held his gaze, grasped his shoulders, then lifted her dress off and tossed it onto the sofa.

Her barely there black bra matched those sexy panties that had set him off earlier. He could see her nipples through the sheer fabric and he reached up, teasing each bud through the material of her bra.

She gasped, then hissed. "Yes. More."

He undid the front clasp of her bra and she shrugged it off, giving him access to her nipples. He pulled her forward and sucked one into his mouth. He needed to touch her, to taste her, to feel her, and as she slid down over his cock, he sucked her nipple harder, breathing in the whimpering sound she made as she began to rock.

She held him against her breast as she moved back and forth, then lifted up and down, torturing his cock in ways that made his balls tighten.

When she finally pulled back and popped her nipple out of his mouth, he'd never seen a woman look more beautiful. The deep dark bronze of her skin glowed in the overhead light. He wanted to lick every part of her, to touch every inch of her. She never looked away, always at him, and his cock swelled at the raw, sexual honesty in her eyes.

This was his woman, from her glorious black hair to her perfectly painted pink toenails. And no one would ever threaten that.

He lifted his hips and rubbed her clit. She dug her nails into his shoulders and cried out with her climax. He felt his own tunneling through every nerve ending and he let it loose, a wild spurt that seemed never ending as he poured everything he had into her. He grasped her hips and held on, rocking into her over and over again until he was emptied.

When he caught his breath, he picked her up and carried her into the downstairs bathroom. They cleaned up and got dressed, then he went into the living room to pick up the pieces of the checkerboard he'd tossed onto the floor.

Harmony kneeled on the floor to hand him a few checkers, her shoulder brushing his.

"Fun game," she said with a wry grin.

He kissed her. "I enjoyed it. Especially since I won."

She leaned back on her heels. "In what universe did you win that game?"

"It was obvious."

"I think not. You ended the game prematurely." She righted the game, then refilled their wineglasses. "Now we start over—regular checkers this time."

He took a long swallow of wine, then leaned over the board. "Sure, if you feel like losing again."

She slanted a glare at him. "Barrett, I'm going to kick your ass."

He laughed. "Game on."

THIRTY-FOUR

BARRETT HAD PUT OFF THAT IMPORTANT CONVERSA-
tion with Drake all week.

He couldn't put it off any longer.

They were at Mama Diane's house tonight for dinner. Tomorrow they'd leave for the road game against Dallas.

It was a light crowd tonight. Just Drake, him, Harmony and
her friend Alyssa, and a couple of the guys from the team. Mama
Diane's sisters weren't here, and neither were a few of her friends
who usually showed up.

It would be a good night to talk to Drake. They'd had awesome
practices all week. Drake was confident about the team and in a
really great mood.

Barrett figured now was the time. He was in love with Harmony and he needed to tell Drake so his relationship with the
woman he loved could be out in the open.

Hell, he needed to have that all important conversation with Harmony. He hadn't yet told her how he felt about her.

But first he had to get things straight with Drake.

He pulled Drake away from the crowd of other players. "Hey, Drake. I need to talk to you."

"Sure."

"Let's grab a couple of beers and step outside."

Barrett caught the concern on Harmony's face as he and Drake headed for the door, but he hoped Harmony didn't interfere. This was between Drake and him.

"What's up?" Drake asked, as he sat in the patio chair.

Barrett cradled his beer in his hands, trying to hide his nervousness. It was like asking permission to date a man's daughter. In a lot of ways, that was the case. Since Harmony didn't have a father, Drake was the closest thing to that, and had been since the two of them were kids.

"It's about Harmony."

"What about her?"

The words hung, and he didn't exactly know how to say them. "I've been seeing her."

Drake frowned. "What do you mean, you've been seeing her?"

"She and I . . . We've been seeing each other for a while now."

Drake laid his beer on the patio table. "What the hell are you talking about?"

"I'm in love with your sister, buddy."

"I don't understand. You're sleeping with Harmony?"

He'd blown right past the part where he'd admitted he was in love with her. And the tone of Drake's voice spelled trouble. Barrett stood. "It's not like that, man."

"Then you tell me what it is like. You tell me you've been seeing her. How long?"

"A couple of months."

He saw the anger tighten Drake's features. "A couple of months? And you didn't tell me about it? Why not?"

Drake's voice was getting louder, and Barrett knew his best friend well enough to read the escalation in it. "Because of the way you're acting pissed off about it right now."

"I'm pissed off about it because you didn't have the decency to tell me you wanted to date my sister when it first started. I thought we respected each other. What did you do? Start screwing her and decide if it didn't work out, no harm no foul? I didn't need to know?"

Shit. He reached out for his friend. "Drake. It's not like that."

Drake slapped his hand away. "Fuck you. It's exactly like that. I can't believe you. I thought we were friends."

Barrett mentally counted to ten. His friendship with Drake was important, and he didn't want to get into a fight with him, but Drake wasn't seeing things clearly.

"This is between Harmony and me. It always was. We wanted to keep it between us at the beginning. I'm sorry that hurts you. That's not what I intended."

"No, I know exactly what you intended. You intended to screw her, then screw over our friendship by not telling me you were seeing my sister. Hell, you didn't even ask me what I thought about it. What the hell, man?"

Barrett threaded his fingers through his hair. "It really was between Harmony and me. I'm telling you now."

"You're telling me too late."

Now Barrett was angry, and he knew it was the wrong thing, but goddammit, he didn't need to ask Drake's permission to date Harmony.

He stood. "Look. I know you're pissed, and you have a right to be because I should have talked to you about Harmony when things first started up between us. But I didn't need to ask your permission to see her."

He started to approach, and Drake shoved him.

And that was enough. Barrett shoved back.

He was trying so damn hard to keep his cool. "Come on, man. We don't need to get into this."

Drake had a fistful of his shirt in his hands. "Fuck you, Barrett. You know what? I trusted you, and I don't trust a lot of people. Damn you for violating that."

"You can fucking let go of me now."

The door flew open and everyone spilled out, from his teammates to Mama Diane to the last person he wanted out here— Harmony.

"Drake," Harmony said. "What the hell is wrong with you? Let him go."

Drake sent a scathing look to Harmony. "Stay out of this."

Their teammates got in the middle of them and pulled them apart.

"It's okay," Barrett said to them. "It's okay. We're okay."

"Leave me the hell alone," Drake said to the other guys.

But Harmony didn't leave him alone. She shoved at Drake's chest. "Are you out of your mind?"

"What is wrong with you, Drake?" Mama Diane asked. "Barrett is your best friend."

"Is he? Ask him what he did to Harmony."

Mama looked over at Barrett, then to Harmony. "What is he talking about?"

"Could we please not do this in front of . . . everyone?" Harmony asked.

"All of you, go inside," Mama Diane said, shooing them with her hands. "This is family business."

After she cleared the patio, she stood between Barrett and Drake. "Now, talk."

"He's screwing Harmony," Drake said.

Harmony rolled her eyes. "It's not like that, Mama."

"It's exactly like that," Drake said. "And it's been going on for months."

"I told you that's not how it is, Drake." God, this had been such a bad idea. He should have gone to Drake's house to have this discussion. They might have gotten into a brawl, but at least Harmony wouldn't be embarrassed. "What happened between Harmony and me shouldn't have been your business in the first place. I didn't need your permission to do anything with her."

Drake lunged for him, but Harmony stood between them. "This is ridiculous. It's not the Dark Ages. I do not need you to come between me and any man."

"He's not the right one for you," Drake said.

"Drake," Mama Diane said, her voice low and warning. "Mind your words."

"Really," Barrett said, deciding he'd had just about enough. "And what makes you think that?"

"Because any man who would screw his best friend's little sister has no honor. And she's just as bad as you."

And just about became more than enough. He moved around Harmony and went for Drake, pushing him against the wall and pinning him with sheer force of will and strength. "Do not ever fucking talk about Harmony that way again."

Drake threw a punch, connecting with Barrett's shoulder. He felt the shock of pain, and retaliated with a punch of his own to Drake's head. Drake shoved him hard and he fell, and suddenly Drake was on top of him.

He didn't hear anyone else. It was only him and Drake rolling around on the ground together, shoving each other but not getting any more punches in, since they both had death grips on each other.

He finally heard Mama Diane yelling, and suddenly their teammates were on them, pulling them apart.

The first thing he saw when he was pulled up off the ground was Harmony, tears streaming down her face. Her friend Alyssa had her arms wrapped around her.

Barrett pulled free of his teammates, but it wasn't Drake he wanted to go to. It was Harmony.

"Harmony," he said, but she took a step back.

Drake went toward her as well. "Hey, baby sis. Don't cry. This asshole isn't worth it."

She held up both hands and shook her head.

"Stop. I'm sick to death of both of you." She looked at Drake. "If you weren't so obsessively overprotective, Barrett and I wouldn't have had to hide our relationship this entire time and none of this would be happening."

Then she turned her attention on Barrett. "And if you weren't so afraid of ending your friendship with Drake, you might have actually had the balls to face him and tell him we were seeing each other.

"I don't even want to look at either of you right now."

She turned and went inside. Barrett saw her grab her purse, then she and Alyssa left.

Mama Diane turned to Drake. "For God's sake, Drake. What is wrong with you? Your sister is a grown woman more than capable of running her own life. You need to let it go. It's time to let *her* go. I'm ashamed of your behavior toward your sister and your best friend."

Then she turned to Barrett. "Harmony's right, you know. This is not the way someone who claims to care about my daughter should act. I know you love my son. No one has been a better friend to him than you have. But this."

Mama Diane shook her head. "You handled this whole situation poorly, Barrett. I'd like you to leave now, while I have a few more words with Drake."

He'd never once been asked to leave Mama Diane's house. He felt like someone had shot a hole in his heart.

For more reasons than one.

With a short nod, he walked inside, then out the front door, feeling like he'd just lost an entire family of people he loved.

And the woman he loved right along with them.

THIRTY-FIVE

BARRETT WENT HOME, BUT HE DIDN'T FEEL SETTLED. He needed to talk to Harmony.

He called her, but she didn't answer. He texted her, but she didn't answer his texts, either.

No way was he going to leave town tomorrow without seeing her, so he got in his SUV and drove over to her town house. When he knocked at the door, Alyssa answered.

"She doesn't want to talk to you right now, Barrett."

He inhaled, then let it out. "I just need five minutes."

Alyssa opened her mouth as if she had a very definite opinion about him needing five minutes, but then she just shrugged. "I'll ask her."

She shut the door in his face.

He waited, pacing the small front porch until the door opened again. This time, it was Harmony.

"What?"

Wow, she was really mad. He deserved it.

"I'm sorry. Can I come in?"

"No."

He raked his fingers through his hair. "Harmony, I don't want to do this on the porch. Please."

She sighed. "Fine."

She opened the door and he stepped in. Alyssa stood just behind Harmony, arms folded like a warrior bodyguard.

"Alyssa," Barrett said. "Can we have a minute, please?"

Alyssa looked over at Harmony, who gave her friend a short nod.

"I'll be upstairs. You holler if you need me."

Alyssa gave him a look that told him not to upset her best friend, then went upstairs.

"Can we sit down?" Barrett asked.

"I'd rather stand. Plus, you're not staying long."

Okay, so it was going to be like that.

"I'm sorry. I picked the wrong time and place to talk to Drake."

"You think? You knew he wasn't going to react well, and to do it in front of my mother?"

"I know. I need to have a conversation with your mother—to apologize to her."

"No, I'll have a conversation with my mother. I think you've done enough."

"Fine. Then I'll talk to Drake."

"Right. Because that went so well the first time."

He threw up his hands. "What do you want me to do, Harmony?"

"I don't want you to do anything. No, what I want you to do is turn back the clock, man up and tell my brother we were together when we were first together, like you should have."

"You know that wasn't the right time."

"Why wasn't it the right time? Because you just wanted to fuck me then, and if it didn't work out, then your friendship with Drake wouldn't have been tested? What about me, Barrett? What about my feelings? You've been hiding me away like some ugly secret for months now, and I've gone along with it because I thought you and I might have something worth working toward. But you know what? I'm done with that. And I'm done with you."

Cold dread settled in the pit of his stomach. "You don't mean that. And I told you before I never thought you were an ugly secret. We agreed—"

"*We* never agreed. I reluctantly settled because that was the way you wanted it. But no more. If you'd cared about me, if you'd respected me, none of this would have happened. I'm done."

He reached out for her. "Harmony, there are things I need to tell you."

She held out her hand. "I don't want to hear anything else you have to say. Please leave."

He heard the finality in her voice. The tremble and the hurt. He hated to have been the one to put that pain there. And by the words she said, it sounded a lot like "this is over."

He wanted to say the words, to convince her he loved her, but she looked so hurt, her arms wrapped protectively around herself, that he knew anything he said right now would roll right over her.

She wouldn't believe him. She wouldn't hear him.

In a lot of ways, she was just as stubborn as her brother, especially when her back was up.

Now wasn't the time for a declaration of love. First he had to fix the damage he'd caused.

He turned and walked out the door, feeling like the absolute asshole that he was.

He had to find a way to make this right.

THIRTY-SIX

HARMONY HAD SPENT THE PAST TWO DAYS FEELING absolutely miserable. She'd held on to the anger all day Friday, which had gotten her through the workday in one piece.

By Friday night, the anger had dissolved and the hurt had wedged its way in, followed by miserable tears.

She hated crying over Barrett. He so wasn't worth it.

But he was. She loved him. She didn't want to love him, but she did.

She also highly disliked him at the moment.

Along with her brother.

Deciding not to think about the male gender at all, she'd brought paperwork home and was buried in spreadsheets and pretty designs when her doorbell rang. She knew it wasn't Alyssa, because although her best friend wanted to camp out with her and hold her hand through this, Alyssa had to work today and Harmony had refused to let Alyssa take the day off to hold her hand.

She didn't need handholding. She could get through this.

She went to the door, surprised to see her mother there. She'd talked to her mom on the phone and assured her she was fine.

"Mama. What are you doing here?"

"I came to see my baby girl. Is that all right?"

"Of course it is. Come on in." She hugged her mother and brought her into the living room.

"Do you want some iced tea?"

"I'd love some."

Harmony fixed two glasses of iced tea, then sat on the sofa next to Mama.

"Now," her mother said. "Since you've been avoiding me with all that 'I'm okay' nonsense, why don't you tell me how you really feel?"

She sighed. Mothers really did know best. "I'm miserable. I miss Barrett, even though I'm so angry with him."

Her mother patted her leg. "Of course you do. And why didn't you tell me about the two of you?"

She shrugged. "I don't know. I guess I kept waiting for the right moment. And that moment just never came around. Until he and Drake got into that awful fight."

"Well, yes. And your brother. He and I had words."

"Did you?"

"Yes. I made it clear that the head of the household has always been me, and that while I appreciate him being protective over you, that nonsense has to stop. You're not a baby anymore and I'm tired of seeing him act like a bully. And if he doesn't stop this behavior he and I are going to have more than just words next time. It's a pattern, and an ugly one and I won't have it from my son. I think I got my point across this time."

"Thank you for that."

"But as far as the rift between Drake and Barrett? I'm afraid the two of them will have to fix that."

She shrugged. "I don't even care anymore. Barrett should have told Drake about us right from the start. Or I should have. I don't know." She rubbed her forehead where a dull ache had made its home for the past day.

"It's complicated. You have two men who have been friends for years. And trying to date a best friend's little sister is complicated."

Her lips curved. "That's an understatement. Especially where Drake is concerned."

"Give the two of them time and space to make things straight with each other, and don't interfere in that. You and your brother have to get right with each other, too."

Harmony nodded. "I know that. And we will. Eventually. I'm just so mad at him right now."

"And you have a right to be. But you two will fix things."

"I'm sure we will—eventually." Mama wouldn't allow anger to fester between Drake and her. She'd have to make up with him. But not now.

"And how about you and Barrett?"

She teared up just thinking about it. "It's over."

"Why is it over? Because he and Drake fought? Honey, that's nothing to break up about."

"Because he waited too long to tell Drake about us. Because he felt it necessary to keep us a secret. Because . . . I don't know. I guess because he didn't put me first."

Her mother nodded. "I can understand that. You have a right to be mad as a poked hornet about that. Maybe Barrett's just not the one for you."

"Oh, he was the one, Mama. I love him. That's why this hurts so much."

Her mother sighed. "Baby girl, my heart hurts for you. I hope you and Barrett can work this out. God knows I love that boy."

Mama pulled her into her arms and held her. It didn't matter how old she was, there was nothing better than being held by her mother. She took comfort in the solid embrace. It might not fix things, but at this moment, she felt loved.

And for now, that was good enough.

THIRTY-SEVEN

THE GAME AGAINST DALLAS HADN'T GONE LIKE BAR-
rett had wanted it to. Offense had been stagnant, putting up only
seven points. Defense had been crusty, slow on getting off their
marks.

He and Drake, not even speaking to each other, hadn't been in
sync and it had showed.

He'd tried to talk to Drake at practices and before the game and
Drake wouldn't have it. Every time he'd approached him Drake had
walked away.

The tension had been noticeable even to their defensive coach,
who had told them both that whatever was going on between them
needed to be resolved, and it sure as hell better not affect their
game play.

Barrett wasn't sure if that's what had accounted for their shitty
game against Dallas, but it definitely hadn't helped.

They'd lost, fourteen to seven.

He hated losing, especially a game that was close enough they could have won.

He needed to fix things between Drake and him. He needed to fix a lot of things.

He drove to Drake's condo on Monday. It was an off day, and he knew that if he let this simmer between them it was only going to get worse. He rang the bell, and Drake answered.

His expression was still one of anger.

"What the hell are you doing here?" Drake asked.

"We need to talk."

"I got nothing to say to you, man."

"Then you can listen and I'll talk. We've been friends since college. We've been teammates for four years. I love you like a brother, Drake. Don't let this come between us."

Drake opened the door to let him in. That was a start.

He walked in and Drake shut the door. What happened next would be telling.

"You want a water?"

For the first time in five days, that tight band around Barrett's chest started to loosen.

"Yeah. Thanks."

They walked into the kitchen and Drake pulled two waters out of the fridge, then handed one to Barrett. He opened it and took several long swallows to coat his nervous, parched throat.

"I owe you an apology," Barrett said. "You were right when you said I should have respected you enough to come to you and tell you when Harmony and I first started dating. You and I have been friends a long time, and I should have trusted that you would be open and understanding, and know that I have enough respect for your sister to never mistreat her."

Drake nodded. "That's right, you should have known that.

You're not one of those assholes she typically dates. You're my best friend. You would never hurt her."

"But now I have hurt her. I hurt her all along by keeping this secret from everyone she cares about. I hurt her, I hurt you and I hurt your mother. And for that I'm deeply sorry. I ask you to forgive me. And then I'm going to go ask your mother to forgive me. After that I'm going to beg Harmony to forgive me. I'm in love with your sister, Drake. And I'm not giving up on her until she lets me back in."

Drake breathed in, then let it out. "Man. You're in love with my sister."

"Yes." He was going to stand there and take whatever Drake handed out.

"I have to own some of this because I have a rep as a Class A dick where she's concerned. All of it has come from a place of love. I've felt the need to protect her since she was a baby. But Mama has finally opened my eyes to the fact that Harmony is now a grown woman. And she can make her own choices, even if those choices end up with her getting hurt. And if she ends up getting hurt, I need to learn to stand by and support her without getting involved."

Drake's lips ticked up. "It's obvious she loves you, or she would have never put up with this bullshit from you, man."

"This is not making me feel better," Barrett said.

"Good. I respect you for coming here and laying this down with me. I love you, man. I don't like things to be off between us."

"I don't, either." Barrett took a step forward and put his arms out.

Drake hugged him, and they slapped backs.

He'd never felt more relieved.

"We're good?" Barrett asked.

"Yeah. We're good. Now you need to go make it right with my sister."

"I intend to. And we need to figure out how we fucked up that game with Dallas so that shit never happens again."

Drake nodded. "You got that. We'll be back in the game in no time. Now that we got our personal shit settled."

"Almost settled. I have to go get the woman I love to forgive me."

Drake laughed. "Good luck with that, my man. Harmony's tough."

Yeah, he knew that. It was one of the reasons he loved her.

THIRTY-EIGHT

HARMONY HAD DECIDED TO PAINT ONE OF THE WALLS in her living room to give the room a pop of color. No doubt it was some form of breakup therapy.

She had tarps down, the baseboard was taped, and there she was on a Tuesday night, wearing her raggiest set of shorts and T-shirt, wielding a paintbrush.

She was halfway through when the doorbell rang.

Dammit. She laid the brush against the roller tray, grabbed the rag to wipe her hands and went to the door, shocked to see her brother there.

She hadn't yet gotten past her anger.

"Hey," she said.

He had the decency to look crestfallen. "Hey yourself, baby sis. Okay if I come in?"

"I guess." She stepped aside and led him into the living room.

Drake surveyed the living room wall, then looked over at her. "Doin' some painting?"

"A little. What brings you here, Drake?"

He turned to face her. "I'm here to apologize for acting like such an ass around you for so long. I guess I have to realize you've grown up, and I haven't come to terms with that. I was wrong to attack Barrett, but more importantly, I've been wrong about you for a lot of years now. I need to let go and let you live the life you choose."

Big admission coming from Drake. "I appreciate that. But words only mean so much to me, Drake. It's actions that'll mean more. Which means that you need to step back, let me make mistakes, let me make choices that might hurt me. Because I need to own my life."

"I know that. And I'll work on it, I promise. But you know that if you need me, if you're ever in trouble, I'll always be here for you."

She realized then that he was afraid for her, just as he'd been afraid for her when she was a little girl and she'd crawled into his lap and cried when she'd fallen down and bloodied her elbow. He loved her and he always would.

She walked into his arms and hugged him. "I love you, Drake."

He wrapped his arms around her. "I love you, too, Harmony."

Tears pricked her eyes. She really did love her brother. And when he squeezed her tight, she realized how much he loved her, too.

She pulled back and he smiled at her.

"We'll always be the devilish duo, like Mama used to call us."

He laughed, and she saw tears in his eyes. "Hell yeah."

"Did you and Barrett talk?"

He nodded. "Yeah. We're good."

"I'm glad."

"He come talk to you yet?"

"No. I'm not sure that can be fixed."

He reached out and took her hand. "Sure it can. Give it some time, and when he calls, listen."

She shrugged. "We'll see."

"Well, I gotta go. Got a hot date tonight."

She rolled her eyes. "Don't you always?"

He grinned as she walked him to the door. "Got a rep to maintain, ya know."

They hugged again at the door and she closed and locked it.

Okay, she felt marginally better now that she and Drake had straightened things out.

She went back and picked up the roller, attacking the wall again. Not twenty minutes later, the doorbell rang again.

What the hell now? She laid the roller down, grabbed the rag to wipe her hands and went to the door, looking out to find Barrett there.

She wasn't sure she wanted to answer it. She'd had enough emotional upheaval already tonight.

But finally, she pulled the door open. "What are you doing here?"

"I'd like to talk to you."

"I'm busy."

He arched a brow. "You have paint all over you."

"Aren't you the observant one. I said I was busy."

He looked around her. "Painting the living room?"

"I'm painting a wall. And if you don't mind, I'd like to get back to it."

"Are you painting because of me?"

"Of course not."

He arched a brow.

She lifted her chin. "I'm giving the living room a pop of color."

"Sure you are."

"Is there something else you need, Barrett, or are we done now?"

"I could help you paint."

"I don't want your help."

"Oh, come on. Painting is fun."

Before she could shut the door in his face, he was inside.

"Barrett." She followed him into the living room, where he was examining the wall color.

"This is . . . interesting. Purple? Really, Harmony?"

Okay, so it had been a rash decision. "It's not purple. It's called Plentiful Plum."

"Looks purple to me."

She was about to shred the rag in her hands. "Why are you here?"

He pulled his attention from the wall and onto her. "I want to talk to you."

"I think we've said enough to each other."

"No, we haven't." He took the paint rag from her hand and took her hands in his. "I haven't told you how badly I messed everything up between us. I haven't told you how I should have told your mother and your brother from the very beginning that you and I were seeing each other. That was my mistake. I should have put you first, because you've been the first thing I think about when I wake up in the morning, and the last thing I think about before I go to sleep at night. Your eyes are my sunset and your smile is my sun. You make my heart beat faster every time I lay eyes on you. Having you sleep next to me is like having the other half of me feel like a whole.

"I didn't even know anything was missing in my life until you came into it. You're in my heart, Harmony Evans. I'm in love with you and I'm so afraid of losing you that I can't even take a deep breath. I don't deserve your forgiveness for screwing this all up, but I hope like hell that you'll offer it."

Harmony's breath held, her pulse raced and she wasn't sure if she was breathing or not. As a declaration of love, it was one she'd spent her entire adult life dreaming about.

"You love me."

"One hundred percent. Though I've done a shitty job showing it. I promise I'll do better in the future if you'll give me the chance. I've had a talk with Drake, apologized to him for not being straight with him from the start. He and I are good now. I apologized to your mother as well, because I should have talked to her, too. You were the last person I came to because you're the most important person in my life, Harmony. You're the woman I love, the one I want to spend my life with. You're my future."

Tears pricked her eyes. "Dammit, Barrett. I'm painting my wall."

His lips curved. "I can see that. Do you need to finish it?"

"You don't understand. It's my way of getting over you."

He looked over at the wall, then back at her, giving her a look of utter sympathy. "It's a pretty awful color."

"I know." She let out a sob and fell against him. He wrapped his arms around her and held her tight, and God she needed that.

When she pulled back she lifted her gaze to his. "I love you, Barrett."

He brushed her tears away with his fingers. "Forgive me?"

"Yes."

He kissed her, and her world spun right on its axis again. Having his lips on hers had always made everything right.

He swept her into his arms and carried her upstairs to her bedroom.

"I need to make love to you," he said, lifting her tank top and bra off and flicking his tongue over her nipples.

She threaded her fingers into his hair. "Yes."

He pushed her down on the bed and pulled off her shorts and underwear. "And I need to tell you that you're the most beautiful woman I've ever known."

He always made her feel beautiful, and when he touched her body with his hands and his mouth, cupping her sex and making her ready for him, she felt worshipped.

He stripped, spread her legs and entered her, his amazing body rising above hers. She snaked her hands down the corded muscle of his arms, reveling in this man who was hers, who would always be hers, as he lifted and drove into her, taking her into a spiraling orgasm that made her cry out his name. And when he went with her, she wrapped her legs tightly around him and claimed him as he shuddered within her.

After, they lay together, entwined together. She rested her head against his chest and let her fingers travel over his expansive chest.

"What now?" she asked.

"Before I royally fucked everything up, I was going to ask if you'd be interested in moving into my house."

She splayed her hand over his chest. "I don't know. I really like my town house, especially with the new purple wall in the living room."

He raised his head. "Really?"

She laughed. "No. Are you kidding? I'd love to move into your house. I love that house. I might have even subconsciously designed it with the thought of someday living there."

"It's the steam shower, isn't it?" he asked.

She grinned. "Of course."

He laughed, then rolled her over onto her back, kissing her so thoroughly her body ached for him again.

"It's yours. I'm yours, Harmony. Forever."

An unexpected rush of love and tenderness filled her. "And I'm yours, Barrett. Always."

THIRTY-NINE

DINNER AT MAMA'S HOUSE WAS CHAOTIC AS USUAL. The guys had an away game this weekend, which meant it was a full house tonight. Everyone wanted home cooking before they headed out on the road.

Mama and the aunts had made meatloaf and mashed potatoes, along with salad and green beans. Aunt Paula had baked homemade biscuits.

Harmony was starving. She'd put in a full day of work, and though she'd snacked all day, she hadn't had a full lunch, so she was more than ready to dig in.

Plus, tonight was the first night Barrett was going to be here as her man, out in the open, no skulking around. She intended to enjoy every minute of that.

She laid her purse on the table by the door and made a beeline for the iced tea in the kitchen. Alyssa was already there and, as soon as she saw her, she poured her a glass.

"You're my savior," she said, hugging her friend.

"You look worn-out," Alyssa said.

"Long day."

"Hey, baby sis," Drake said, coming up next to her and giving her a short hug.

"Hey yourself. How did practice go today?"

"Good."

"Where's Barrett?"

"He texted me a little while ago and said he had to make a stop on the way, but he should be here soon."

"Okay. And did you bring the entire team with you tonight?"

Drake laughed as he looked around the living room. "Seems like it, huh?"

She went into the dining room and gave her mother a kiss on the cheek. "Hi, Mama."

Her mother gave her a sweet smile. "Hello, baby girl. How was your day?"

"Intense. And I'm hungry."

"Go get yourself a snack. Dinner will be ready in a little while."

"Okay."

She went over to the refrigerator and opened it up. Inside was a white envelope with her name on it.

"Okay, this is weird."

"What's weird?" Alyssa asked.

"There's an envelope in here. And it has my name on it."

"What?" Alyssa got up and looked over her shoulder. "What is that?"

"I have no idea."

"Well, open it."

She grabbed the envelope and opened it. Inside was a plain white card that read: *Walk out to the front yard.*

"Huh." She looked up at Alyssa. "What do you think this means?"

Alyssa shrugged. "I have no idea."

She was going to go over to her mother to ask, but her mother had disappeared. So had everyone in the house.

"What the hell is going on?"

"Again," Alyssa said. "I have no idea."

Something strange was going on. And she was tired and hungry and cranky as hell.

"I'm going to get to the bottom of this." She went to the front door and opened it.

And there, on her mother's front porch, was Barrett. In the yard stood her mother and Drake and—wait. Barrett's parents? And was that Mia, too?

What were they all doing there?

And everyone held white balloons in their hands. And Barrett was dressed—really nice—in black slacks and a white button-down shirt.

Her throat went dry.

Alyssa gave her a warm smile and pushed at her back. "Go on outside, honey."

She gave a quick glance over her shoulder to Alyssa and then took a step onto the porch.

Barrett stepped up to her and smiled. "Hi, Harmony."

"Hi, Barrett. What's going on?"

"I started off our relationship on the wrong foot. Instead of shouting to the world how I felt about you, I made you keep it secret. And I kept it a secret. And that was a big mistake, because the way I feel about you is something I want everyone to know. So in front of everyone who's important to me—your family and mine, and our friends—minus my brothers, because they're all off playing baseball and football, I want everyone to know how I feel about you."

She shook her head. "This isn't necessary, you know."

"It is necessary, because I have a very important question to ask you."

Oh, God. "Barrett."

He rubbed his thumbs across her hands. "Harmony Evans. I love you. I fell in love with you from the minute you asked me to date you. And I should have known it right then, and I should have acknowledged it right then, but you know how guys are sometimes. We're a little slow to pick up on the obvious. Like how your hair picks up the sunlight and glows like midnight at noon. And how your smile makes my stomach clench, and how smart you are and how talented you are and how you've made a beautiful home for both of us to spend the rest of our lives in."

She could not breathe right now.

He pulled a black velvet box out of his pocket, and then he got down on one knee. And at the same time, everyone turned those white balloons over, and written on them was "Barrett loves Harmony."

"I love you, Harmony. Will you do me the great honor of marrying me?"

She finally exhaled, tears pooling in her eyes. "Yes. Oh, God, yes, I'll marry you. I love you, Barrett."

He put the most beautiful diamond ring on her finger amid the cheers from her family and his family and their friends. Then he stood, pulled her in his arms and kissed her.

And it was the best kiss of her life.

She looked forward to getting a lot more kisses like that in the years to come.

LOOK FOR THE NEXT PLAY-BY-PLAY NOVEL

RULES OF CONTACT

COMING IN THE FALL OF 2016
FROM BERKLEY BOOKS!

TURN THE PAGE TO READ
A SPECIAL EXCERPT FROM
THE NEXT HOPE NOVEL BY JACI BURTON . . .

DON'T LET GO

AVAILABLE SOON FROM JOVE BOOKS!

BRADY CONNERS WAS SPENDING THE DAY DOING ONE of the things he enjoyed the most: smoothing out dents in a quarter panel of a Chevy. As soon as he finished, he'd paint, and this baby would be good as new.

It wasn't his dream job. He was working toward that. But with every day he spent working at Richards Auto Service, thanks to Carter Richards, he was pocketing money that got him closer to his dream. And someday he'd open up his own custom motorcycle paint shop.

Somewhere. Maybe here in Hope. Maybe somewhere else. Probably somewhere else, because this place held memories.

Not good ones.

A long time ago—a time that seemed like an eternity now—he had thought maybe he and his brother Kurt would start up a business together. Brady would do bodywork and custom motorcycle paint, and Kurt would repair the bikes.

That dream went up in smoke the day Brady got the call that his brother was dead.

He paused, stood, and stretched out the kinks in his back, wiping the sweat that dripped into his eyes. He took a step back and grabbed the water bottle he always stored nearby, taking a long drink through the straw, swallowing several times until his thirst was quenched.

Needing a break, he pulled off his breathing mask and swiped his fingers through his hair, then stepped outside.

It was late spring, and rain was threatening. He dragged in a deep breath, enjoying the smell of fresh air.

He really wanted a cigarette, but he'd quit a little over a year ago. Not that the urge had gone away. Probably never would. But he was stronger than his own needs. Or at least that's what he told himself every time a strong craving hit.

Instead, he pulled out one of the flavored toothpicks he always kept in his jeans pocket and slid that between his teeth.

Not nearly as satisfying, but it would do. It would have to.

He leaned against the wall outside the shop and watched the town in motion. It was lunchtime, so it was busy.

Luke McCormack, one of Hope's cops, drove by in his patrol car and waved. Brady waved back. Luke was a friend of Carter's, and while Brady wasn't as social as a lot of the guys he'd met, he knew enough to be friendly. Especially to cops.

Samantha Reasor left her shop, loading up her flower van with a bunch of colorful bouquets. She spotted him, giving him a bright smile and a wave before she headed off.

Everyone in this damn town was so friendly. He mostly kept to himself, doing his work and then heading to the small apartment above the shop at night to watch TV or play video games. He had one goal in mind, and that was to save money to open his business.

He saw his parents now and again since they lived in Hope, but the strain of Kurt's death had taken a toll on them.

Nothing was the same anymore. With them. With him either, he supposed.

Sometimes life just sucked. And you dealt with that.

His stomach grumbled. He needed something to eat. He pushed off the wall and headed up the street, intending to make a stop at the sandwich joint on the corner. He'd grab a quick bite and bring it back to the shop.

He made a sudden stop when Megan Lee, the really hot brunette who owned the bakery, came out with a couple of pink boxes in her hands. She collided with him and the boxes went flying. She caught one, he caught one, then he steadied her with his other hand.

She looked up at him, her brown eyes wide with surprise.

"Oh, my gosh. Thank you, Brady. I almost dropped these."

"You okay, Megan?"

"Yes. But let me check these." She bent down and opened the boxes. There were cakes inside. They looked pretty, with pink icing on one and blue on the other and little baby figurines in strollers sitting on top of the cakes. There were flowers and other doodahs as well. He didn't know all that much about cake decorations. He just liked the way they tasted.

"They're for Sabelle Frasier. She just had twins." She looked up at him with a grin. "A boy and a girl. Her mom ordered these for her hospital homecoming. I spent all morning baking and decorating them."

He didn't need to know that, but the one thing he did know was that people in this town were social and liked to talk. "They look good."

She swiped her hair out of her eyes. "Of course they're good."

He bent and took the boxes from her. "Where's your car?"

"Parked just down the street."

"How about you let me carry these? Just in case you want to run into anyone else on your way."

Her lips curved. "I think you ran into me."

He disagreed, but whatever. He figured he'd do his good deed for the day, then get his sandwich.

He followed her down the street.

"I haven't seen much of you lately," she said.

He shrugged. "Been busy."

"I've been meaning to stop in the shop and visit, but things have been crazy hectic at the bakery, too." She studied him. "How about I bring pastries by in the morning? And I've never brought you coffee before. How about some coffee? How do you take it? Black, or with cream and sugar? Or maybe you like lattes or espresso? What do you drink in the mornings?"

He had no idea what she was talking about. "Uh, just regular coffee. Black."

"Okay. I make a really great cup of coffee. I'm surprised you haven't come into the bakery since it's so close to the auto shop. Most everyone who works around here pops in." She pressed the unlock button on her car, then opened the back door and took the boxes from him.

Man, she really could talk. He'd noticed that the couple of times they'd gone out. For someone like him who lived mostly isolated, all that conversation was like a bombardment.

Not that it was a bad thing. The one thing he missed the most since his self-imposed isolation was conversation. And Megan had it in droves. He just wasn't all that good about reciprocating.

After she slid the boxes in, she turned to him. "What's your favorite pastry? You know, I've dropped muffins off at the auto shop. Have you eaten any of those?"

He was at a loss for words. He always was around her. A few of his friends had fixed the two of them up before. Once at Logan and Des's dinner party, then again at Carter and Molly's wedding. They'd danced. Had some conversation. Mostly one-sided since Megan had done all the talking.

He wasn't interested.

Okay, that wasn't exactly the truth. What heterosexual male wouldn't be interested in Megan? She was gorgeous, with her silky light brown hair and her warm chocolate eyes that always seemed to study him with interest. She also had a fantastic body with perfect curves.

But he was here to work. That was it. He didn't have time for a relationship.

He didn't want a relationship, no matter how attractive the woman was. And Megan was really damned attractive.

"Brady?" she asked, pulling his attention back on her. "Muffins?"

"What about them?"

She cocked her head to the side. "Oh, come on Brady. Everyone has a favorite pastry. Cream puffs? Donuts? Scones? Cakes? Bars? Strudel?"

He zeroed in on the last thing she said. "Apple strudel. I used to have that from the old bakery when I was a kid."

She offered up a satisfied smile. "I make a killer apple strudel. I'll bring you one—along with coffee—in the morning."

He frowned. "You don't have to do that."

She laid her hand on his arm and offered up the kind of smile that made him focus on her mouth. She had a really pretty mouth, and right now it was glossed a kissable shade of peach.

He didn't want to notice her mouth, but he did.

"I don't mind. I love to bake. But now I have to go. Thanks again for saving the cakes. I'll see you tomorrow, Brady."

She climbed in her car and pulled away, leaving him standing there, confused as hell.

He didn't want her to bring him coffee. Or apple strudel. Or anything.

He didn't want to notice Megan or talk to Megan or think about Megan, but the problem was, he'd been doing a lot of that lately. For the past six months or so he'd thought about the dance he'd shared with her. The conversations he'd had with her. She had a sexy smile—not the kind a woman had to force, but the kind that came naturally. She also had a great laugh and she could carry a conversation with ease. And that irritated him because he hadn't thought about a woman in a long time.

For the past year and a half since his brother had died, he hadn't wanted to think about anything or anyone. All he'd wanted to do was work, then head upstairs to his one-room apartment above the auto shop, eat his meals and watch TV, and on the weekends do custom bike painting. Keep his mind and his body busy so he wouldn't have to think—or feel.

Women—and relationships—would make him feel, and that wasn't acceptable. He'd noticed that right away about Megan, noticed that he liked her and maybe—

No. Wasn't going to happen—ever. He needed to get her out of his head.

He only had time for work, and making money. He had a dream he was saving for.

And now he barely had time for lunch, because he had a Chevy to get back to.

Jaci Burton is a *USA Today* and *New York Times* bestselling author of the Play-by-Play series, including *All Wound Up*, *Quarterback Draw*, *Straddling the Line*, *Melting the Ice*, and *One Sweet Ride*, and the Hope series, including *Make Me Stay*, *Love After All*, *Hope Burns*, *Hope Ignites*, and *Hope Flames*. Visit Jaci at jaciburton.com.